A CHRISTMAS WISH: I'LL BE HOME FOR CHRISTMAS & COME HOME TO ME

A COMING HOME DUET BOX SET

THE COMING HOME SERIES

JESSICA SCOTT

THIRTY ONE FOX BOOKS

A goofball soldier hiding his pain behind a quick smile. A worried Army wife. A Christmas miracle that brings them back together again.

"*Buy it. Read it. Have lots of Kleenex on hand. Scott's stories are always powerful and emotional but they're honest, she doesn't jerk you around or manipulate you. The power of the stories and of the characters emotions gets into you and sweeps you away.*" - Bea's Book Nook

Meet the lovable smart ass who can always crack a joke and the woman who loves him more than life itself.

Vic Carponti always has a joke — no matter how bleak the situation might be. He's the guy who can make jokes in the middle of a firefight in Baghdad or when he's getting sewn back up after getting blown up. But his sense of humor hides a fierce loyalty to

the men he serves with and a devotion to his wife who he loves more than life itself. But there's nothing funny about war...

But as he prepares to leave on his latest deployment into the violent throes of the Surge in Iraq, his jokes don't seem as funny to his wife. Nicole forces herself to laugh at his redeployment antics but behind her laughter hides the darkest fear of every Army wife — that the knock on the door may be the news that destroys her world.

They both try to make the best of the deployment but when the phone doesn't ring for a few days, Nicole starts to worry. And when the dreaded call comes telling her he's been hurt, she'll move heaven and earth to be there when her husband wakes up.

"I won't spoil it, but it will give you hope, laughter and tears!" ~ *Romancing Rakes*

THE COMING HOME SERIES
Because of You
I'll Be Home for Christmas: A Coming Home Novella
Anything For You: A Coming Home Short Story
Back to You
Come Home to Me: A Coming Home Novella*
Carry Me Home*
A Place Called Home*
Take Me Home*
Homefront
After The War
Last One Home*

Note – these books are fiction. Any resemblance to real people or events is purely coincidence

Learn More At...

http://www.jessicascott.net
Follow Jessica on Twitter
Like Jessica on Facebook
Sign up for Jessica's Newsletter

Author's Note

The Coming Home series and Homefront series were originally published as separate series. I have rebranded them to get things organized as they were originally intended.

Come Home to Me: A Coming Home Novella* was originally published as part of the Homefront series

Carry Me Home* was originally published as **Until There Was You** as part of the Coming Home series

A Place Called Home* was originally published as **All for You** as part of the Coming Home series

Take Me Home* was originally published as **It's Always Been You** as part of the Coming Home series

Last One Home* was originally published as **Find My Way Home** as part of the Homefront series

USA TODAY BESTSELLING AUTHOR

JESSICA SCOTT

I'LL BE HOME FOR CHRISTMAS

A Coming Home Novella

*To Donna
Because these books wouldn't be here without you.*

1

Fort Hood, Texas
Early 2007

Sergeant Vic Carponti paused outside his company operations office, taking a deep breath. It was funny how their corner of Fort Hood felt deserted the night before a deployment. The company colors had already been cased. They would uncase them in a few weeks, once they got settled into their new home across the ocean in the middle of the war.

He didn't know why this deployment was bothering him so much. It wasn't his first time heading off to war, so he knew what to expect when the shit hit the fan in combat. But there was something hanging over his head this time. A fear that maybe this time his luck would run out.

He sighed and rubbed his face with both hands before walking into the company ops. The only thing they'd left up was the plaque that bore the names of their fallen brothers from the last deployment. The commander—Captain Trent

Davila, a man Carponti had known for years—was planning on carrying that with him personally so it couldn't ever get lost.

And so no one would ever forget. Carponti reached up and took it gently off the wall, then strolled into his company commander's office with a nonchalance painted on his face that he damn sure didn't feel. But people expected him to laugh and joke and make them forget the bad shit all around and so that's what he was going to do.

"Don't forget this," he said, placing the plaque on Trent's desk. He plopped down in a chair, then kicked his feet up on Trent's desk. "Are you coming out with us tonight?"

Captain Trent Davila lifted one eyebrow at Carponti's feet and said nothing. Carponti looked at his commander and longtime friend, then at the plaque next to his boots.

"Fine," he said with a sigh, dropping his feet to the floor. "So answer the question."

Trent sighed. "I can't go out with you guys. I'm the company commander. I'm not allowed to have fun," Trent grumbled. "Besides, my boss would have my nuts in a sling if anything happens while I'm there."

"It's the last day before our deployment. You're allowed to have fun. You can just say you're supervising all of us miscreants." Carponti took the last Dr. Pepper out of Trent's fridge. "The deployment hasn't even started and you already look stressed the hell out. You should be working your lieutenant to death instead of trying to do everything yourself."

Trent shook his head and pushed his glasses to the top of his head. "Yeah, well, my new executive officer seems to think he's God's gift to the Army. He's good but he's not as good as he thinks he is."

"Oh, the boys just love him," Carponti said.

"Really?"

"No, not really. He's an arrogant fuck who believes his own

press. Personally, I can't stand him, but luckily I don't have to deal with him much. I just sic Sarn't Garrison on him."

Trent grinned and reached for the plaque, sliding his hat on top of it so he wouldn't forget it. "Yeah, Garrison has a way with words."

Garrison was Carponti's platoon sergeant. Garrison and Trent had been squad leaders many moons ago when Trent had still been enlisted. In Carponti's world, it meant a whole lot that Trent had stayed close with his enlisted friends even after he'd crossed over to the dark side and become an officer.

"I'm swinging by his place on my way home. He needs to go out before someone shoots his grumpy old ass. He's been a complete buzz kill since his wife left him."

"Your sympathy is astounding," Trent said dryly. He grinned and shook his head. "Why do we put up with you?"

"Because I'm charming and funny and good in a firefight?" Carponti said with a grin.

"Pretty much. You can make anyone laugh."

"It's an important life skill. Like balancing a checkbook. So seriously, find a babysitter and come out with us. Your wife could use some fun before she has to spend the year dealing with all the spouses in the Family Readiness Group and chasing your kids around while you're off on another fun adventure."

"I wouldn't exactly call going to combat a fun adventure." Trent rubbed his chest. There was a scar there, Carponti knew. A scar that had damn near killed Trent several years ago. Carponti wondered just how much stress his commander was carrying and not telling anyone. Trent's face flushed when he realized Carponti had caught him rubbing his scar and he tapped the pencil hard enough to snap the eraser off. "You know, you're right. Let me see if we can't find a sitter."

"Excellent. We'll be congregating by the bar when you get

there. Now I just have to go convince Garrison to come out with us."

"Good luck with that," Trent said, pulling his glasses down. "He's on the verge of becoming a warrior monk."

"Not if I have anything to say about it," Carponti mumbled as he strolled out of his commander's office. He wished he hadn't seen the flicker of worry that flashed in his commander's eyes when he'd mentioned his wife. He'd thought that Laura and Trent were one of the strongest couples he knew. She'd put up with him deploying back to back to back since he'd almost died a few years ago.

But that flicker of worry? Yeah, Carponti hadn't missed it. There were problems there, hopefully small ones that Trent would take time to fix after this rotation into the sandbox.

Carponti looked down at his own wedding ring. It was his last night home and his last night with his wife.

He was glad he'd convinced her to come out with him and the boys. That way he could make sure they had a most excellent party and spend time with Nicole at the same time. He was going to spend part of the night chaperoning his guys to make sure they made the most of it— which meant making sure no one ended up in jail—but then? Then the time he had left was going to be spent making his wife laugh.

Because try though he might, he couldn't shake the quiet dread that settled in the pit of his stomach that tonight was the last night of normalcy he had on this earth.

NICOLE CARPONTI BREATHED DEEPLY and fanned her eyes, trying to stop the burning of hot tears. She leaned against the wall of the bathroom in *Ropers* and tried to stuff down all the churning emotions chained to the fact that her husband was leaving for war tomorrow. Again.

The first time he'd left she'd been scared, but then the war, the deployment...the waiting...it had all been unknown. She'd worked on finishing her degree and kept herself busy and waited by the phone like all the military wives who had gone before her.

The second time he'd left, she'd known better what to expect. The long waits between phone calls. The silence when he couldn't talk long. The quick e-mails saying "I'm alive" that once upon a time would have been too little, but during the war were more than enough to keep her going.

But this time? This time was different. The Surge was different. They were sending in massive amounts of soldiers to try to quell the Iraqi insurgency. It was bloody and deadly and soldiers were getting attacked at higher rates than at any earlier time during the war.

And Nicole was terrified.

She had to hide it, though. She'd agreed to come out with him tonight just because it gave her a chance to pretend that she was fine. She had to keep everything in check until after he left. She couldn't let him know how much she worried this time.

Fanning her eyes once more, she stepped out of the bathroom and into the rowdy country bar. A place like this was guaranteed trouble on a normal night, but tonight her husband's platoon was rolling deep. Which was either going to be a really good thing or a really bad thing for her future job at the Army's Criminal Investigation Division, depending on how cantankerous tonight got.

She spotted her good friend Laura Davila at the bar with a cute blond woman Nicole had met in the bathroom a little while ago. She had already completely forgotten the other woman's name. She was terrible with names.

She wound her way through the pulsating crowd until she

reached them. Laura grinned at her and she exclaimed, "I can't believe you came out tonight."

"You've already said this twice," Laura said. They had to shout to hear each other.

Nicole flagged down the bartender and leaned around Laura to her friend. "I'm a terrible person but I already forgot your name. I'm Nicole Carponti."

The petite blond held out her hand. "Jen St. James."

"Nice to meet you, Jen. I won't forget this time," Nicole said with a smile.

Laura leaned toward Nicole. "I'm trying to get her out of her shell. She had cancer and she's been struggling with her self-esteem ever since."

Nicole frowned, glancing toward Jen, who was now trying to get the attention of the bartender. On the other side of her, though, was Garrison, her husband's platoon sergeant. He was a big man and he was currently leaning down to talk to Jen. "How's that for a self-esteem boost?" Nicole said, gesturing toward the two.

Laura glanced over, then quickly looked away before she was caught. Her eyes lit with a brilliant smile. "Oh, that couldn't be more perfect if I had planned it."

Nicole studied her friend through narrowed eyes. "Did you plan it?"

"I wish. But let's just see how this little situation develops, shall we?"

Nicole raised her beer in mock salute to her friend. "You, m'dear, are a devious and loyal friend."

"I'll drink to that," Laura said. "So how's Carponti taking this deployment?"

Nicole heard the undercurrent in her friend's voice. "You know how he is. Always cracking jokes, which I suppose is a good thing. I'm terrified, though."

"Yeah, I know. I've been talking to some of the spouses. The

Surge has everyone terrified. One of the spouses told me it was a death sentence." Laura took a sip from her beer, scanning the bar.

Nicole scoffed quietly. "How's that for melodramatic?" But she didn't voice her own fear that this deployment was going to be worse than the previous ones. "I don't envy you as the Family Readiness Group leader."

"Oh, come on, don't you want to volunteer? You can be responsible for keeping me from going crazy. It's a primary duty position, you know."

Nicole laughed. "Not in this lifetime," she said. "I always feel out of place once the spouses find out I'm pretty much a cop."

Jen leaned over, rejoining their conversation as Garrison wandered off in the direction of Laura's husband. "What's going on over there?" she said, pointing at Laura's husband.

Nicole sighed heavily and took another drink. "Oh joy. Looks like Trent is giving one of his lieutenants some love. Couldn't have the rest of the night without drama, could we?" She glanced back at Laura and Jen. "We should go interrupt before the second round of fireworks go off."

Earlier, Vic had gotten into an argument with Lieutenant Randall and now it looked like Laura's husband was finishing things off with the arrogant prick. The LT made Nicole's skin crawl and she wasn't looking forward to another bar fight. Not two in one night, that was for sure.

But whatever had happened was over now. She watched as LT Randall made a beeline for the door. Out of the corner of her eye, she saw Garrison talking to Jen again. And Laura? Once Randall was gone, she and her husband moved off to a dark corner of the bar and were deep in conversation.

She hoped it was a good one. She didn't like the worry she'd seen in her friend's eyes when she talked about her husband.

She snuck up behind Vic, sliding her hands over his hips

and up under his t-shirt and the smooth hard skin of his body, placing a kiss at the indentation between his shoulder blades.

He turned and wrapped his arms around her shoulders. "There you are." He kissed her fiercely, reminding her of how much she loved this man. "I was about to send out a search party for you in the little girls' room."

Nicole wrapped her arms around his waist and lifted her chin to meet his eyes. He was leaner than he'd been when he'd come home last year. His body was more solid from long ruck marches and hard training for this deployment. His eyes, though, were the same bright, mischievous green that they'd always been and she counted herself lucky that whatever he'd gone through in the war, he'd come home okay so far. She just prayed their luck held.

"No search party required," she murmured against his lips. "I was talking to Laura. I'm impressed that you got Garrison and Trent to come out."

"You should be," Vic grumbled, biting her bottom lip gently. "I had to guilt both of them into it. It's like they both turned thirty and amputated their fun genes or something."

Nicole laughed against his mouth. "Dance with me?" she asked.

"What in our history makes you think I know how to dance?" he grumbled even as he allowed her to lead him onto the dance floor.

"You'll figure it out," she said, sliding her arms around his neck. She rubbed her body against his, sensuously moving her hips in time with the music.

He dropped his hands to her hips, guiding her exactly where he wanted her. "Keep that up and we'll have to sneak out to the car," he said, his breath hot on her ear.

She nibbled on his bottom lip, biting it gently. "I think you're trying to seduce me," she whispered. She dug her fingers into his back, her blood humming with latent arousal. God but she loved this man.

"I'm absolutely trying to seduce you," he said. He angled his thigh between hers, pressing close to the juncture of her thighs. The pressure sent vibrations through her body and straight to her core.

"I'm kind of ready to go home." Her words were a gasp as he rubbed his thigh against her swollen center. "Before you get into any more fights with your lieutenant."

"Can we not talk about work when I'm trying to turn you on?" he mumbled. He slipped his hand beneath the hem of her shirt, stroking his thumb down the centerline of her back. A shiver ran through her.

"You don't want to talk about work? That doesn't turn you on?" She undulated against him, grateful for the crush of bodies that swayed around them and enabled them to be lost in the crowd.

"No, trying to get you naked turns me on," he said. "We really need to get out of here." His breath traced over her ear a moment before he bit her earlobe gently, a fierce burst of pleasure in the pain.

"That sounds like a brilliant idea."

He sighed as a commotion cleared a corner of the dance floor. "I hate being one of the responsible adults." He kissed her hard. "Let me get everyone out of here first? That way no one goes to jail on our last night in the States."

She kissed him fiercely. "I'll be waiting over here for you to get done being all caveman."

"I'll show you caveman later," he said with a grin before wading into the crowd and diffusing the situation between Garrison and Trent.

It took the better part of an hour before they'd shuffled everyone off to their respective cabs and vehicles. Nicole talked with Laura and Jen and tried not to notice how Jen kept watching Garrison.

It felt like forever before her husband strolled across the parking lot and scooped her up, carrying her toward their vehicle.

Their car was parked deep in a shadowed corner of the parking lot, and the moment her husband closed the door, Nicole crawled into his lap on the passenger's seat. He pulled her close, kissing her hard and fast. Pouring a thousand unsaid things into that kiss. His hand threaded into her hair and he slanted her mouth until he owned her—all of her—and she was lost in his taste, his touch.

Then he broke off abruptly. "What the hell?"

"What?"

"Who is that with Garrison?"

Nicole twisted around in time to see Garrison, one of Carponti's oldest friends, lean in to kiss Jen.

"Oh, now that's interesting," Carponti whispered.

Nicole spun around. "Don't you say anything to him," she said.

"Why not?"

"Because this is the first time Garrison has done anything for himself since his wife left him. Leave him alone."

Carponti blinked innocently. "What makes you think I would say anything?" he said. His words slurred and Nicole grinned before fishing around in his pockets for his car keys. "A little more to the left."

Nicole laughed then climbed into the driver's seat as Garrison stepped back, letting Jen walk to an ancient sedan. "She's cute. She's friends with Laura."

Laura, who was being carried across the parking lot by her husband. She hoped for Laura's sake the happiness lasted longer than just tonight. The war was taking its toll on everyone, and Nicole had noticed more than once that there was a strain in her friend's voice when she talked about her husband.

Vic just looked at her. "Oh really?"

Nicole drove them away before her husband could interrupt what had looked like something very sweet between Jen and Garrison. She'd known Garrison as long as she'd known her husband and it was long overdue for him to find someone that made him happy outside of the Army.

She glanced at her husband, who had closed his eyes the moment the vehicle started moving, a lazy smile on his lips. Something warm bloomed inside her.

She wished Garrison could find the kind of happy that she had with Vic.

2

"Hey, babe, can you find my socks?"

Nicole narrowed her eyes in the direction of the bedroom. Since the night they'd first met six years ago, she'd learned to tell when he was up to something. And he was always up to something. The man didn't know how to be serious and it was the thing she loved most about him.

But she hadn't known it that night she'd pulled him and a couple of his buddies over and arrested him. She'd been a young military police officer, eager to make a difference and her very first traffic stop at her new duty station had been a car full of smart-mouthed infantrymen, fresh out of basic training.

She'd walked up to the driver's side window and had been greeted by...a sock puppet. A sock puppet that had asked her out on a date after she'd threatened to put him in the back of the police car. Her lips curled at the memory.

Yeah, most people had romantic stories about how they met their husbands. Nicole? She had a sock puppet. She'd learned that night that when Vic's voice sounded funny, he was up to something.

And right then, standing in her living room, his socks in her hand, she paused because her husband's voice sounded a little too funny.

And that was never a good sign.

"What's wrong?" she called, stuffing his socks into the bag that would keep them protected from the desert weather.

He was deploying for the third time later today and Nicole was doing her best to stay busy, to help him pack. She was determined not to spend the last few hours she had with him crying. She'd done this all before, right? This was nothing new. Nothing different. So why did it feel like her heart was breaking in her chest? She blinked rapidly and breathed deeply. She wouldn't cry. Not today.

No, she'd save that for later, after he was gone. Today, she would laugh at his jokes because he needed her to laugh. She'd help him pack and savor the last hours she had with him.

Later, after she'd kissed him goodbye, the year would start and her countdown would begin. One day at a time, trying not to let the worry and the fear and the sadness crush her.

"Nothing's wrong. I just need you to come here for a second."

The odd catch in his voice made her instantly suspicious. Still holding the gallon bag of his t-shirts and socks she'd been packing for him, she rounded the corner into their bedroom.

And stopped short. Blinked. Then doubled over laughing.

Her husband—a decorated infantryman—stood in the middle of their bedroom wearing her panties. And not her time-of-the-month granny panties. No, not her husband. He'd managed to squeeze into the tiny little patch of white lace.

She doubled over and clutched her sides and tried not to pee her pants.

"Oh my god. I can't breathe," she said, trying to stop laughing.

He turned around and wiggled his ass. "Does this make my butt look big?"

Nicole gasped for air. "There's something the matter with you."

"Does this get you horny, baby?" She caught the edge of shadows in his eyes despite her own tears of laughter. They were both trying so hard to laugh away the sadness of the night. She loved him even more for that. Something so simple but so important.

She swiped her fingers beneath her eyes, glad at least that she had a moment to hide the well of sadness that had surged behind the laughter. She would miss his sense of humor when he was gone. Nothing seemed as funny when Vic deployed. It was like he took funny with him every time he got on that plane. Still laughing, she crossed the small space, dropping the gallon-sized bag of t-shirts on the bed before sliding her arms around her husband's neck. "You know that you wearing my panties always gets me horny."

He pulled her close and she arched into him. He nuzzled her lips with his. "I'm not really sure what that says about you or me but I'm not going to complain."

She reached between their bodies and wound her hand beneath the fabric, clearly not meant to contain male anatomy, and found him—flaccid.

"I think we need to get you out of these. They're inhibiting your performance," she said, hooking her thumbs in the waistband.

"I think that's an excellent plan."

He shimmied out of the panties and then surprised her by scooping her up and tossing her onto the bed.

She bounced once then opened her arms for him.

She held him close for a long moment, savoring the feel of his body on hers, knowing it was going to be the last time she would have him with her for a long while.

She knew the fear she would live with for the next year. And she hated it.

But she loved her husband and he loved being a soldier. She'd never planned on making the military a career. Vic? Vic wanted to stay forever. And because she loved him, she'd wait for him. No matter how much it hurt.

She blinked rapidly, trying to hide the tears that burned behind her eyes, and pressed her face into his neck. Her no-crying plan was failing miserably. She swiped at her eyes and tried to keep him from seeing the tears that ran down her cheeks.

CARPONTI MIGHT BE a smart-ass but that didn't make him an idiot. His wife was crying. He hated it when she cried. It was worse because he knew it was his fault—he was leaving again. No matter how much he tried to make light of the situation, no matter how ridiculously he behaved to coax a laugh out of her, this deployment was different and everyone knew it. He shouldn't have been surprised that Nicole was having a hard time with it. Even Trent and his wife looked like they were having a hard time.

Everyone was—her, the guys, the guys' wives. Carponti and his boys were getting ready to head downrange into the Surge, a shit hole time in a shit hole war that didn't make a damn bit of sense to anyone. This war sucked.

But that didn't make saying good-bye any easier. And Nicole, God bless her, was doing her best to put on a brave and happy face. He felt her shudder beneath him and he tightened his arms around her a little more.

He didn't want her to cry. He hated it when she cried because it usually meant he'd screwed something up. He tried not to do that on a regular basis. He never wanted to give her a reason to realize that she could do better than a redheaded infantryman. Nicole was so far out of his league, every day he woke up wondering if today would be the day that the love of his life left him for someone better. The day she would stop laughing at his jokes.

Because, let's face it, he wasn't much of a catch. Scruffy redhead with a penchant for saying the first thing that came to mind, Carponti knew his weaknesses. And still, his wife, his beautiful, talented wife with a degree in criminal justice, chose him. He'd married her as fast as he could just to keep her around. Even when she'd gotten out of the Army to pursue her degree, even when she could be with someone smarter, better looking—not better in the sack, though. Carponti had always taken care of her that way. He marveled at the ways he could bring her pleasure—just like the sound of her laughter, the sound of her coming was its own special pleasure.

All because she'd pulled him over for driving like an ass and said yes to a date with a sock puppet. He was the luckiest son of a bitch on the planet.

He lifted himself on his arms and looked down at her, stroking her blond hair out of her face and cupping her cheek. Her eyes were a little bit red and she was trying to hide it and failing badly.

"Don't cry, babe," he whispered.

"I'm trying not to." She pressed her lips to his. "Sorry."

He grasped for anything to say to make her laugh and came up empty. She shifted then, her body rubbing against his, and he smiled slowly, stroking his thumb over her damp cheek.

"We are really wasting this opportunity," he said, kissing the side of her lips.

"What's that?" Her mouth curled into a faint smile, the remnants of her laugh trembling through her body.

"I'm naked. What other opportunity did you think I was talking about?"

He loved it when she laughed. Her eyes lit up and her

whole face smiled. He laughed and shifted, rocking gently against her. "It's a shame you've got on so many clothes."

She lifted her arms for him as he dragged the t-shirt over her head, leaving her in a bra and her jeans. She reached between them to unhook her pants but he stopped her, his hands covering hers. He shimmied down her body. "That's my job," he whispered, then he flicked his tongue over her navel.

He loved the little sounds she made as he tugged her pants off. "Your panties look so much better on you," he said.

"I'm glad you approve." There was laughter in her voice. She threaded her fingers through his hair, her nails tracing his scalp with tiny bites of electricity.

He framed her hips in his hands and pressed his lips to her center. She arched beneath him and shifted her thighs, opening to his touch. He held her there, his thumbs holding the fabric in place when she tried to shuck out of her panties. "I want to try something."

She pushed up onto her elbows, looking down at him, a tiny frown knitted between her brows. "What, the night before you leave, now you want to get creative?"

He met her gaze, his eyes not moving from hers, and traced his tongue over the swollen mound beneath her panties.

"Oh, I am definitely going to miss your tongue when you're gone." She gasped and her breath caught in her throat. "Where on earth did you learn that trick?" she whispered.

She reached down to cradle his face in her palms and Carponti was lost for a moment in the love looking back at him. His wife, his beautiful, smart, sexy, funny wife. A tiny curl of fear licked at him. What if she got tired of waiting for him?

"I watched this sex in your marriage video with Wilks last weekend on staff duty." Nicole fell back into the bed and cracked up. "The art of making love or something. He's going through counseling with his wife and the therapist is trying to save their sex life first. So I watched it with him. See if I could pick up any pointers."

Nicole sighed and turned her head to look down at him. "You are a strange, strange man," she said, smiling. But there was a fear beneath her smile. Fear that someday, the deployments would be too much. That the distance and the time spent apart would change them. That she'd stop wanting to make love, stop loving him enough to wait for him. Garrison, Carponti's platoon sergeant, had recently gotten divorced. They both knew it was because Garrison had been gone too much.

Carponti shoved aside the melancholy, focusing instead on her body. Her touch.

"And you're wasting an opportunity to use that talented tongue of yours." She arched into him, lifting her hips in silent offering.

The laugh snuck out of him and he rested his forehead against her thigh until he could control himself. "This has got to be the corniest thing we've ever done," he said, stroking his thumb over the seam of her panties.

She scraped her nails over his cheeks, gently. "It beats spending the morning crying," she whispered.

A lump rose in his throat and he crawled up her body, capturing her face in his hands. He kissed her then, fiercely, pouring a thousand unsaid things into that one moment. He wasn't good with words or big gestures. There wasn't a way for him to tell her how much he was going to miss her. How much he worried that she would be alone, that she might go through a day without laughing because he was gone. And the unspoken fear that he would leave her alone forever. He kissed her like a dying man, peeled her clothes from her body like it was the last time he would feel her writhe beneath him— because he was terrified that it was. He paused a moment before he slid into her body, desperately grasping for something funny to say to lighten the moment, to make her laugh.

But he had nothing as he fell into her embrace, sliding into her body and completing his soul.

He savored her in those final moments before her release crashed over her, shuddering through them both and taking him under with her.

"You're not serious."

Carponti turned around, his shoulders covered in flecks of red hair. "What?"

Nicole grinned as she leaned against the door. "Garrison is going to kill you."

"Garrison is going to love my new haircut. It looks just like his."

Nicole arched one blond eyebrow. "Except for the bright red fuzzy patch in the center of your head."

Carponti shrugged and rubbed his hands over his freshly shorn scalp. "I can't wait to see what the sergeant major says."

"Isn't he going to be mad?"

Carponti brushed the hair off his neck. "We're going to war. My hair isn't on the list of things he's going to worry about."

Nicole looked down at the pile of hair on the floor and sighed. "Then why do it?"

Carponti smirked. "Because it'll get a rise out of him and I live to make his blood pressure go up."

She laughed. "You need a hobby. Other than blowing things up."

He sidled across the room and hooked his thumb into the waist of her jeans and tugged her close until their hips met. "I have a hobby. Keeping you well satisfied."

She sniffed but her lips curled at the edges. "You're going to be derelict in your duties for a while."

"But I'll be home soon enough and then I'll make up for it."

"I think I'm going to need a deployment boyfriend."

He grinned wickedly. "Did you already get one?" He backed her up against the wall, his body hard against hers. God but she loved this man. "Can I see it?"

A slow flush crept over her face and she tried to look away. He threaded his fingers with hers and lifted her arms over her head. Her back arched with the movement.

"Please?" he whispered against her lips. "That would be an awesome memory to take with me downrange. Just think of me, alone in the middle of the desert. One visual of you with your deployment boyfriend and it could make a lonely night go by so much faster."

Nicole giggled until the laugh overwhelmed her and she was gasping for air. He released her hands and she threaded them around his neck. She buried her face against his throat and laughed.

"There's something really wrong with you," she said when she could breathe again. "I'll send you a video."

He brightened instantly. "Really?"

"Yes. And dirty letters."

"Promise?" He nibbled along the edge of her jaw, guiding her slowly backward toward their bed, stacked high with his two duffle bags and all the crap he still hadn't packed.

But he didn't care. "I promise. And you're going to be late." Her voice caught in her throat.

"Screw it," he whispered. "This is the last chance to make love to my beautiful wife before I have to go traipsing across the desert like Lawrence of Arabia." He nibbled at her earlobe while his hand slipped down her belly to the moist heat between her thighs. "Tell you what. You send me a picture of yours and I'll send you a picture of mine. Maybe I can get him a little horse and saddle and send you a picture. Maybe a Barbie camel. I can put him in a little man dress."

She laughed and Carponti's heart swelled in his chest at the sound of it.

"I'm going to hold you to that." She traced her fingers over his scalp, her body soft and warm against his erection. "I want a picture of him in a man dress in exchange for a video of the deployment boyfriend."

Her legs bumped into the back of the bed and he followed her down. Tangled between the duffle bags and his uniforms, he made love to her one last time before he got on a plane and headed to war.

3

Early December 2007
Northern Baghdad

Carponti walked up behind his platoon sergeant where he sat on his bunk in the wide- open bay that currently served as their home. Someone had put up a small electric Christmas tree in the corner of the bay. It was supposed to be cheery. Instead, it served as a daily reminder that they were stuck in the desert at Christmas. Carponti had thought about it but hadn't had the heart to take it down. It wasn't like the stupid little tree made a difference to anyone. Least of all his platoon sergeant.

Garrison was stressing the hell out lately and there wasn't much Carponti could do about it. Except try to make his boss laugh. He had an idea he couldn't resist. He fought the urge to laugh as he walked up behind Garrison. "Sarn't G, the XO is looking for you again."

Garrison turned his head and came face to face with Carponti's thumb sticking out of his pants.

"Carponti, what the hell is wrong with you!" Garrison

reached across the small space for Carponti's pillow and threw it at him. But he cracked a grin, which was more than he'd done in the last two days.

"Mission accomplished." Carponti removed his hand and buttoned his pants. "What's your problem? You need a hug?"

Garrison sighed heavily, scrubbing his hand over his face. "I'm not in the mood to deal with the XO right now."

"When are you ever? Just go find him before he shows up here and kills all the fun." Garrison lifted one eyebrow and stared at him until Carponti started to squirm. Carponti swore under his breath. Damn it, he needed to get better at lying to Garrison.

"What did you do this time?" Garrison asked.

"Nothing."

"What did you supervise this time?"

Carponti sniffed and his mouth twitched. "Nothing."

"I swear to God, Carponti," Garrison growled. "What did you see happening and not stop?"

"Did you know we have some very talented artists in our platoon?" Carponti couldn't stop himself from laughing because this was the second time someone had defaced the latrine with Lieutenant Randall's ugly mug. "One of the troops drew a new picture of the XO on one of the latrine walls. It's really a work of art. You can completely see the freckles on Randall's nose and everything." Carponti blinked innocently.

"Carponti!"

Carponti pointed over his shoulder. "The XO will be here any minute. I saw him walking into the latrine a few minutes ago."

Garrison laughed quietly, scrubbing his hands over his face. "You're not right in the head." Garrison shook his head and swore beneath his breath. "I really don't want to deal with him today. I'm liable to shove his ego down his throat the next time I see him."

"That would be terrible, just terrible," Carponti said.

"You're not going to go find him, are you?" Garrison said. His leg was bouncing again.

"I mean, if it means that much to you, I'll swing by the company ops and see if I can find out what he wants. But really, we both know I'm just saying that to make you feel better because the almighty executive officer won't deign to talk to a lowly sergeant like me."

Garrison stood and slung his weapon over his chest. "I'll go find him. Just to keep you out of First Sarn't Story's office for screwing with Randall again."

"Taking one for the team," Carponti said, slapping Garrison on the back. "I can't tell you how much that makes me want to write you a Hallmark card." He swiped his finger beneath his eye dramatically.

Garrison flipped him off as he walked out of the bay. Carponti watched him go, wishing there was more he could do to lighten the load. He would have gone to find LT Randall but it wouldn't have done a damn bit of good and everyone knew it. Randall was an epic and unforgettable douche bag and he was making everyone's life miserable.

Especially his platoon sergeant. Garrison liked to pretend everything was fine but Carponti could see the strain of this deployment. Garrison wasn't sleeping well. Hell, no one was. The Surge, as deployments went, sucked. They were getting blown up every time they rolled outside the gate; they were down a half dozen guys who'd gotten hit at various times and well, shit was just ugly.

Carponti was in the not-happy-but-sleeping group of soldiers that included him and…well, him. Everyone was wound too tight, waiting for the next influx of horrible shit to happen and fill up their rucksacks with even more bad news.

Carponti stuffed his hands in his pockets, slung his weapon across his chest, and headed out of the hundred-man bay, where his platoon was stacked up like sardines in a smelly can. The guy in the bunk next to him needed to take a goddamned shower. Carponti was willing to bet that stinky bastard hadn't bathed since the initial invasion back in '03. That was the only way to explain the smell.

Carponti adjusted his weapon and headed toward the company ops. Someone had decorated First Sarn't Story's door with bright red and silver wrapping paper. Story wasn't exactly a jolly type of fellow and he'd sworn something fierce when he'd discovered the defacement. But he'd left it up.

He didn't knock before he entered Trent's office. He walked in to find Trent flipping through a folder, his feet kicked up on his desk. Carponti studied his feet for a moment then decided against saying anything.

Trent looked like he hadn't slept in at least twenty-four hours and possibly more. There was a dirty coffee cup steaming with fresh caffeine near his knee and his hands shook from a combination of too much coffee and not enough sleep. There were dark circles beneath Trent's eyes that his glasses didn't hide.

"You look like shit," Carponti said by way of greeting.

Trent grunted, then a moment later looked up. "Huh?"

"Dude, you need to get some sleep before you pass out."

Trent frowned and tossed the file onto his desk, pushing his glasses up onto his head. "Sorry. Long night. Two more patrols got hit."

"I thought no one got hurt?" Carponti folded his arms over his chest.

"Yeah." He motioned to the wall, a large map of their sector spread across a corkboard. There were pins in clusters surrounding the soccer stadium in their area.

"All the attacks still following the same pattern?" Carponti asked.

"No; that's what's funny. They're decreasing in number," Trent said.

"This isn't exactly a bad thing," Carponti said dryly. "I'm not really a fan of getting shot at."

Trent grinned and took a sip of his coffee. "What brings you by?"

"I'm here to bitch about your executive officer. Why else would I be here?"

Trent's expression shuttered closed. "Randall's not a bad guy."

"He's a raging douche bag and he's not even an effective douche bag. Do you know he was down in the platoon bay demanding we do a weigh-in? We're running patrols every twelve hours and he wants us to do a weigh-in?"

Trent cleared his throat. "Yeah, sorry about that. That decree to conduct the weigh-in has come from on high."

"Are you fucking serious?" Carponti didn't even try to make light of the situation. "The boys are whipped and the powers that be want to do a weigh-in? I think we should be more worried about oh, I don't know, fixing broken weapons and vehicles instead of worrying about whether or not the boys are having too many Twinkies."

Trent held up his hands. "Preaching to the choir. Believe me, I argued and lost. So let's just shut up and color, okay?"

Carponti swore beneath his breath. "Fine." He glanced at his watch. He still had a few minutes before his next hit time.

"Somewhere to be?" Trent asked.

"Calling home. I've got a, um, arrangement with one of the commo kids."

"Is it something I'm better off not knowing about?" Trent asked dryly.

"Probably." Carponti shifted in his chair. "When's the last time you called home?"

Trent frowned. "Not sure."

"You need to be sure," Carponti said quietly. He stood, noticing there was a timeline on the wall behind Trent. He wanted to ask but the shadow that had fallen across Trent's face when he'd brought up calling home worried Carponti. "Speaking of which, I'm late for my own call home."

Trent had more than enough going on but something in his expression made Carponti worry that home was a bigger worry than he let on.

HE CROSSED behind the tactical operations center and pounded on the door of one of the commo shelters. The door swung open slowly, then when the kid inside saw it was Carponti, he opened it all the way.

"Hey, Sarn't C." Jackson was a chubby kid who had an addiction to Oreos and Monster energy drinks. He had a wife who ran around Killeen in a 2006 Escalade, which meant Jackson was always in short supply of cash.

Carponti was not above bribing the kid for a few minutes of alone time with Nicole. Not at all. Carponti slipped him a twenty and Jackson slid it into his pocket.

"You've got thirty minutes until the evening briefing is over. So the network is clear for you."

"You're a great American, Jackson." He patted Jackson on the back as the husky kid climbed out of the shelter.

"Make sure you lock the door, will you? I really don't want to explain to my sergeant why you're whacking it in our shelter."

"Jack, Jack, just 'cause I'm calling my wife and want some privacy doesn't mean..." Jackson shot him a baleful look as Carponti laughed and climbed into the shelter. "I won't leave any evidence."

He closed the door in Jackson's mildly horrified face and flicked the lock into place.

He turned to the terminal and pulled up Skype on the network that had no firewalls to keep him from seeing his wife on the other end.

He waited for her to pick up. Hoped she would pick up. Hoped she wasn't out on an investigation and was actually home. He was damn proud of her that she'd started the new job with the Army's Criminal Investigation Division before he'd left. She was the perfect agent for the job. She looked like someone who belonged on TV instead of investigating the Army's worst of the worst.

But she loved what she did and he wouldn't complain.

He was about to give up hope when she picked up. The screen flickered and darkened and he prayed the network would hold.

Finally, she came into view. Her hair was draped across one shoulder, her eyes sleepy. She'd turned on the bedside lamp so her face was cast in soft light and gentle shadows. God but she was beautiful.

"Damn I miss you," he whispered.

Her smile was sleepy and sexy. "Hi, baby." She leaned up and propped her head up on her palm, slowly waking up. "How are you?"

He swallowed the lump in his throat. He could tell her about the IEDs and the injuries but what was the point? He'd learned on his first deployment that telling her all the bad only made her worry. So he focused on making her smile, on calling enough to make sure she knew he was okay and not rocking in a corner somewhere crying. Sometimes, though, he just wished he could tell her how pointless it all felt. How he thought about coming home and never leaving again.

But his boys needed him and he hoped, he prayed, that she

could continue to understand that. "I'm good. Blowing shit up, just like always. How's the job?"

"I'm good. We're on a new case. I can't tell you too much about it but it's really crazy the things soldiers will do for a very small amount of money."

She was waking up now. Her eyes were bright and he felt like she was actually looking at him now. His heart swelled and a little bit of the bad in his rucksack emptied out, and was replaced with something good from thousands of miles away: his wife's smile.

"Oh, you have no idea. I just paid the commo kid twenty bucks to give me some private time in his shelter while I talk to you."

Nicole grinned, covering her mouth with a yawn. "That's just so wrong."

"But so right." He shifted in the seat, leaning a little closer to the screen, wishing he could crawl into it and end up in their bed. "So I got your last letter."

The first time he'd deployed had been just this side of hell but his wife had figured out how to make it better. He'd been in a big fight in Najaf and had been damn near dead on his feet when the mail had come. And in it had been the first dirty letter she'd ever written him. For a moment, just a few, the war had fallen away as he'd slipped into the fantasy she'd written him. He'd slept like a baby that night and dreamt about his wife and her touch instead of the chaos and smoke of the war.

So it had become a deployment ritual for them. A way to stay connected through the distance and the silence that often came with deployments.

Her smile warmed. "Yeah? Did you like it?"

"Oh yes. It was inspiring." Carponti shifted to ease the tension in his pants.

I want to feel your lips on my sweet, swollen...

He sucked in a deep breath. His cock stiffened.

"Yeah?" Her hand drifted down her throat, sliding slowly off camera. "Which part did you like the best?"

Carponti cleared his throat, wishing he could see where her fingers went. Wishing they were his instead. "The part where you pulled my underwear off with your teeth."

She laughed but he kept thinking about the hand that had disappeared, wishing he could see where it had gone. The way her chest moved as her breath quickened. "What are you doing?" he whispered.

"Touching myself." Her voice was thick, sultry.

Carponti stopped breathing as all the blood rushed to his cock and it strained against his uniform pants. "Holy crap, warn a guy, will you?"

Her laugh was throaty. Sensual and sleepy mixed together. "Want to know where?"

He cleared his throat again. "Where?"

"Say it," she whispered. "I want to hear you ask me."

"Where are you touching yourself?" He flicked open his uniform pants, freeing his cock, and thanked the powers that be that Jackson kept paper towels and hand sanitizer in his shelter. It wasn't exactly the most romantic setting in the world but he'd take whatever time with his wife he could get. God but he missed her.

He closed his eyes as he fisted his cock, waiting for her answer. "Between my legs. I'm wet. Thinking about you gets me so wet, Vic."

He swallowed, his throat dry as he slid his hand over his erection, wishing it were her hand, her touch.

"Tell me what to do?"

"Slide a finger inside yourself," he whispered when he could remember how to talk.

They didn't get to do this often enough. Hell, he'd do it every night if he could but he didn't like waking her up. Right then, though, with her words wrapping around him, he could almost close his eyes and pretend he was home.

"I want you inside me, Vic." Her voice was a whimper. A plea in the middle of the night that spanned the gulf between them and brought him home, just for a moment. "I want you here."

Her voice broke but she covered it quickly. "I want you here, I want you filling me, deep. Fast." She gasped. "Hard."

"Finish," he whispered, urging his wife to her own climax before he reached his own. "Stroke yourself. Pretend it's my lips sucking on you."

She whimpered again, and her back arched off the bed. She shivered and bit her bottom lip, a smile spreading across her face as she came. He gripped his cock tight as his orgasm ripped through him, tearing out a piece of his heart as he came hard and deep.

"I needed that," she whispered. "I miss you."

"I miss you, too." He licked his top lip, not wanting to get off the computer but knowing she needed to sleep. He smiled at her as he cleaned himself up. "I love it when you do that for me," he said quietly.

She shifted and he could see the swell of her breasts against the tank top she slept in. "It makes me miss you more," she said.

He swallowed, the glow from his orgasm fading as reality crept back in. "I miss you," he said suddenly. He felt the creeping presence of the clock, ticking down, reminding him that he had to go before he got caught. He needed these moments with Nicole more than she knew. "Stay safe at work?"

"I will. I have a new partner and a new case. I've been working out of Waco a lot." Carponti frowned. "What's in Waco?"

"Can't tell you over a nonsecure line but it's an interesting case, that's for sure."

"Be careful? You're not allowed to get shot or anything. I can't promise I won't end up in jail without you in my life."

"It's not like that." She grinned and covered her mouth with her hand as she yawned. "Have you heard anything more about whether you get to come home in a couple weeks?"

Carponti swallowed hard. "I'm trying. Christmas is a hard time to try and get out of theater."

He wished he didn't see the disappointment flicker over her face. "I know you are."

She'd lost her father last year and while her dad had never really liked Carponti, his loss had really done a number on Nicole. Her mom? Her mom was traveling the world and drowning her sorrows in the life of a luxury travel agent to the stars, which meant Nicole would be alone.

Christmas was important to her and Carponti had missed more than he'd been there for. He needed to be there for her this year. If the damn war would cooperate.

"I'll talk to Garrison about it again. See where I am on the list. I'll e-mail you what I find out."

She smiled and it warmed her eyes. Damn it, he wished he was home, curled around her body. Feeling her breathe. He missed her so badly it hurt.

His watch beeped as the timer went off. "I've got to go."

"Call me again when you can?" she asked.

"I will. I love you," he said.

"I love you. Be safe, okay?"

He grinned. "Of course. And don't think I've forgotten about the video promise. I'm still waiting."

Across the miles, she flushed. "I'm working up the courage."

"Work harder. At this rate, the war will be over before you send me that video. It'll be the highlight of my tour."

She laughed and he wanted to kiss her. He loved making her laugh. God but he missed her. "I'll call soon, okay?"

She nodded. "I love you."

"You, too, babe."

He sat in the silence after the connection died, putting all the happiness from a few moments alone with his wife back in its place, a place the war couldn't touch. He loved her, more than he could ever tell her.

Because when he stepped out of that commo shelter, the war would be back to the top of the list of shit he was focused on.

4

Nicole walked into Target and felt the festive cheer of the holidays. Beside her, Laura scolded her son for running off for the seventeenth time. Ethan—who looked like a miniature Trent—was completely contrite for all of about six seconds before he was lured away by the brightly colored Christmas decorations on yet another end cap. Bright red sales signs advertised Christmas specials and silver tinsel lined the shelves. Of course, it wasn't really Christmas without snow in Nicole's opinion, but they'd lived in Texas for a couple of years now and somehow, she'd gotten used to Christmas in the South.

"I think I'm going to have to adopt this early shopping plan more often," Nicole said. "Even if this is a ridiculous hour to be out of bed on a Saturday morning."

Laura handed Emma a pen and notebook so she could doodle while she sat in the cart's basket. "It's the only way I can manage. All the crowds drive me crazy."

"I can understand that. I can't beat my husband out of the house on payday in Killeen." She pulled out the list of stuff she needed for Vic and tucked her hair behind one ear. This would be the last package she could send him if she wanted him to get it before Christmas. In case he might not get to come home, she still wanted him to have something to open on Christmas. "Does Trent have anything specific he needs?"

Laura sighed. "I wouldn't know because he hasn't called me."

She mumbled the words so that her kids couldn't hear but Nicole didn't miss the worry beneath the bitterness in her voice. She placed her hand on Laura's shoulder. "I'm sure he's just busy," Nicole said quietly.

"When's the last time Vic called you?" Laura said.

"This morning," Nicole admitted.

"And Vic doesn't have a phone on his desk." She blinked rapidly. "I thought I could wait for him to get whatever he's running from out of his system." She bit her lip. "I just don't know how much more I've got in me."

Laura ducked down the office supply aisle and Nicole headed toward the junk food section, giving her friend a moment to collect herself while she gathered junk food and other distractions for Vic. He'd developed a recent addiction to almonds for some reason, so she dropped a couple of tubs of trail mix and mixed nuts into the cart.

For a man who ate like hell, he was an amazing physical specimen. He never went to the gym but his body was toned and tight from long hours on his feet. Unlike Nicole, who had to hit the gym every day or else.

She turned down the Christmas aisle and bit back a twinge of sadness. God but she hoped he made it home. She wasn't sure she could do Christmas alone. The last couple of times he'd been gone for Christmas, she'd gone home to see her dad. But her dad had left her last year. He'd gotten sick and within four weeks he was gone. His death had stunned her. And Vic? Vic had been her rock during the whole fiasco of sorting her father's affairs, while her mother tried to take everything he had.

She blinked rapidly and felt her phone vibrate in her purse. She dove for it, digging furiously, hoping it was Vic.

It wasn't. It was work. Nicole let it go to voice mail. She wasn't in the mood to talk shop.

Laura found her meandering near the Christmas aisle. Ethan, apparently, had not gotten the message about running off and so was constrained in the shopping cart with a coloring book. Laura looked much happier, despite pushing a heavier cart.

"So, I've got this Christmas party next week for the families and two of my key volunteers decided to go into labor and have babies. I'm shorthanded. Can I please, please, please beg you to help me manage this chaos?"

As a rule, Nicole tried to avoid the Family Readiness Group. It was great for spouses who needed help and guidance and mentorship, but Nicole always felt out of place. Not like she was better than everyone else, but she always felt like she didn't belong when some of the wives would start talking about Pampered Chef or arts and crafts and Nicole couldn't stop thinking about her latest case at work. She wasn't the only spouse who worked but she was the only one in law enforcement.

But this was Laura and she knew Laura was going through her own bad stuff right now with her husband. Nicole had meant to ask Vic if there was anything going on with Trent but she'd forgotten when he'd called. She blamed him for the distraction. She smiled. His call had been a great distraction.

"I guess," Nicole said with a dramatic sigh. "What do you need me to do?"

"Help with the food?"

Nicole arched one eyebrow. "You realize I burn water, right?"

"You can order it. I've got the FRG checkbook." Laura looked relieved and Nicole was glad she could say yes. If only to help her friend.

"So let me buy you coffee and you can talk me through everything you need me to do." Nicole stopped in front of a small Christmas gnome. It had a bushy red beard and bright cheeks. There was a twinkle of mischief in his eyes. Her throat tightened and she swallowed quickly, missing her husband badly.

"Do you know of a coffee shop that has a play area for two small children?"

"No, but that is an amazing idea for some entrepreneurial soul," Nicole said. "McDonalds?"

"Done." Laura sighed. "Thank you so much, hon."

"No problem. Let me finish getting stuff for Vic? I want to get it in the mail this weekend."

"Sure. I've got to pick up a few more things then I'll meet you there."

Nicole nodded as her friend wandered off again in search of the things on her own list. Nicole studied the gnome with the bright red beard.

He was on sale this week. She held him in her hands, wondering what would become of the little fella if she sent him to her husband. She was tempted to keep him here. Put him on the fireplace.

She still had to decorate the house.

Her eyes burned and she breathed deeply to keep the sadness at bay. She wasn't quite ready to do that alone. Not yet. Maybe tomorrow she'd climb into the attic and get the decorations down. She put the little gnome back on the shelf and finished picking up stuff for her husband.

∽

The door to the first sergeant's office slammed as Garrison stepped into the small hallway. Carponti flinched but didn't move from where he stood at parade rest, waiting for the ass chewing of a century.

Lieutenant Randall apparently had no sense of humor.

He dared to glance at Garrison, who stood for a moment in the silence that echoed after the slamming door. "Well, that was fun," he said. "Let's go."

Carponti frowned and glanced back at the first sergeant's festive door. "He doesn't want to see me?"

"Oh he does," Garrison remarked. "But we should really get going before he changes his mind."

Carponti grinned as he followed the big platoon sergeant out of the company ops. "That's a hell of a Jedi mind trick you've got going there. I'm impressed."

"You should be," Garrison said roughly. "He threatened to have you busted all the way back to private."

"He can't prove it was me. I have no artistic talent whatsoever." Carponti grinned. "But you have to admit, the mural on the latrine wall is some really great artwork."

Garrison shot him a long-suffering look. "So great that unless I send the kid who drew it to brigade to work on the t-wall mural, both of our asses are going to be explaining things to the sergeant major."

"I am confident that Tigger will be happy to volunteer his talents to leaving our mark on the Iraqi t-walls." It was tradition that whenever a new unit arrived in theater, they painted their unit crest on a t-wall or jersey barrier.

Garrison sighed heavily. "Look, just stop getting in trouble for a while? We're heading out on patrol and when we get back, I would really like to go to sleep instead of have to bail your ass out of a sling again."

"But you love me so you'll do it," Carponti said.

"I love that you're a fucking machine in combat and I can

always count on you," Garrison said. He paused. "And you're damn funny, too."

Carponti sniffed dramatically. "You really should write Hallmark cards."

Garrison grinned. "Shut up and get everyone ready. We're leaving on patrol in two hours and I want everyone's head in the game. Our high value targets are holed up near the soccer stadium. Maybe if we get these guys, we can get some intel on why the attack patterns are dropping."

"The soccer stadium that keeps getting blown up? Lovely." Carponti sobered. "You'd think we wouldn't be complaining about this. Fewer attacks are a good thing, last time I checked."

Garrison shot him a sidelong look as they walked through the maze of jersey barriers back toward the platoon bay. "Normally I'd agree with you but there's such a sharp drop-off that Trent thinks there's another reason. Might be building for a massive attack or something. He's worried about the changing pattern."

Carponti grunted. "He should be worried about calling his wife."

"Yeah." Garrison was quiet for a long moment. "I guess he figures Laura will always wait for him. She's waited this long."

"No woman can wait that long." Carponti drummed his hands on the butt of his rifle. "Hell, I call my wife as much as I can and I'm still worried she'll leave me for her deployment boyfriend. Or worse, a real boyfriend."

Garrison slapped him on the shoulder. "Nicole is the one woman on the planet with a sense of humor enough to match yours. She'll never leave you."

"From your lips to heaven's ears," Carponti said.

He watched Garrison walk off. He hoped that maybe after they got back, Garrison could get some sleep. Carponti buried the niggling worry that taunted him, whispering on the back of his neck. He headed off to start rounding everyone up, wishing he had time to call his wife before they headed out on patrol.

He wanted to hear her voice.

Needed to.

She was his personal good luck charm. As long as she was there in the world, things would be okay.

5

Nicole's phone vibrated next to her bed, dragging her out of her fitful sleep. She blinked and glanced at the alarm clock. Three in the morning. She groped for the phone and saw a mass text message from Laura, sent to everyone on the Family Readiness Group roster.

We have information about an attack. There are injuries but no casualties. Please stay off social networks until we have confirmation of who has been hurt. I will do my best to keep everyone informed.

Nicole sat up, instantly awake, and wiggled the mouse on her computer. Once upon a time, she would have thought it was strange sleeping with a laptop next to her bed, but now? Now it was an easy way for Vic to call her, so she left Skype logged in.

But tonight, her inbox was empty. Nicole swallowed the fear and dialed Laura's number. "Hey," Laura said.

"You don't sound like you've been to sleep."

"I haven't." Laura sounded exhausted.

"How can I help?"

Laura sighed quietly. "You can't. There's nothing we can do right now but wait for more information. And even then, it'll take time for the casualties to be sent from Germany to here. My inbox is going nuts right now."

"That's understandable." Nicole rubbed her eyes. "We're all scared."

"Yeah," Laura admitted. "Me, too."

"Still no word from Trent?" God but Nicole's heart broke for Laura. Her husband was still in silent mode and Laura? Laura's patience was reaching a breaking point. She'd never seen her friend more upset.

"No."

Nicole clicked refresh on her inbox, wishing an e-mail would magically appear and tell her that Vic was okay. She fought the blind panic at his silence.

"I'm sorry," she said to Laura. "I'm so sorry."

Laura said nothing for a moment and Nicole was almost positive her friend was biting back tears. "Me, too. Listen, I've got to get some sleep. Can I call you if I need help?"

"Yeah. Absolutely."

The line went dead and Nicole sat there for a long moment, clicking refresh on her inbox. Just a couple more times. She looked down at the phone and flicked the vibrate off. If Vic called, she wanted to hear it.

She curled up onto her side, staring at the blinking cursor on her computer screen. Her eyes burned, but the fear was too raw, too real. She blinked the tears back, trying her damnedest to keep the ragged fear from breaking free. She stared at the empty inbox as her vision blurred. And clicked refresh again and again as the tears spilled down her cheeks. Just once more before she gave up and tried to go back to sleep.

CARPONTI SAT NEXT to Garrison's bed in the open bay of the combat hospital. The hospital was eerily quiet, the silence smothering and oppressive. The chaos and noise and static that had been buzzing around the hospital bed was gone now, leaving nothing but the septic silence. His ribs ached and his chest throbbed but he wasn't in the hospital for his own—comparatively minor—injuries.

They'd gotten blown up. They'd captured their high value target, but the cost? The cost had been really fucking high. The soccer field had been blown all to hell and had taken out Garrison and damn near taken Carponti out, too. His ribs hurt where that rocket had knocked him off the truck. Thank God and Army contractors for body armor that worked. And for guys with shitty bomb-making skills.

There was a tube down Garrison's throat and they were getting ready to move him to the airfield for his flight to Germany. Because the rest of him was pretty banged up. He lowered his head to the bed again. His throat wasn't working right and it was hard to breathe. He blamed his bruised ribs. Couldn't be the raw sadness threatening to overwhelm him. Nope, couldn't be that.

Carponti tried to talk but every time he opened his mouth, his throat closed off again.

There was blood on the floor. They hadn't gotten around to cleaning yet.

The chaos was gone now but for Carponti, the only thing he heard was the steady, rhythmic beep of the heart monitor over the black tattoos on Garrison's chest.

"So listen," Carponti said. "When you wake up—" He cleared his throat roughly. "When you wake up," he tried again. His voice broke but he kept talking because otherwise, he was going to sob like a fucking baby. He scrubbed both hands over his face. He reached for Garrison's hand. The one that hadn't gotten all blown half to hell along with the rest of him. It was warm and listless. Missing the strength and courage of the man Carponti looked up to and wanted to be when he grew up.

"Listen, you're going on a flight. And you're gonna wake up at some point. Be nice to the nurses. 'Cause they're going to take care of your grumpy old ass until you get better. And you need to hurry the hell up and get healthy because you know who they're bringing in to replace you? That asshole Iaconelli from battalion." He dropped his head to his hand where it covered Garrison's. They hadn't waited a day to bring that fucking guy down to the platoon, still reeling from the complex attack that had taken out their fearless platoon sergeant and a couple of the other guys. "So you need to get back here really soon because he's liable to throw my ass out of the Army."

"Sergeant?"

Carponti pinched his eyes before looking up. There was a major wearing scrubs at the end of the bed. She looked like she hadn't slept in about three weeks but there was a sharpness in her eyes. This was a familiar routine for her. Carponti wondered how the hell she—how any of them—kept going when all they had around them were the broken and the bleeding.

She'd done this too many times to be upset by another mangled GI. But Carponti would never get used to it.

Not this.

"We're getting ready to go." She took a step closer and put her hand on Carponti's shoulder.

It took everything he had to keep from shattering from that single, human gesture. He swallowed a couple of times before he could speak. "So you're not going to chop off any body parts while he's unconscious or anything?"

She smiled gently. "We hope not."

Carponti snorted quietly. "That wasn't really a helpful answer." He tried to offer up a smart-ass grin and failed. "He'll be okay, right?" he managed.

"We'll do our best." Her hand squeezed his shoulder gently. "It's time for you to go."

He nodded and stood. He patted Garrison's hand awkwardly. "Don't die, all right, old man? 'Cause there's no telling the amount of trouble I can get into without your old ass keeping me in check."

He walked out then, before his voice broke any more.

Couldn't let the boys see him cry. They had another mission in twelve hours. So he stuffed all the emotion down and bolted it closed.

He'd face that fear and sadness and everything else some other time. Another time when hopefully there would be lots of booze to ease some of the pain. But for now? Now he stuffed it down and went back to work.

Because that's what Garrison would expect him to do.

"SERGEANT CARPONTI!"

Carponti kept walking, ignoring the voice of that hell-spawned lieutenant. He wasn't in the mood to deal with LT Randall on a good day and today was definitely not a good day.

"Sergeant, I'm talking to you!"

Carponti's temper snapped and he rounded on the XO. "What the fuck do you want, LT?"

"Watch your fucking mouth," Randall snapped.

Carponti sighed dramatically. "You weren't hugged enough as a child, were you?"

"I'm not in the mood for your smart mouth, sergeant."

"And I'm not in the mood for yours."

Randall stepped into his face. "Your buddy Garrison isn't around to protect you now. I'm going to have your ass before this deployment is over."

Carponti smirked. "You can't do anything to my ass. That's a violation of Don't Ask Don't Tell."

"You think you're so funny."

"I know I'm funny. You, on the other hand, have no such redeeming quality." He patted the XO's chest. "What the fuck do you want? I've got a squad of men waiting for information on their platoon sergeant, who just got blown all to shit. Oh, but you wouldn't care about that because you don't know the meaning of the word 'care'."

"I need your paperwork on the sensitive items report."

Carponti swore and stalked off.

"I wasn't done talking to you, sergeant." Randall grabbed his arm.

"I'm done talking to you, LT. Go find my platoon leader for that officer bullshit." Carponti rounded on him, yanking his arm free. "And if you put your hands on me again, I'm going to break your fucking hand."

He stalked off, needing to get away from the XO before he really did something stupid. Because as much as he hated LT Randall, the bastard was right about one thing: Garrison had kept Carponti out of a ton of trouble. If Randall wanted to make an example out of Carponti, now was a prime opportunity.

He really didn't want to call home and tell his wife he'd gotten busted. Maybe he should start watching his mouth.

He grinned bitterly and swiped at his eyes.

Yeah right.

"Everyone tracking?" Carponti straightened from where he'd been leaning over the sand table and looked around at his boys.

Half of them looked dead on their feet. The other half looked shell-shocked from the attack two days ago. And the one after that. And the one after that. Things hadn't stopped since Garrison had gotten hit. Somehow, they just seemed worse without him.

Their company had endured three more attacks but no more serious injuries. No one was taking things well but in Carponti's platoon, everyone was acting like Garrison had died and he hadn't. There was no way he could take the guys out on the road like this. No one had their head in the game.

Goddamn it.

"All right, look. We had a bad mission but Sarn't G is going to be all right so y'all need to stop moping like a bunch of crybabies." He folded his arms over his chest. "Besides, he's going to be so pissed off when he wakes up. He's got this tube in his dick like, this long." He held his hands shoulder-width apart. "I mean, it's ridiculous."

"How the hell do you know?" Wilks asked.

Carponti forced himself to grin like it was just another day. "Because I drew a smiley face on it before he left."

"Bullshit." This from a skinny kid they called Tigger because he bounced when he played whatever video game they'd stolen from the commo geeks. Tigger was six and a half feet tall and weighed a buck fifty soaking wet but he had some pretty amazing porta pottie artist skills. Not that Carponti was going to tell anyone that. He'd take that shit to his grave before he threw Tigger under the bus for drawing that picture of Randall doing something untoward with a goat.

Carponti placed his palm over his heart. "Hand to God. He's going to get an awesome Christmas present when he wakes up in Germany or the States or wherever they ship his old ass."

Chuckles scattered through the group and Carponti figured it was best not to push his luck. "Everyone rack out. No computers or shit. Just get some fucking sleep. We're going to be busy as hell tomorrow and I don't want Tigger falling asleep in the turret again."

Tigger flipped him off. "One time and I'll never hear the end of it."

Carponti blew him a kiss. "Go to bed, sweetheart. If it gets cold, I'll come snoodle with you."

He waited until everyone was racked out before killing the lights. The hundred-man bay descended into darkness, lit only by the emergency exit lights near the doors and the occasional flashlight as someone ignored the directive to go to sleep. Carponti couldn't summon the energy to care about the few rebels.

"You're not crashing, Sarn't C?" Wilks's bunk was at the foot of Carponti's.

"Nah. I gotta go find LT Miller and the new platoon sergeant and some other shit." Wilks didn't leave. Carponti sat up. "What's wrong?"

Wilks swallowed hard a couple of times. His Adam's apple bobbed in his throat. "Sarn't G's going to be okay, right?"

"Yeah, man. I saw him. He's gonna be fine. Now go the fuck to sleep." The emotions he'd tried to lock down were surfacing, threatening to break free. If the boys saw him fall apart, there was no telling the chaos that would unleash.

So he'd lied. And now he needed to get the hell away from all of them because he was this close to losing his shit completely.

Carponti stalked away from the bay, away from his boys who were all racked out, sleeping off the adrenaline from the constant chaos.

He didn't care where, he didn't know where, he just needed to get away.

Garrison was gone. Jesus Christ, putting Garrison on that MEDEVAC was the most godawful thing he'd ever done.

He slammed back against the nearest barrier, sliding down the concrete. He ground the heels of his hands into his eyes, fighting the grief that ripped through him, tearing and slashing and cutting.

His ass collided with the ground and he pulled his knees to

his chest and finally let the grief come, ignoring the pain in his ribs. He wept bitterly for his friend, his mentor, his *brother*. The tears tore out of him, ragged and raw and bitter.

He hadn't been able to get an update on Garrison. Nothing from that fuckwad lieutenant Randall, nothing from the CO. Trent had been more busted up than Carponti at Garrison's condition.

For the first time he could remember, Carponti had no jokes, no smart-ass comments. He'd gotten his boys racked out like Garrison would have expected him to do.

And now this? Garrison would whip his ass if he saw Carponti fall apart like a crybaby in some deserted sector of the base where only the camel spiders congregated. But he couldn't stop. Jesus, he couldn't stop.

He didn't know how long it was before the tears stopped coming. He sat there as the moon slid over the top of the barrier and illuminated the smoke and the dust swirling beneath the stars. Distant explosions echoed in the night.

He should get up.

He should head back. He wanted to call his wife but the words he needed were just...they were gone. He had nothing. No way to tell her what had happened. It was better that she didn't know anyway. She'd worry about him and the last thing she needed to do was worry about him.

He'd call her soon. Whenever he felt like he could bullshit his way through a conversation without telling her everything that had happened. He wanted to call her and just listen to her voice, telling him about something at work or griping about the line at the grocery store. God, he'd give anything to go grocery shopping with her. Something so simple.

He just wanted time with his wife. Just a few minutes alone, listening to her talk. Feeling her breathe on his chest. He'd been gone so much.

He'd call her. Soon. But not today. Because as badly as he

needed to hear her voice, she'd hear the sadness in his and she'd worry. He didn't want her to worry. He was terrible at lying to her. Every time he tried to surprise her with flowers or a date night, she caught him.

He dragged his hands over his face. His eyes felt raw and swollen.

He needed to get back. To find LT Miller and check on him. Check on Trent. To *do* something. Anything other than sit there sobbing.

But instead, he sat there, staring up at the stars. He wasn't a praying man. But he sat there, looking at the night sky, unable to think of anything except how tore up Garrison had looked in that hospital bed. A whispered plea crossed his lips.

"Please, let him be okay." His voice broke. His eyes burned.

And after a while, when he was empty and raw, he wiped his eyes, brushed off his pants, and went back to work.

NICOLE STEPPED BACK and looked at the tree. It tipped slightly at the top but for the most part, it was straight. She reached for her cell phone in the breast pocket of her husband's dress shirt and checked it for the umpteenth time that morning. It wasn't on vibrate. Vic just hadn't called. She slipped the phone back into her pocket and studied the tree.

She didn't think she was going to be able to make it any straighter than it already was. Folding her arms over her chest, she simply stood there for a moment and tried to find the courage to climb into the attic and pull down the decorations.

She sighed hard and reached for the glass of wine she'd poured herself before dragging the tree in off the roof of her husband's truck and into the living room. The scent of fresh pine needles filled the air.

She hadn't gotten a dreaded phone call from Laura, either,

which meant that Vic was probably busy, not hurt. She could console herself with that. She didn't really have a choice. The wine was sharp and crisp across her tongue, sliding smooth and easy down her throat.

Her laptop was on the kitchen table. No new e-mails from Vic the last fifteen times she'd checked it. She knew he was okay. But she still wanted to hear it in his voice. Something.

But no matter how many times he'd deployed, she'd never been able to explain to him how hard it was to wait for news. She always worried about sounding like a nag. Like he was over there, dodging roadside bombs and she was bitching at him about a phone call. She knew all she was asking for was a phone call but, sometimes? It felt like she was asking too much.

She took another look at the slightly tippy tree and took another drink of her wine. The silence from her husband made her miss him; that was all. She hadn't had a good laugh in, well, forever.

She padded over to her inbox, looking for the last note from Vic.

Sorry I haven't called much. Been insane over here. I'm fine. We're all fine. Just busy. Will call as soon as I can.

I love you

PS still waiting for that video you promised.

She smiled. The note was from a week ago. She looked at the box on her kitchen table, filled with junk food and five-dollar previously viewed movies.

She could make him a video, right? It wasn't much different from having a glass of wine and writing him a dirty letter.

She swallowed the rest of her wine even as her blood warmed at the thought of touching herself for him. She thought of how surprised he'd be—and how thrilled. She smiled.

She was going to need more to drink.

6

"Why the fuck aren't your optics tied down to your weapon, soldier?" Carponti looked up as Tigger attempted to stand up straight while the new platoon sergeant, Sergeant First Class Iaconelli ripped him a new asshole.

Carponti tossed down what he was doing and strolled over.

"What's the problem here, Sarn't Ike?" Carponti said, and stepped between him and Tigger. He hated the nickname Ike, which was why Carponti made every effort to call him that.

It must have looked a little strange having a five-foot-ten ginger kid step between two men who were easily six feet tall but, then again, Carponti wasn't exactly counting on having to get into a fight.

But he damn sure wasn't going to sit there and let Iaconelli treat Garrison's boys like they were fucking morons, either.

"Mind your own business, sergeant," Iaconelli snapped.

Carponti tipped his chin. "Tigger is in my squad, ergo this is my business, *sergeant*. So I say again, what seems to be the problem?"

Iaconelli glared down at him and Carponti couldn't miss

the fact that his eyes were rimmed with red. Either Iaconelli wasn't a big sleeper or there was something else wrong.

"His optics aren't tied down."

Carponti looked over his shoulder at Tigger's weapon. "They're tied down just fine."

"No they're not. It's not done like this." Iaconelli held up his weapon, which had some intricate mixture of five-fifty cord and hundred mile an hour tape securing his optics to his weapon. "This is how we do it in my old platoon."

"Well," and Carponti turned and held up Tigger's weapon, "this is how we do it in Garrison's platoon."

"This isn't Garrison's platoon anymore," Iaconelli snapped.

Carponti handed Tigger back his weapon. "If you have a new standard, tell us. Don't come in here and get your panties in a twist and start yelling. That's not how we do things here."

Iaconelli looked shocked that a junior ranking sergeant would be so openly defiant but then again, Carponti didn't actually give a shit. Maybe someday his mouth would get him in trouble but right then, with the guys still reeling from losing Garrison, the last thing he was going to let the new guy do was become another LT Randall. Fuck that.

"You'll do things the way I say we'll do things. This is the Army, not a democracy."

Carponti smiled coolly. "Were you potty trained at gunpoint?" He held open his arms. "Come here, big guy, let me give you a hug."

"If you fucking touch me..." Iaconelli stuck his finger in Carponti's face and Carponti seriously considered planting a kiss on the tip of it. He wondered if Iaconelli would punch him and how much it would hurt. Considering Iaconelli was a fucking giant who spent way too much time in the gym, Carponti would probably lose a couple of teeth before it was all said and done. "Fix the goddamned optics," Iaconelli snapped.

Carponti offered a mock salute. "Yes, master."

"Carponti..." Iaconelli's word was a growled warning. Carponti couldn't have cared less as Iaconelli stomped off.

He turned back to the platoon, who looked somewhere between amused and slightly horrified. "You heard him, ladies. Let's fix the optics so Uncle Ike doesn't have a reason to yell."

Carponti set the guys to work taping down their optics and went back to work on his own project. He wanted to take a few minutes to go see if Jackson would let him call home but lately, the network had been sucking and Jackson had been too busy to let Carponti steal a few minutes.

He hoped Nicole would understand. Goddamn he missed her.

"What are you doing?"

"Oh goody, you're back." Carponti looked up into Iaconelli's face and kept his own expression as innocent as he could. It was an expression Carponti had perfected at the age of six. "I'm sewing; what's it look like?"

"You're sewing?" Iaconelli's hands shook as he folded them across his chest.

"Yep." Carponti could have screwed with him about his hands shaking. He could have asked when was the last time the mean son of a bitch had had a drink.

But he did none of those things. Iaconelli had come on board yesterday, two days after Garrison had gotten sent back to Germany. Carponti had finally gotten the most useless status update ever from Captain Davila: They had no flipping idea how long Garrison was going to be there before he'd get shipped back to the States.

So Iaconelli, the poster boy for interpersonal hostility, was in charge. And to say that Carponti and Iaconelli had differing opinions on things...well, there was a better chance of peace in the Middle East than Iaconelli and Carponti getting along.

He hadn't meant to get into a pissing contest with Iaconelli right off the bat but well, things just kind of happened that way.

Until the incident a few minutes ago, Carponti had bitten his tongue because he hadn't felt like being the leader of the insurgency. But he drew a line when someone screwed with his men.

He had other things to worry about. He sat there and sewed the little strip of fabric. It centered him. Reminded him that there was still something good out in the world—his wife.

He hadn't called home in a few days. Every time he thought about it, he felt empty. Cold. He wanted to hear Nicole's voice but he didn't want to talk.

He didn't know what to say. So he said nothing. Maybe he'd still get out of there in time to make it back to Texas for Christmas. He tried to ignore the shadow of Iaconelli standing over him. He wasn't sure he could leave the guys alone with him right now. Carponti didn't trust him and as badly as he needed to be home with Nicole for her first Christmas without her dad, he wasn't sure he could live with himself if something happened to the guys while he was gone.

He couldn't tell her that, though. She'd loved him through choosing the Army so many times, this was the one time she needed him to choose her. He needed to be there for her this Christmas. Less than two weeks away. He could see her soon.

He was holding on to that hope like a lifeline.

"Yes, I'm sewing. Everyone has a hobby. Take Jax over there. He's playing World of Warcraft with a girl in Scandinavia. At least that's what 'she' told him. I suspect it's some bored fat slob on another base somewhere here in Iraq but you can't tell him that. He swears they're getting married."

Iaconelli's face flushed and Carponti could see him trying really hard not to lose his temper. "You're sewing," Iaconelli repeated.

Carponti lifted both eyebrows. "You seem to be hung up on this fact but the simple fact is that yes, I am sewing."

It was almost comical watching the myriad of emotions

flash across Iaconelli's face as he tried to find some kind of cogent response. "Have you been to the shrink lately?"

"Clean bill of health after my last explosion."

"Obviously someone missed something if you're sewing," Iaconelli snarled. "Okay, smart-ass, I give up. Why are you sewing?"

"It's for my wife." Carponti grinned in pure innocence. He didn't need to tell Iaconelli what he was sewing. "So she'll send me a dirty video."

Iaconelli's expression twisted into some form of modified horror. For a man who had been on the initial run to Baghdad, that was saying a lot. Carponti smiled and blinked.

Iaconelli held up one hand when Carponti opened his mouth to speak. "Just. Stop."

"What?"

"Not another word. Put the goddamned cross stitch away and get ready to go to a mission brief."

"Do I have time to go call my wife? It's almost Christmas and I want to see if I can get her to talk dirty to me." Iaconelli thought he was kidding. Carponti didn't need to correct him.

He was enjoying Iaconelli's horrified reaction a lot. It had probably been a long time since someone didn't cower at the big platoon sergeant's feet.

Iaconelli started to argue but relented. "I don't give a shit but if I find you whacking off anywhere near my bunk, I'm cutting your dick off."

Carponti smiled. "I love you, too, Sarn't Ike."

"Carponti, I'm not fucking kidding." He looked ready to blow a gasket. Or maybe have a heart attack; Carponti wasn't really sure. Iaconelli choked and turned a slightly different shade of purple. Which was really hard considering his skin was already darker from being in the constant sunshine. It might be almost Christmas but it was still hot as balls and sunny as hell during the day. The nights?

The nights, he froze his ass off. He'd tried to crawl into Iaconelli's bunk the other night— with his sleeping bag—and Iaconelli had threatened to kill him. There was nothing wrong with grown men snuggling to keep warm but apparently Iaconelli would rather freeze than partake of body heat. About five of them had piled into the middle of the bay to keep warm because they hadn't been given enough fuel and well, when the gas ran out, so did the generators that powered the heat in their bay.

So they'd frozen together. And Iaconelli, being the charming SOB that he was, had stayed in his own cot, missing out on a prime bonding moment with his new platoon.

Sarn't Iaconelli had not seen the humor in the situation.

Carponti continued to sew. There was something about the repetition of the needle. He could see why women did this sort of thing. Not that he was going to take up fashion design or anything. He glanced up at Iaconelli. "Did the XO find you?"

Iaconelli sighed heavily. The fact that Lieutenant Jason Randall was a raging asshat was the single point of agreement between the two of them. And neither one of them was about to admit it.

"No. I'm avoiding him. That little fuckweasel can kiss my ass." He zeroed in on Carponti's sewing. "And you need to put that shit away." Carponti could have sworn he heard Iaconelli mutter *It's creeping me out* but that couldn't be right.

Silence hung on between them for a long moment. Carponti didn't like Iaconelli because he wasn't Garrison. Iaconelli didn't like Carponti because he wasn't properly respectful. Carponti thought it wise not to mention that he'd failed basic customs and courtesies in infantry school. Things could be worse.

They could have Randall as the platoon leader. It was bad enough trying to ignore him as the executive officer. For the life of him, Carponti couldn't figure out why Trent hadn't fired

Randall's sorry ass yet, but that was officer business and Carponti tried to stay far, far away from that stuff. So things weren't as bad as they could be. It could be worse but Carponti wasn't in the mood to test the fates.

"Yeah, well, if you don't go find him, then the rest of us are going to have to suffer through him coming in here and honestly? LT Randall smells funny." He looked up at Iaconelli with his best innocent expression. "So would you please go find out what he's complaining about so we don't have to smell him?"

Iaconelli growled and stomped out of the tent, mumbling something about missing his old platoon and whiny little bastards. Carponti grinned and tucked the little stitch of cloth in his pocket and headed across the FOB to the commo shelter and hopefully, a call to his wife, then figured he'd stop by the company ops and check on Trent on his way.

The closer Christmas came, the more depressing the sad little decorations looked. Someone had decorated the counter in the company ops now and there was quiet Christmas music playing as Carponti stepped into the dusty office.

Carponti froze in the doorway.

Lieutenant Randall stood far too close to the only female in the company, PFC Adorno.

Carponti cleared his throat and strolled in, noting the way Randall jumped back. "I thought you worked in the motorpool," he said to Adorno.

She flushed and tucked her cropped dirty blond hair back behind one ear. "I did. I've been pulled up to work in the company."

Carponti frowned, watching Randall attempt to slink away. Oh, wasn't that interesting. Relationships between officers and enlisted were forbidden but Randall was attempting to sleep with one of his direct reports? Interesting, indeed.

He looked at the XO. "Sarn't Iaconelli is looking for you."

Randall sniffed. "He knows where I work."

"God, you are one charming bastard, you know that, LT?"

"Sergeant—"

Trent wasn't in the company so Carponti left before the XO could launch into another diatribe about Carponti's military bearing and disrespect. Couldn't have witnesses around when he told the XO to kiss his ass, now could he?

He dreaded her answering the phone. As much as he wanted to hear her voice, a tiny, selfish part of him didn't want her to pick up.

He didn't have the energy to find a way to make her laugh. He was tired. Bone tired. The kind of tired that made him want to sleep for a week. Maybe then things would be okay.

Maybe then he'd find his missing sense of humor.

"Hey." Her voice slid over his skin, a balm over all the ragged exposed wounds.

"You awake?"

Nicole's voice was tired. "I'm working."

"Oh yeah?"

"Yeah." Her smile was soft and sexy. "It's that case I can't really tell you much about. I'm with my partner and we're on the way back from Waco."

"He's keeping his hands to himself, right? I don't have to come home and like, unleash my PTSD on him, do I?"

She laughed quietly. "No, honey. David isn't going to violate your precious."

He smiled, wishing they were alone so he could tell her how much he missed her. But they weren't. So small talk it was. "So did you decorate the house for Christmas yet?"

"I started but...it's hard without you. Have you heard anything else about R&R? Are you still trying to get home?"

He swallowed the lump in his throat. "I'm on the list for next week. If the fates align, the planets are all in conjunction and Sarn't Ike doesn't get his period, it'll work out." He paused, unable to tell her that he was thinking about pulling his leave until things settled down. It felt wrong to think about leaving his platoon over the holidays. But instead he said, "I really want to be there for you. I know this Christmas is going to be hard."

"Yeah." A rustle of fabric. "I want you home, honey."

"I know. Trust me, I'm having a blast on my vacation over here in the desert. It's so much fun getting blown up every day."

"Not funny." She sniffed. "Is it that bad?"

He shrugged, even though she couldn't see it, and leaned forward, cupping his face in his hands. "It's not that bad. It could be worse."

"How?"

"We could be getting attacked multiple times a day."

"Not funny."

He smiled. "It's a little funny."

"No, it's not." She was serious. Shit. He hadn't actually meant to freak her out.

"Hey, so I made something for you."

"Made something? What, do you have arts and crafts hour between patrols?" The laughter was back in her voice but there was an edge. Something sharp and wary. A barrier he didn't want between them but a barrier he couldn't scale nonetheless. Not then. Not at all.

Because his rucksack was just too full of bad news for him to force any sarcasm through.

"Yeah. I'll give you two guesses."

"I have absolutely no idea."

"Really? Think back to the night I left."

She sighed and he heard the exasperation in her voice. Shit, he wasn't usually this inept with her. "Man dress."

She laughed. But it wasn't the same. Probably because

dickwad David was in the car. He shouldn't hate the man but Carponti was tired and feeling slightly peevish. David could have been Mother Teresa's great nephew twice removed but at that moment, he was taking time from Carponti and his wife.

He rubbed his thumb between his eyes, needing to tell her all the bad shit. Wishing he could unload some of it and she could tell him something good to replace the bad.

Maybe he should have told her about Garrison but if she knew he was hurt, she'd worry. And she needed to focus on her job right now, not worry about what her husband was going through downrange.

So he kept quiet and the silence grew on the line. Finally, his patience snapped. "Look, I know you can't talk much right now. I'll try to call again soon?"

"Yeah. Hon?"

"Yeah?" He frowned and waited, his breath catching in his throat.

"I really hope you make it home for Christmas."

He swallowed. "Yeah, me, too."

He disconnected the call before he let his temper get the better of him and walked out of the shelter and back toward his bay. Nicole didn't deserve him being a douche bag at the moment but he'd really hoped she'd laugh at the man dress costume.

And when she didn't...okay, she had but not like she would have if she'd been alone.

He dropped the little piece of fabric on his bunk as he grabbed his kit and headed toward the mission brief, trying to smother his disappointment. His one skill in life was making his wife laugh and tonight he'd fallen flat on his face. He tried not to let it bother him. He wanted to brush it off.

He failed. The one thing he'd needed, badly, was to hear her laugh. To replace some of the miserable strain of the goddamned war with something good and pure.

He barely listened as Iaconelli briefed the plan, his thoughts a thousand miles away, missing his wife.

NICOLE STARED at her cell phone in the dim lights inside the car and fought the urge to cry. The whole conversation was stunted and...off. Fear curled up inside her heart. Something was wrong. Vic was never serious unless something was wrong.

She flipped the phone in her hands, unable to put the emotions churning inside her back in the box. God but she didn't want to cry. Not at work.

"You okay?" David's gentle voice broke the silence. He was older than she was by at least fifteen years.

"Not really," she said, hoping her voice wouldn't break.

"Deployments are tough duty." He drummed his fingers on the dashboard, the movement creating little shadows in the interior lights. "I'm sorry you're having a hard time."

"I'm worried about my husband," she whispered. "He's scaring me."

"I deployed on the initial invasion into Iraq," David said after a while. "Desert Storm, not the Thunder Run. The news made it sound like we sliced through the center of Iraq and woke up in Baghdad. It really wasn't that easy." He paused. "It was the first time my wife and I had ever been apart. She wanted me to call home every chance I got."

Nicole looked at him. His weathered face was cased in shadows, his dark skin lined with experience. "Did you?"

He shook his head. "No. I couldn't. There was stuff I couldn't talk to her about. There's still stuff I don't bring up. And it's hard because she wants to know what the war was like. I can't talk about all of it." He glanced at her quickly. "Going to war isn't all PTSD and trauma. It's just some stuff is hard to talk about."

"How did you make it through?" Nicole asked quietly. His words had struck home. She did want to know. She hated not knowing. It hurt her, knowing that Vic wouldn't talk to her but David's words sank in. Maybe he *couldn't* talk right now.

"I talk to her when I can. Try to share some things with her. But mostly, she listened when I told her there was some stuff I just couldn't talk about and I asked her to be patient with me."

"Is she?" She admired David. He was a mentor and a friend. It was difficult to picture him as less than a perfect gentleman.

"She gets frustrated with me. I shut down sometimes. But yeah, she's there for me." He reached forward and turned down the air conditioner. "I don't know what would have happened to me if she hadn't stuck with me. Even when I was drinking myself stupid every night."

"You drink?" This was new information.

"I quit. Wrapped my car around a tree about six years ago. CID stood by me and supported me while I went through treatment. So did my wife." He pulled up in front of her house. The outside light shined like a beacon in the darkness. "So I can't tell you what to do but if you still love him, hold on until he gets home. Give him some time to process everything."

Nicole swallowed the sadness blocking her throat and nodded. "Thanks, David."

"For what it's worth, I'm sorry you're going through this."

She closed the door quietly behind her. It was reassuring that he didn't pull off until she closed her front door and clicked off the outside light. The Christmas tree stood in the corner, a dark unlit shadow. She hadn't managed to get the lights on it yet. Every time she started, she just got too sad.

She turned her phone off vibrate and plugged it in next to the bed. Then she turned on the computer and logged in to Skype, hoping, praying that her husband would call her back.

She slipped out of her clothes and into one of Vic's shirts. She tried not to cry as she sprayed his cologne on her wrists, needing the familiarity of his scent even if she was missing the warmth of his body in the bed next to her.

But when she slipped between the sheets and pulled a pillow to her belly, she let the tears come. Great, wracking silent sobs broke through and she cried until she couldn't stop.

"I just want him home."

But it was a plea to the darkness that no one heard.

7

Iaconelli's hands weren't shaking. Carponti watched his new platoon sergeant as he talked with their platoon leader LT Miller just to be sure. Nope, no shaking.

Which meant one of two things: either Iaconelli's DTs had finally eased back or he'd gotten his hands on some alcohol.

Carponti wasn't a betting man but he was willing to bet Iaconelli had found some booze. Any and all sins were available in Iraq; you just had to know where to look and be willing to pay for them. He supposed it was just like America after all.

Carponti took a pull off his Dr. Pepper and debated his actions. It had been less than a week since Garrison had gotten sent home and Iaconelli was no more integrated into the platoon than he'd been at the start of this little adventure.

It didn't help that two more guys were getting stitched up at the aid station. But they were coming back with a prescription for Motrin and a good night's sleep. Carponti couldn't blame Iaconelli directly for them getting hurt but that didn't mean he wasn't going to try. He couldn't keep drinking on the patrols. He didn't care how much of a functioning alcoholic the man was; his drinking was going to get someone killed.

It could have been worse. He kept reminding himself of that. He reached his hand into his pocket and felt the little piece of fabric that made up the man dress.

It had been funny when he'd started on it a few months ago. He'd sat on his cot and thought about taking pictures and sending them to his wife. Now, after that last phone call, he started to think it was just stupid. He'd wanted to call her back but every time he'd tried to break away, something had come up.

He felt like an asshole leaving the last conversation like he had. It wasn't her fault she'd been working that night. Carponti had been a shit and he knew it. He wanted badly to call her back, damn it.

But if he was honest with himself, and he really didn't make much of a habit of telling himself lies, he was terrified to pick up that phone. He was afraid she wouldn't answer. That maybe the distance on the line hadn't been his imagination.

That maybe, this time, she'd finally gotten tired of waiting for him to come home.

Things were weird between them this deployment. He knew it was him not calling as much. Putting space between them. He didn't have it in him to pick up the phone and listen to her talk about work. He used to love hearing her talk about nothing at all. Now? Now he just couldn't summon the energy to care. He was too tired. Too worn down. The war was kicking his ass and he didn't know how to be normal on the phone with her. Maybe that made him a prick but the war—the war was taking everything he had right then.

He hoped she'd understand. Maybe he'd get to go home next week after all.

The thought of getting on a plane and leaving his boys, though... He wasn't sure he could do it. He knew the commander would let him stay if he told him he wanted to push back the R&R dates. Captain Davila wouldn't argue, especially not since he'd just lost Garrison as one of his key leaders.

"Sarn't Carponti!"

Carponti stuffed the fabric back into his pocket and pasted on a bored expression as he turned. "Yes, your highness?"

LT Randall's skin tightened over his bones as he kept coming and stepped right into Carponti's personal space. "You will call me fucking 'sir', you arrogant little bastard."

Carponti didn't really think about what happened next. He blinked and the next thing he knew, strong hands were dragging him off the LT. Iaconelli's big hand shoved him backward. "Cut the shit, Carponti," Iaconelli growled.

But Carponti wasn't done. He squared off with the lieutenant, ignoring Iaconelli's attempt to pull him off. "Don't fucking talk to me like that, you scumbag motherfucker."

"Goddamn it, Carponti!"

They were nose to nose. Randall's face was swollen, just like his fucking ego, but there was triumph in his eyes. "You just crossed the line. I'm going to have your rank for this, Carponti," Randall snapped.

"Good luck with that," Carponti spat.

"That's not how this works, *Sergeant*." Randall spat the word. "You will respect my rank."

Carponti shoved Randall a step backward. "That's exactly how it's going to work. Stop harassing my guys because of your incompetence, lieutenant. You lost the fucking equipment, you find it. But leave my goddamned men alone."

The veins in Randall's neck stood out against his skin. Carponti was reasonably certain the man was going to have a coronary.

It would have been one memorial ceremony he'd have been happy to attend.

Iaconelli finally moved his hand off Carponti's chest and

stepped into the fray, shoving Carponti back and stepping between them. "LT, what's missing?" he asked.

Carponti frowned as one of the guys came up to watch the fireworks. It was Neal Sloban, a guy who'd been with Carponti since the middle of the last rotation.

"Since when did Iaconelli become a voice of reason?" Sloban muttered.

Carponti shrugged. "I have no idea. Maybe his horoscope told him to play nice today."

Sloban shook his head and walked off as Carponti continued to watch the de-escalation between the two, like Iaconelli was some kind of lieutenant whisperer. Randall finished gesticulating wildly and stomped off. Iaconelli hesitated a moment before he walked back toward Carponti.

"That was impressive," Carponti said as Iaconelli walked back to the waiting convoy.

"I have my specialties."

"You have to tell me how you did that." It was a strange truce between them. Half the time, Carponti was certain that Iaconelli was going to whip his ass if Carponti made one more smart-ass comment. Which of course, Carponti did. Iaconelli never laughed, though.

"I threatened to knock his front teeth out if he didn't stop fucking with my platoon."

Carponti laughed and stuffed his hands in his pockets. The piece of fabric made him think of his wife. Something slipped out, something briefly happy in the midst of the fucking sadness that had been haunting him since he'd watched them put Garrison on the plane.

He needed to call home. Right then, before they rolled out the gate. He glanced toward the company ops.

He didn't have time. Damn it, he didn't have time.

He brushed his thumb over the fabric in his pocket. He'd call her when he got back to the FOB.

He swallowed and pulled his helmet on. He'd finish sewing when he got back to the base.

It would have to be good enough. He'd been an ass and he really needed to hear her tell him that she still loved him.

Carponti ducked behind the tire of the truck that was currently the only thing providing even a smidgen of cover for the last half of their convoy. Rounds exploded overhead even as Tigger manned the fifty cal and tried to lay down suppressive fire.

Their convoy had gotten hit exactly one block outside the base. Carponti would be pissed off later. Right then, he needed to get his boys set on the defense and figure out if anyone was wounded back in Sarn't Iaconelli's truck.

Iaconelli, in the trail vehicle, had been hit by the IED that had blown the front end of his truck all to shit.

Carponti ducked and rushed from his own vehicle to where Iaconelli was leaning on Carponti's seat, blood running down the side of his leg and talking on the radio. "Sarn't Ike, you realize you've got blood pouring out of your ass?"

"Shut the fuck up, Carponti. I'm trying to call this in." He paused, his face going grey for a brief moment. "Where's the LT?"

Carponti glanced toward the front of their patrol, where he saw Miller directing some of the guys. "He's getting the lead vehicle out of the kill zone."

"Security?"

"Security is set. I've got Foster and Sloban manning the rear position. LT is going to recover the downed vehicle or blow it in place, then we're going to get the hell out of here."

Iaconelli was leaning against Carponti's truck, the hand mic from Carponti's radio in his hand. "Casualties?"

"None, other than your ass, apparently."

Iaconelli looked like he wanted to punch him. A piece of concrete blew off the building and Carponti ducked. It bounced off his eye pro and he jerked his head, cracking his helmet on the side of the vehicle.

"You're going to want to apply pressure to that," Carponti said when his vision had cleared up. He reached for Iaconelli's first aid kit.

Iaconelli slapped his hand away as he listened to the radio. "Not in this lifetime."

Carponti stood there for a second, completely speechless. Then he started laughing.

"Then you need to let the medics check you out, because that's a shitload of blood and you're so pale you look like the Emperor on *Star Wars* right now, which, for a brown guy, is pretty fucking pale."

Iaconelli shot him a dirty look. "Are you ever serious?"

"I try not to be. Bad things happen when I'm not making jokes. It upsets the cosmic order of the universe or something." He glanced around at Iaconelli's bloody uniform. "Still bleeding. And the sergeant major is calling you."

Iaconelli sighed heavily and lifted the hand mic to his face so Carponti could get the bandage from his first aid kit. Carponti grinned as he pulled the bloody uniform away from Iaconelli's ass. "You have such firm, round..."

"Carponti, I swear to Christ—" He broke off listening to the radio.

"What? I was giving you a compliment." He pulled the fabric away from Iaconelli's ass, tearing the rest of his uniform all to hell. "Well, it could be worse," Carponti mumbled.

"Stop the goddamned bleeding and get the hell away from my ass," Iaconelli growled. "Roger that. Reaper Main. Two vehicles."

Carponti focused on the task at hand, which started with

cutting a bigger hole in Iaconelli's trousers. He pulled the end off his Camelbak and flooded the wound with water so he could see what he was dealing with.

"Oh, you're not going to like this," he said.

There was a piece of metal sticking out of Iaconelli's buttock. A small one the size of a penny, but still. It was a sharp penny.

"What?" Iaconelli twisted to look over his shoulder.

"Are there any arteries in the ass cheek?" Carponti asked.

"You're kidding, right?"

"Nope. 'Cause I can put this dressing on your wound but, well, I'm thinking it's going to hurt worse than if we wait for the medics to pull this thing out of your ass." He beamed as Iaconelli glared at him. "I've always wanted to use that phrase in a sentence."

Iaconelli turned purple. Yes, definitely purple. "Just...just use your Leatherman or something and take care of business."

"This is going to hurt." Carponti chuckled and pulled his Leatherman out. "One. Two. Two and a half..."

"Just fucking do it," Iaconelli snapped.

But Carponti had been counting on irritating Iaconelli with the countdown. The minute he'd snapped, Carponti had seized the shrapnel and tugged.

Iaconelli hissed and swore between gritted teeth. The shrapnel popped free. Blood flowed freely but he got the pressure dressing in place. Kind of. "There's really no good way to tape something to your ass this way," he muttered, more to himself than to Iaconelli. He started cutting strips off Iaconelli's tattered uniform to tie the bandage in place. "It's going to take more than a Band-Aid."

He leaned around Iaconelli. "You want to save this?" He held the piece of metal in the tongs of his pliers.

Iaconelli grunted and waved Carponti off. He plunked the

metal into Iaconelli's pocket. He'd want that later. Maybe. If not, he could sell it on eBay or something.

You've reached Nicole Carponti. Leave me a message and I'll call you back.

Carponti's heart sank in his chest as her voice mail beeped. "Hey, baby, it's me. Just got back from taking a piece of metal out of my platoon sergeant's ass. I think this means we're BFFs now." He sighed and rubbed his eyes. "Sorry I missed you. I'll call again soon."

He hung up, breathing deeply to push aside the disappointment in his chest. He walked away from the call center, back toward the open bay where he and the guys were bunking, and figured he'd try to get some sleep.

Hopefully, he wouldn't get blown up in the middle of his nap. That would suck. One of the life support areas had got hit last week. Luckily, the guy who'd lived in that trailer had been banging the division commander's aide de camp across the base at the time so he hadn't been home.

It was nice to just sweep a bunch of shit into the trash instead of having to attend another ramp ceremony saluting a flag-draped coffin on its final flight. God but he hated those ceremonies. He swallowed and stepped into the bay.

There was mail on his cot. From a few feet away, he could see his wife's neat handwriting on a small package.

He suddenly couldn't breathe. He sat down, back to the rest of the bay. Iaconelli had taken over Garrison's cot but he wasn't there right now. He was busy getting his ass stitched back together. It was as close to privacy as Carponti could get without asking Jackson to use his commo shelter, and Jackson was on a mission down at Camp Victory or something so he wasn't about to go ask one of the other kids.

His hand shook like a schoolgirl's as he sliced the top off and pulled out the letter and...

And a CD. In neat block letters was the word *private*.

He opened the letter.

I swear to God if the rest of your platoon sees this, I'll divorce you.

He could almost hear her scolding him with a smile on her face. Every emotion he'd locked down came tumbling out and he blinked hard and quick against the wetness in his eyes. He'd guard that CD with his life.

Okay, now that we've got that clarified, I made you a Christmas present in case you can't come home. Well, two presents (read the next page). I really want you home, Vic.

I miss you. I'm not going to moan on and on (next page) but I just need to tell you that. I love you, more than anything else. So I don't care what you have to do, just come home to me, okay? Because I'm going to be really upset if you die. Just so you know. Now go someplace private and read the next page. I love you.

Nicole

Carponti sat for a long moment, just reading her letter again and again. The sound of her voice in his head was as clear as if he was on the phone with her.

He wasn't sure if he dared to read the letter. It wouldn't be cool if he started walking around with a raging hard-on in the middle of a bay full of dudes. Then again, it would probably piss Iaconelli off to no end. He laughed. He should leave a crumpled up, wet paper towel on Iaconelli's cot just to screw with him.

It would be funny to watch him freak the hell out.

'Course, he might actually knock Carponti's teeth out. That would certainly put a damper on things. Go home after the war and talk to his wife like the Gopher on Winnie the Pooh.

Carponti read his wife's letter once more, then slowly turned to the next page.

I miss you. I lay awake at night, thinking about you. I miss the little things. The sound of you getting up at night. The feel of your body in bed with me. I sleep in the middle of the bed when you're gone.

Sometimes, I can almost pretend you're here with me. I wear your cologne to bed and close my eyes. My nipples tighten. I imagine it's your fingers teasing them.

Your tongue tasting them.

I miss the way your mouth feels on my body. The way your fingers could slide between my thighs and make me wet. My fingers slide down my stomach. My nipples brush against the cool sheets. I'm wet for you, Vic. I can feel your fingers stroking my pussy. I want you to fill me. To touch me the way only you know how.

My back arches as you fill me. Make love to me, Vic. I miss you so much. I miss the way you move inside me. I'm wet, so wet. I want you. Faster. Inside me. Harder. I want to feel you all around me. My breath catches as I come around you, vibrating, shaking, surrendering to your touch.

I love you.

Carponti was going to embarrass himself if he stood up. It was going to be damn near impossible for him to stand up, let alone make it to the latrines a quarter mile away without anyone seeing his erection. He pulled his pillow over his lap and just sat there, reading her words again, hearing her voice in his head.

He smiled and couldn't care less. His wife loved him enough to violate several federal laws and a couple of general orders, and send him a dirty letter and better yet, a dirty video.

He curled into his bunk and onto his side. For a brief moment, he shut out the world and thought about his wife. For a moment, he forgot about the shit war in the shithole country and all the bad things that had been happening recently.

He closed his eyes, and let his mind drift back to the States. To the beautiful sexy woman waiting for him.

NICOLE STEPPED out of the shower and wrapped her body in a towel. She was exhausted after pulling thirty-six hours of duty. She'd barely managed to stay awake long enough to shower but the entire time she'd been in there, she'd been listening for the sound of her phone.

She padded through their bedroom toward her phone.

Missed call.

Damn it, damn it, damn it.

The voice mail notice vibrated in her hand. Tears welled in her eyes as she listened to Vic's message.

He sounded terrible. Her heart cracked in her chest and she sat down on their bed, giving into the exhaustion and the sadness. She was so tired of the war.

She curled into a tight ball and wept bitterly. Vic's voice was so off. So tired. He was avoiding her. He always did that when bad things happened. She knew it but she still didn't like it.

She'd prayed he'd call, that she'd get to hear his voice. But she heard his voice. And it wasn't enough. Damn it, it wasn't enough.

She listened to his voice mail again, cursing herself for forgetting to turn the vibrate off.

She pushed up off the bed and wiped her eyes, then went back into the bathroom. She found his cologne and sprayed it on her wrists and chest. A lonely ritual but one that kept her sane.

Then she pulled on a pair of his old sweatpants and climbed onto his side of the bed, hugging a pillow close and breathing in his scent, and trying to ignore the breaking of her heart in her chest.

8

"Hey, Carponti."

Carponti frowned. He'd been having an amazing dream about his wife, her deployment boyfriend and a bottle of lotion. He really didn't want it to end but damn it, someone was poking him in the back.

"Unless you're checking my kidneys, stop touching me," Carponti mumbled.

"Wake up, man. You gotta hear this." It was Tigger.

Carponti groaned and sat up. "What the hell is so important you had to wake me up?"

"We're on lockdown."

Carponti frowned, scrubbing his hand over his face. "Why?"

"There's a bunch of shit going down about some missing optics."

Something sank in the vicinity of Carponti's heart. Missing optics were on par with missing weapons systems. As in, really not good. "What missing optics?"

Tigger shrugged. "I don't know but everyone's talking about it. Randall's apparently got to go get sworn statements from some of the guys back in the States. And there're rumors that the commander is going to get fired."

"Why the hell does the LT need to go back to the States to get statements?"

"It's what everyone's saying. I figured you knew."

Carponti shook his head. "No, I haven't heard anything. And for the record, news about that fucktard Lieutenant Randall was not important enough to wake me up from dreaming about my wife."

Tigger stood, looking completely unfazed. "Yeah, well, something's going on. You might want to find the platoon sergeant and see what's up. I think we're on lockdown until the commander figures this stuff out."

Carponti swore and dragged on his uniform. "I'll go see what's going on," he said. He was still irritated that he'd been woken up for some drama at the company but he'd lied when he'd told Tigger it wasn't important enough to wake him up.

Missing optics was definitely on the list of things to wake someone up for.

He crossed the base quickly, walking into the company ops. Since the new soldier had started working up there, the ops had gotten decorated with more and more Christmas stuff. Someone needed to give the ops clerks more to work on before it exploded with Christmas cheer.

He walked into the commander's office without knocking. Trent was busy typing away and motioned for Carponti to sit while he finished whatever he'd been working on.

"So what's this I hear about you firing the XO?" Carponti asked.

"Sadly, I'm not firing him." He tossed his glasses on the desk. "I don't have any cause to fire him."

"Missing equipment seems like it might be a good reason," Carponti said.

"Yeah, well, he's investigating said missing equipment, not the cause of it."

"Sure. Whatever you say."

Trent frowned. "What's that supposed to mean?"

Carponti looked around the office, searching for the words he needed. "I'm just thinking that Randall's got some integrity issues, that's all."

"Anything you can prove?" Trent asked cautiously.

"Nothing other than supposition and rumor," Carponti said. "But is he really being sent home?"

"If he can't find the stuff here, yeah." Trent grinned humorlessly. "And on top of all of that, I have to report to the commander that we've done a hundred percent weigh-in. So are you ready to go get a class on how to properly evaluate body fat?"

"You're serious?"

"Yep. We've got professional development class in..." He glanced at his watch. "Five minutes. I get to be the guinea pig for first sergeant to demonstrate the proper conduct of the Army's body fat test."

Carponti sighed dramatically. "I'm quite confident I have never been to war before when garrison broke out. You realize this is stupid, right?"

Trent stood, circling the desk. He slapped Carponti on the shoulder. "Oh yes. Very much so."

Nicole stood in the lounge at her office headquarters and scanned the news ticker for any information about her husband's base. She flicked the vibrate button on her cell phone. On and off. On. Off.

"Hey, Nicole, we're going out for drinks to celebrate. Are you...?" Major Olivia Hale stuck her head in the door then paused and came all the way into the break area. "Are you okay?"

Nicole offered a smile and hoped it passed for a reasonable facsimile. "I'm fine. Just waiting for news, that's all."

"Yeah, it's been a bad week for attacks across the board." Olivia glanced at the TV. "I'm sure your husband is fine," she said quietly.

"I know. I just, I worry, that's all."

Olivia sighed and tucked her hands into her pockets. "A few of us are going out to drink to celebrate putting that sex offender in jail. Want to join us?"

Nicole glanced down at her cell phone. Somehow, it felt wrong going out to the bar while her husband was deployed, suffering through God only knew what. She shook her head slowly. "I'll pass, thanks. I've got some last minute Christmas stuff to do."

"Christmas isn't for another ten days. You obviously don't know the meaning of the phrase 'last minute'," Olivia said dryly.

Nicole looked down at her phone.

"Ah shit, honey, I'm sorry," Olivia said quietly.

Nicole covered her mouth with her hand and tried to keep the tears at bay. "I'm okay," she said finally. "I'm gonna go." She offered an apologetic hug. "Sorry. This Christmas is just really hard."

She left before Olivia could talk her into staying. She felt out of place and off kilter since she'd missed Vic's call, and as Christmas cheer spread, her mood only sank further into unhappiness.

She tried to tell herself he'd be home if he could. That he'd call if he could. That everything was fine; it was just the war.

She thought about going home but instead detoured to Laura's office. She wasn't sure she wanted to be alone right now. Maybe she should have just gone out with everyone from work but she was confident she'd have just been alone in the crowd of celebratory cheer.

She knocked on Laura's office door a few minutes later. Her friend looked up from her computer and Nicole was rocked by how upset and tired her friend looked. "I was coming to see you for moral support but it looks like you might need it more than I do," Nicole said quietly.

Laura swallowed and said nothing for a long moment. Then she handed Nicole a plain manila folder.

Nicole read the first page before she nearly dropped it like she'd been burned.

Laura Davila, Plaintiff—

"You can't be serious, honey," Nicole said.

Laura was trying hard not to cry but her eyes rimmed with red anyway. "He's breaking my heart," she whispered. Her voice broke.

Nicole closed the door behind her then walked around the desk, pulling her longtime friend into a tight hug.

God damn the war that did this to them.

To all of them.

"I haven't heard from him in weeks. Weeks. I'm the Family Readiness Group leader and I don't know what's going on. I can't tell any of the spouses that. We've got attacks daily and I don't know if he's hurt or if anyone else is." She pulled out of Nicole's embrace. "But the worst part is the emptiness. I can't keep crying myself to sleep over him. It's been years." She swiped at her eyes. "I keep waiting for him to come home from the war." She sighed quietly. "I don't think that day is going to come," she whispered.

Nicole looked down at the divorce papers on Laura's desk. "You can't... Just wait. Give him more time. There's got to be a good reason."

"You know what the rumors are? They say he's cheating on me." She smiled pitilessly. "But the worst? The worst fucking thing I've heard? He's been volunteering. Every single deployment he's been on, he's volunteered for." She pressed her lips together. "I can't keep having faith in a man who gives me no reason to believe in him," she whispered.

Nicole pulled her close again, offering nothing more than silent support. If she was going to do this, Nicole would support her.

But fear was a powerful thing and it slithered beneath her skin, whispering that nothing and no one was safe from the strain of war.

～

"No, you can't use my camera."

"Come on, Tigger, please?" They had a mission in less than six hours. Carponti needed a damn camera and the world was conspiring against him.

"No."

"I'll pay you." Carponti couldn't find his camera. He was convinced that LT Randall had stolen it but he couldn't prove it and so he kept the allegation to himself. That sneaky bastard had been caught with one of the soldiers' iPods a few months ago and had denied stealing it.

The commander had told him to give it back and let the matter drop. But that didn't make anyone any more trusting of the LT. Randall was the epitome of a toxic leader, the Army's favorite new buzz word. He practically came with a biohazard warning.

He'd finished the man dress he'd been sewing and now he wanted to send the picture home to his wife. He'd woken up that morning with a feeling of sick dread tying his guts in knots. Sending the pic home to his wife was suddenly the most pressing task he needed to accomplish.

Ever since Garrison had gotten hurt, Carponti hadn't felt

right. He knew it was grief and all that other shit the counselors liked to say, but this felt different. He *had* to send that picture home to his wife. Something was hanging over his head that if he didn't get that picture sent home, something bad was going to happen.

He hated when he got those feelings because, damn it, something bad always happened. And he *hated* being right about crap like this.

They were heading out on a mission later tonight and damn it, Carponti wanted that picture in Nicole's inbox when she woke up.

At least that way, if he died, she'd always have a picture of a little outfit he'd made with love to keep with her instead of whatever was left of him that they sent home.

And wasn't that a depressing thought. It was enough to make him need a hug. He glanced toward Iaconelli, busy cleaning his weapon. He doubted Iaconelli was the hugging type.

Shit, he was feeling melancholy.

He tried again to get Tigger to let him borrow his camera. "I'll sanitize it before I bring it back."

"I said fucking no," Tigger snapped and rolled over in his cot.

"You could have just said so," Carponti grumbled.

Damn it. He stalked out of the bay and headed to the company ops. Maybe he could convince Trent to let him borrow the company camera.

'Course, he'd have to figure out how to delete the picture. Or maybe he'd leave it on there. Oh, to be a fly on the wall when the ops sergeant used the camera next time. That would be awesome.

Carponti grinned as he pushed through the plywood and two by four contraption that constituted the door to the company ops.

"Roger that, sir. I understand."

Carponti frowned and stopped by the door, not sure who Trent was talking to. Whatever it was, it didn't sound good.

"Roger, sir." Trent looked up then motioned for Carponti to come all the way in.

"Roger."

Trent hung up the phone and looked at it for a long moment, then, as though remembering Carponti was present, shook himself.

"So, I need to borrow your camera, sir." It felt weird calling Trent 'sir'. They'd served together in Germany when Carponti had been a private and Trent had been his platoon leader. Carponti, for one, was grateful that Trent was his commander. Carponti doubted he'd have gotten away with half the stunts he'd pulled had it been some other pencil neck officer in charge.

Trent frowned and sat down at his desk. "Can I ask why?"

Carponti grinned. "You may not really want to know the answer to that question. But I'll tell you if you really want to know."

"Let's just stop there while I can still cherish my innocence." Trent shook his head and kicked his feet up onto his desk. "Change of subject away from your delinquency. How's Iaconelli working out?"

Carponti thought about the booze and then decided he really didn't give a shit. Iaconelli wasn't getting drunk, which meant he was a functioning alcoholic at the very least. So long as he kept performing and keeping the guys out of the hospital, Carponti couldn't really argue the means. There was enough shit going on that he didn't need to get the commander spun up on that. Not when LT Randall was out of control and they were potentially missing optics. "He's not Sarn't G, that's for sure."

"Not many people could step into Garrison's shoes."

Carponti frowned. "Well, that would be gross. Do you know what kind of fungus is growing around here?"

Trent pushed his glasses up onto the top of his head and leaned back. He didn't laugh. Carponti took that as a very bad sign. "So listen. There's some bad shit going on."

"And you're telling me something I don't already know because...?" Carponti said. He tapped his fingers on the butt of his weapon.

"Look, I know you took Garrison getting hit hard but there are other things going on. If I get pulled out of this job, I need you to keep things running smoothly, okay?"

Carponti looked at the rank on his chest and ignored the thousands of questions skipping through his brain, about why his commander might get fired and why he was talking to one of his squad leaders about it. "You realize I'm a buck sergeant, right? As in, pretty low on the list of people you should expect to run things if you're not here. And where are you going, anyway?"

"I'm not going anywhere if I can help it." Trent swung his feet to the floor and leaned forward on the desk. "You've got influence, whether you see it or not. The guys look to you to gauge whether shit is really bad. If you're still around cracking jokes, then everyone else tends to just keep rolling along."

Carponti held up his hands. "Obviously you've been drinking too much coffee because you're a little intense right now. Why would you get fired?"

"It's a long story that requires a significant amount of alcohol." He glanced at his computer. "You're heading home on R&R in a few days, right?"

"I wanted to talk to you about that." Carponti shifted in his chair uncomfortably. He wanted nothing more than to go home and see his wife and forget about the war for a few days but the feeling of dread that gripped his insides turned the thought of leaving his boys for the holidays into something sour. It felt like he was abandoning them. And as badly as he needed to connect with his wife, with as badly as he needed to know she was still there for him, he...he couldn't bring himself to leave. Not with everything going to shit around them.

Nicole would kill him if he didn't come home. Goddamn, he knew how hard this Christmas was going to be for her. It was breaking his heart to even think about asking to skip his R&R but his guys were having too hard of a time right then. God, but he hoped she'd understand. "I don't think it's a good time to go. The guys are still off kilter from Sarn't G getting blown up and all and well..."

Trent held up one hand. "You're going," Trent said flatly.

Carponti looked up.

"You're going. As much as you like to think you are, you're not the Energizer Bunny. You need to take a knee and unwind just like the rest of us."

Carponti frowned and started to argue but the small piece of fabric in his pocket was suddenly heavy. It was a stupid thing, this desire to tease his wife with a picture of a stupid costume but suddenly, he very much wanted to do it in person. He wanted to watch her double over in laughter. He wanted to feel her laugh when he was inside her. There was nothing better in the world than hearing her laugh. Nothing better than feeling her body tremble when he touched her.

The pressing need for the camera flittered away. He could show her the man dress in person in a few more days.

He swallowed and nodded. "I get that. I don't like it but I get it."

Trent opened his mouth to say something, then paused before he spoke again. "You're not going to argue?"

"Nah. There's something I really want to give my wife. I was going to send her a picture but I can do it in a couple of days when I get home."

A strange look passed over Trent's face. "Yeah, you need to take care of her. Don't let her forget you."

"When is the last time you talked to Laura?" Carponti asked quietly.

Trent shook his head and reached to turn on his computer. "Just...when you go home, if you see my wife..." He bit his lip and Carponti had never seen his friend more unsteady in all the years he'd known him. "Tell my wife I love her?"

Carponti wanted to press Trent on what the hell was going on but the phone rang and Trent waved him out of the office. Things had gone to hell in a relatively short period of time. Garrison had gotten blown up, Trent was missing equipment and potentially facing an investigation...and the rumors... The rumor mill was breeding faster than a barn full of unsupervised bunnies.

He was suddenly glad he'd be getting on a plane and heading home soon. Carponti slipped from the tactical operations cell and headed back to the bay to prep for the next mission. One last mission before he got to see his wife.

9

"So we're going to provide the blocking force here and here," Iaconelli said, drawing an x in the sand. "This intersection that sits squarely in a bad part of town."

Carponti reached for the stick before Iaconelli could snatch it out of his hands. "And by bad part of town, Sarn't Ike means the locals would rather slit your throat than feed you to the dogs. Which is pretty bad, all things considered."

Iaconelli snatched the stick out of Carponti's hand and looked like he wanted to beat Carponti with it, completely unimpressed by Carponti's sarcasm. Carponti scowled. He must be losing his touch.

"Someone hasn't had their daily pick me up," Carponti grumbled. A couple of the guys laughed until Iaconelli glared at them.

"The enemy has been very active in this sector," Iaconelli said, ignoring Carponti's jab.

"And we know this because every time we roll through this sector, we get blown up," Carponti added.

"Are you trying to piss me off?" Iaconelli snapped.

Carponti looked up. "Is it working?"

"Yes."

"Then yes."

A few more chuckles from the guys. Iaconelli pointed toward the door. "Outside, funny guy."

Carponti bowed as he exited in front of his platoon sergeant. The guys heckled as Iaconelli practically shoved Carponti through the door. Carponti spat into the dirt and waited. They were all just trying to survive and Iaconelli was making it fucking miserable.

"You need to quit screwing around before you get someone hurt."

It took a lot to piss Carponti off. Like, act of God to really get him going, but right then, Iaconelli's words shot straight to the heart of his temper. Iaconelli was bigger than him by about a half a foot and seventy-five pounds, but well, Carponti had never really thought his actions through.

He shoved his platoon sergeant back against the bay doors with a bang. "Considering you've probably been drinking since before the sun came up, I don't really think you get to lecture me on doing something stupid that might get someone hurt," he said quietly.

Iaconelli broke Carponti's hold easily and shoved him backward. "You don't know shit about me, you little smart-ass."

"Really? You want to play that game? I make jokes to keep the guys from getting too fucking depressed. In case you haven't noticed in your alcohol-induced fog, we've had a pretty shitty deployment. If a joke makes them think about something else, then maybe, just maybe, I'll keep them from focusing on all the bad shit. But I wouldn't expect you to notice that because your coping mechanism is at the bottom of a bottle."

Iaconelli grabbed Carponti by the front of his shirt and cocked his fist back. Carponti puckered his lips up and made a kissing noise. "You only get one shot," he taunted.

Iaconelli pulled back and Carponti realized perhaps this wasn't his smartest move.

Iaconelli swore and shoved him away. Carponti stumbled backward but kept his feet, then smirked and made a show of straightening his uniform. "And so we've reached an impasse. Shall we continue with the war? The one outside the gates, I mean."

Iaconelli jabbed a finger in Carponti's face then bunched his fist and said nothing. He stalked back into the bay.

Carponti spat into the dirt again and followed him back in, threw his arms around Iaconelli's shoulders and grinned. "Yes, yes, boys, we kissed and made up. Now back to your regularly scheduled war."

Iaconelli shrugged him off roughly but otherwise ignored him as he moved on with the mission brief. Carponti wished he could blame the lingering adrenaline from the near fight with Iaconelli but as they rolled out the gate, he couldn't shake the feeling that bad shit was coming. And when Iaconelli insisted on changing up the vehicle locations so that his truck was in front of Carponti's, the bad feeling got progressively worse.

But he kept that to himself. Because he was just being paranoid. Right?

He listened to the radio as they rolled out deep into insurgent territory. Everyone was on high alert.

He tugged on Tigger's leg, reminding him to duck down behind the defilade. Too many soldiers had gotten beheaded from wires strung beneath intersections and across roadways. Garrison had driven that point home more than once.

They passed the soccer stadium without incident and Carponti nearly pissed himself with relief. They were heading toward the Iraqi police station where they were supposed to link up with their Iraqi Army counterparts.

Providing they made it there without getting blown all to—

The blast shattered the windshield on his truck. A moment

later, a cloud of dust and debris rolled through the interior. Instantly, Tigger and the other gun trucks started laying down suppressive fire. When the dust finally cleared, he saw Iaconelli's truck lying on its side.

Oh fuck. If they hadn't changed up the order of movement, that would have been Carponti's truck lying there in the dirt. Shit, he'd known that was a bad idea.

"Holy shit," he muttered. "Tigger, keep suppressive fire going. Wilks, Jax, I need you with me to get them out of that truck before they get blown all to shit."

It was a horrible case of *deja vu*: rushing across the road just like he had with Garrison. He climbed onto the truck and managed to yank the door open.

Inside, Iaconelli and the boys were coughing but everyone looked unhurt. "You girls okay?" Carponti shouted over the chaos.

Iaconelli flipped him off.

"Nice to see you, too, sweetheart." Carponti ducked as a rocket whizzed overhead, grossly off target. God, but he was happy the insurgents had crappy aim. "Y'all want to get your asses out of there? Kind of a hot zone out here."

The driver and gunner climbed out, followed last by Iaconelli. Iaconelli paused in the doorway.

"You're never serious, are you?" Iaconelli asked.

"I thought we already had this conversation."

Iaconelli heaved himself out of the truck. "We need to try to get this thing back on all four wheels."

"Got it covered." The Humvee in front of them was already maneuvering into position to try and drag the flipped truck over. More rounds tinked off the truck's armor and Carponti ducked down behind the door he was still holding. "Shit, that one was close."

"Get off the damn truck before you get blown up," Iaconelli said, leaning over the side of the truck and firing at a group of approaching men armed with what looked like a couple of rocket-propelled grenades.

"Oh goody, the greeting committee," Carponti mumbled.

"Get down!"

It was the last thing Carponti heard.

"Carponti!"

The voice came from very far away. Carponti frowned and tried to open his eyes. They were heavy. Something was burning.

"I hope that's not my balls," he mumbled.

"Jesus, you never stop. Open your damn eyes."

"Am I still in Kansas?" Carponti frowned and managed to blink. His vision cleared slowly and Iaconelli came into view, clearly not happy. "What's that smell?"

Iaconelli glanced at Carponti's side, then his gaze flicked back to Carponti's face. "Don't worry about it."

"Wait, that smell is me?" Panic clutched at him, closing off his lungs.

"I said don't worry about it. We've got the MEDEVAC coming for you."

Carponti tried to sit up and Iaconelli damn near flattened him with a single palm to the chest. He groaned. The pressure made him see spots. "Oh, what the hell? Did I manage to get myself blown up?"

"Little bit."

A slow ache sharpened abruptly, tearing up his arm and down his side like molten fire. "Oh, now I feel it," Carponti said. He no longer tried to sit up. The fire in his arm went from nonexistent to eleven in less than a nanosecond. He winced and breathed out hard. "That stings."

Iaconelli cleared his throat as he continued to do whatever he was doing to Carponti's arm. "Yeah, I'm sure it does."

Carponti reached up with the hand that didn't feel like absolute hell and gripped Iaconelli's body armor. "Give it to me straight. Just tell me if my dick is still intact?"

Iaconelli flushed and finally laughed. "I have no idea and I'm not checking for you."

"Jesus, it takes me getting blown all to hell to get you to laugh? That is seriously fucked up."

He wasn't a fan of the gory details. But he had to know. "Dude, seriously? I can't move my arm to check myself."

Iaconelli's gaze flicked over to Carponti's side again and the source of the pain. Carponti was tempted to look, he really was. But he knew something bad had happened. Nicole was going to be so pissed at him.

"You're fine. Does that help?"

Carponti sulked. The thunder of overhead air support rumbled closer. "Not really, but it looks like my ride is here." He frowned and bit down on his lip as a bolt of pain ripped through his arm and down his side. "Is it bad?" he finally asked Iaconelli as the helo touched down. Dust swirled violently around them. Moments later, he was jolted onto a stretcher. "Ow."

"The docs are gonna sort you out, okay? But I think it's a long way from your heart."

Carponti managed to laugh. "My dad used to say that to me all the time." He blinked and looked up at Iaconelli. "Does that make you my daddy?"

"Fuck off, Carponti," Iaconelli growled. But for once, he didn't sound like he wanted to knock Carponti's teeth out.

Which Carponti took as a very bad sign.

Her phone rang at five thirty in the morning. Nicole was instantly awake, praying it was Vic. "Hello?"

"It's Laura. I need help."

An hour later, Nicole was busy in the emergency room, trying to help Laura keep order in the chaos. Laura's call for help with the Family Readiness Group had been desperate. Someone had leaked on social media that their unit had wounded soldiers coming in from Germany and everyone was gossiping and trying to figure out who was hurt. Normally families would have already been notified if their loved one had been wounded but this was the Surge and nothing was normal anymore. It had happened more than once that soldiers had been wounded and shipped halfway around the world before families had been notified.

Today, apparently, was turning into one of those days when getting a manifest was in the too hard to do category.

The emergency room was crowded full of spouses jockeying for information, and the staff there was doing their best in the middle of abject insanity. Nicole fought for patience as she tried to herd the women and two men into some semblance of order while she waited for Laura to figure out what was going on. She breathed deeply and tried to keep her own fear from paralyzing her.

There was no news from Vic. No e-mail telling her he was okay. No phone call. Fear clutched at her heart as she tried not to hover near Laura and their friend Jen—a nurse at the hospital—who was trying to get the list of names of the wounded from the admin folks.

She almost missed her cell phone vibrating in her pocket. She fumbled for it and nearly dropped it before desperately connecting the call.

"Hey, babe."

Nicole almost collapsed with relief. "You're okay," she breathed. "You're okay."

"Yeah, about that." She froze. Her heart stopped in her chest. "Um, I'm kind of in Germany."

Tears instantly burned behind her eyes, pouring down her cheeks. She swiped at her face. "What? Vic, what's going on?"

He breathed deeply on the phone. "So, I got blown up a little bit." He cleared his throat. "I'm going in for another surgery so I'll call you when I'm out." His voice was strained.

"How bad?"

"I'll see you when they evac me back to the States, okay?"

"My ass you will. I'm getting on a plane." Like hell she was going to sit there and wait. They didn't have a ton of money but her mom could get her a flight. Nicole knew her mom would do that much.

"Nic—"

"Don't argue. I'm coming."

He didn't say anything for a long moment. His silence terrified her but she held it in. "Okay." He paused. "I love you."

Her voice cracked and broke. A flood of fear crashed against her heart. "I love you, too. I'll be there as soon as I can."

She hung up the phone. Laura was right there. Nicole's eyes burned. "Vic's been hurt."

"What can I do?"

"I'm good. I've got to go, okay?" She was this close to falling apart. She needed to get away from the pitying looks from the wives who'd overheard the conversation.

The wives who were grateful it wasn't them. She couldn't blame them. It came with the territory. It was a guilty relief, a terrified fear that maybe next time it might be their loved one.

Right now, none of that mattered. She needed a plane ticket now. She didn't have time to fall apart.

Laura pulled her into a quick hug. "He's okay."

"I know." Nicole wiped beneath her eyes. "I'll let you know as soon as I know something, okay?"

Laura nodded and let her go.

Nicole was on the phone instantly, having her mom make the travel arrangements. She packed a bag in a blur. Somehow she remembered to pack a coat. She didn't even check any luggage. The plane took forever to taxi down the runway.

Her thoughts raced. Her heart drummed in her ears. She didn't do well with sitting on her hands but there was nothing else she could do. She paid the flight attendant for three little bottles of vodka. The first one burned all the way down then spread through her veins like a languid, numbing balm. The second one made her head fuzzy. She pulled the dark blue airplane blanket over her chest and turned her face toward the window so no one would see the tears as they ran down her face.

The third one went down smooth and she forced her eyes closed. She didn't sleep. She couldn't stop the fear that ate at her. Vic was in the hospital. He was alive. She clung to that thought amongst all the chaos in her head on the long hours of the flight to Frankfurt.

Her husband was alive. Whatever else happened, he was alive.

10

It was dark the next time the puffy cloud of morphine let him go. He blinked and tried to open his eyes but they were still too heavy. So he lay there in the dark and waited for the drugs to fade a little more.

He had a vague memory of being sent out of Iraq. The flight on the hospital plane was nothing but noise as far as he could remember.

He frowned as he blinked, hoping his eyes would obey at some point in this century. There was an itch on the palm of his right hand that was driving him crazy. He tried his hand to rub his fingers together to scratch it and felt...nothing.

Going in for surgery.

Carponti swallowed hard against the snippet of memory and breathed deep against the panic in his chest. *Oh fuck.*

He didn't burst awake in a panic. He blinked a couple of times then opened his eyes. Another deep, unsteady breath and he held up both hands. There was empty space where his right hand should have been. His forearm was heavy and numb and wrapped in thick gauze.

His eyes burned. *Oh fuck. Oh fuck.*

He covered his mouth with his hand. His hand. He held it up. His left hand was intact. He made a fist. His fingers closed. Okay. Wedding ring. He needed to find it. Nicole was going to kill him.

He looked at his right hand. Or, rather, the space where his right hand used to be.

The bandage was thick and heavy and extended past his elbow to his mid upper arm. He felt like his hand was still there but the empty space his eyes saw argued with the sensation in his brain.

Alone in his room, Carponti didn't have any smart-ass comments. He couldn't really come up with anything funny to make himself laugh.

He just kind of sat there for a minute and did nothing.

He didn't swear at God. Or get angry.

He just... sat.

It was much harder to wrap his brain around his missing hand than anything else. He was going to have to learn to write with his left hand. Was he still going to be able to shoot? Hell, he was going to have to learn to fire left-handed.

He scrubbed his left hand over his mouth. He stopped looking at the bandage and the empty space. Echoes from before his surgery came back to him.

Infection. We have to amputate now.

Might lose the whole arm if we don't.

He swallowed. All of that was a blur. He remembered making a crack about his balls but maybe he hadn't because the doctors hadn't laughed.

Maybe his sense of humor had been in his right hand and that had been amputated, too.

That was a shitty feeling. Holy crap, Nicole was going to be pissed. Had he called her? He couldn't remember if he'd called her.

What if she freaked out about it? What if she took one look

at the missing appendage and executed an about face and walked out of his life forever and went and found someone who was still a whole person? Someone who hadn't left her alone for years on end while he was off fighting some stupid ass war.

A man with both his hands to hold her with.

Holy hell, he didn't want to call her. He wasn't ready for that. She was going to be so pissed at him for getting hurt. Damn it, how the hell had he gotten himself blown all to hell in the first place? He frowned and glanced down at the bandage. *Residual limb.* Was that what it was called? Where had he heard that?

The silence was closing in on him. He wondered if the nurses would be irritated if he got out of bed. He didn't do well with sitting still. Never had. Hell, he'd driven his teachers nuts when he'd been a kid. The ginger kid with the smart mouth. He'd made everyone laugh. Except his teachers. They had never been amused.

He had a sudden, terrified thought that maybe he was missing more than just a hand. He froze.

Took a deep breath and lifted the blanket.

His legs were intact. A white bandage spread across his hip. Oh fuck. He lifted the gown.

Relief was something cold and wet that slapped across his skin. Everything was still there. His arm buzzed like a low jolt of electricity that hummed over his skin. He lifted it back onto the pillow where it had been resting before he'd started fidgeting.

He had to piss. He could do that by himself, right? He pushed the blanket off his legs. Hospital gowns were so sexy. He cradled his bandaged arm against his chest and gently eased his legs over the edge of his bed.

His head spun and the world tilted. He gripped the edge of the bed for a moment, waiting for the spinning to stop.

There was a quiet knock on the door. His stomach pitched,

imagining Nurse Ratchet coming in to give him hell for getting out of bed.

The door to his room swung open.

And a thousand emotions crashed into him.

His wife stood in the doorway, a small bag over her shoulder. She looked rumpled and tired and so goddamned wonderful. His heart did a funny flip in his chest. Right above the bandaged limb he'd cradled against his hospital gown.

NICOLE STOOD THERE, rooted to the spot. He hadn't shaved. There was at least three days of stubble on his face. A light dusting of red hair. His cheeks were thinner. He hadn't been eating well.

But his hair had grown back.

Tears burned behind her eyes. She felt like she hadn't stopped crying since she'd left the States.

She stood there—her husband a dozen feet away—and she couldn't move. He looked so good. So tired. So strained.

Her gaze drifted down his body, stopping on the bandages wrapped around his right arm. And reminded herself to breathe.

HIS FIRST URGE was to hide his arm. To keep her from seeing what had happened to him.

To run and hide from the fear of her reaction. The worst fear in the world seized him: that she would turn around and walk out that door. Asking her to wait for him had been nothing compared to this: asking her to love him when he was missing a piece of himself.

A thousand options raced through his head. Fear burned

through him. He'd be damned if he was going to cry about it. So he sat a little straighter, despite the dizziness that threatened to pitch him face first onto the floor. And wouldn't that be a disaster?

"Hey, babe." His voice sounded strange to his ears. "Don't be mad. I got a little blown up."

She bit her lips together. Her eyes filled. Fear stabbed him in the heart. She was going to leave. She was going to leave. Oh fuck, she was going to leave.

She dropped her bag and rushed to the bed. It was all he could do to move his bandaged arm out of the way.

And then she was there, her face pressed to his neck, her arms tight around him. A shudder rocketed through her. Grief, happiness, sorrow. A thousand emotions ripped through him, tearing at his heart and blocking his throat.

He froze for a moment, not really believing that she was there, in his arms. For the first time in months, he was holding his wife.

And at that moment, nothing else mattered. Not the missing hand. Not the months he'd spent away.

He wrapped his arm around her and held her tight. Breathed in the scent of her hair. Savored the feel of her body against his. "I'm sorry," he whispered. "I'm so sorry."

And when she crawled into the bed with him, he didn't argue. He held her as best he could and tried not to embarrass himself by crying.

***

Nicole came awake slowly, the steady beat of her husband's heart warm beneath her cheek. She lay there for a long moment, just feeling him breathe, reassuring herself that yes, this was real.

It was morning. She'd fallen asleep after the doctor had

come in and brought her up to speed on Vic's injuries and where he stood. Vic's expression when the doctor had said no sex would have been almost comical if the warning hadn't been so serious. She'd spent the rest of the evening lying with her husband, reading through the pamphlets the doctor had left. She remembered lying there quietly when the nurse came in to take his vital signs.

Her fingers curled over his heart as the tears threatened again. She wasn't normally this much of a crier. At least, she hadn't been before this deployment. It was just fatigue. She'd get some more rest and then she'd be fine.

Vic was alive. She sniffed quietly, trying not to wake him, but his arm tightened around her shoulders.

"Hey," he whispered.

"Sorry." She swiped at her eyes. "I didn't mean to wake you."

He pressed his lips to her forehead and she closed her eyes as the sensation of him touching her warmed her terrified heart. "You didn't," he said.

She swallowed and wiped her eyes, not wanting to move from the cocoon of warmth in his bed. She vaguely remembered the nurse asking her to sleep in the chair. She wasn't sure if Vic had threatened the woman but she knew she'd been allowed to stay.

"Are you hungry?" she asked.

"They already brought breakfast."

She turned her head, and saw the tray sitting off to one side. She brushed her hair out of her face and looked down at him. He looked tired. But he'd never looked better to her. "What time is it?"

"After eight in the morning." He reached up and brushed his fingers over her cheek. "You slept a long time."

"Sorry," she mumbled.

His lips were curled in a funny half smile. "Don't be."

Her stomach rumbled and he smiled. "Eat, if you're hungry."

She looked at him and tipped her chin. "Did you eat?"

Vic shrugged. "Haven't had much of an appetite."

"They're not worried about you not eating?" She sat up, crossing her legs and sitting on the edge of the bed. She felt fuzzy, like she needed a shower. But she didn't want to leave him. It was a stupid fear but she was terrified to let him out of her sight.

"I'll eat if I get hungry." He reached for the tray and pulled it closer. "You eat. I'm good."

She lifted the pale plastic lid of the domed tray. "Wow." Three pieces of French toast, two slices of bacon, and two hard-boiled eggs. She frowned, then immediately changed the direction of her thoughts.

Vic caught her. "What?" he asked.

She hesitated, hating herself for being so unsure around the man who'd always made her laugh. "I was just thinking the hard-boiled eggs were kind of messed up to give to a guy with only one hand."

Vic blinked for a long moment then busted out laughing. He reached for her, pulling her close as he laughed. She smiled and wiped at her eyes.

"You scared me," she said softly. She swallowed. "The next time, can you give me a little more information than *Hey, babe, I got blown up?*"

"Well, I...wasn't really sure what to say. I'm usually not at a loss for words and...well, yeah." He held up his bandaged arm.

Her expression softened. "Does it hurt?"

Carponti snorted. "No. They've got me on so much morphine right now they could probably cut off my other hand and I wouldn't feel anything." He held up his good hand. "Not that I want to test that theory or anything."

Nicole smiled. And his wife, his beautiful wife, cupped his face in her hands and kissed him.

WITH ONE KISS, she banished any awkwardness he'd imagined between them. He didn't want it to be awkward. He wanted his wife to curl into bed with him and... Well, the doc had said he wasn't authorized to have sex yet but that didn't stop his imagination.

She ran her fingers over his cheeks. Something so simple. He closed his eyes and let the tingling sensation run through him.

She cupped his face and he was conscious of the fact that his jaw was covered with bushy red stubble. "But you're okay. And that's what matters."

He just sat for a moment and looked at her. Savored the feel of her hands on his body, even if it was just his face. She was touching him. She was here and she hadn't run screaming from the room at the sight of his bandaged hand. He covered her forearm with his good hand. Her skin was warm and soft and real beneath his.

He was suddenly really glad she wasn't a drug-induced hallucination. "I can't believe you got on a plane that quickly."

She smiled. "It was a long flight." Her fingers drifted over his cheek.

She was touching him. She wasn't horrified by the missing hand. His thoughts kept repeating, over and over. Fear made him still, prevented him from reaching for her and pulling her close again. He was afraid. Afraid she was in shock. Afraid she was still adjusting to the idea of his missing appendage.

Missing body parts were a big adjustment, or so he'd been told. There weren't any briefings that could prepare you or your spouse for this. At least, none that he'd attended before. Maybe there were now.

Nicole looked away and slipped her hands from his face. The loss of her touch physically hurt him.

But he didn't say anything. Because he didn't have the words to bring her back.

She started sorting through the bag of things that had apparently come in with him from Iraq. He had no idea what was in that bag, but he wasn't entirely sure she should be going through it. He didn't want her stumbling across a bloody uniform or worse.

She pulled a small plastic bag out and held it up. His dog tags glittered muted silver in the fluorescent light along with his missing wedding ring. She pulled out his wallet and a clump of fabric. Carponti flushed and said nothing.

Somehow, his sewing project didn't seem funny right then.

"I'm glad you're here," he whispered, holding out his hand for the baggie. He took a deep breath, then dumped the contents onto his lap. His dog tags jingled against his wedding ring. He maneuvered the plain gold band onto his finger, then managed to use his thumb and pinky to get it back where it belonged.

Nicole hadn't noticed but it was a small victory for him. It felt right having his ring on. She turned back toward him, her lips curled faintly. "You didn't honestly expect me to sit in Texas and wait for you, did you?"

"I don't know. We never really talked about something like this."

She glanced down at his bandaged arm, then pushed the tray out of the way and climbed over his legs until she straddled him. And just like that, any chasm he'd imagined between them was gone and Carponti was lost in the sensation of his wife's body against his in all the right places. Okay, maybe not *all* the right places, but close enough.

"So listen," she said, crawling up his body until her knees rested on either side of his ribs. "This sucks but it's not the end of the world."

"You're going to get in trouble with the nurses," he said. He rubbed his hand over her hip, urging her a little closer.

"Since when do you care about following the rules?" She smiled and rocked against him even as she slid her arms around his neck. "I missed you so much, Vic."

The block of fear around his heart melted and thawed.

"So the good news is that everything from the waist down is still intact." He smiled wickedly up at her. "Want to take it for a test run?"

She rocked against him gently and cupped his face in her hands. "I'm sure we'll figure it out," she whispered against his mouth. "But no sex until after the wound is healed. I'm not violating any doctor's orders and risking you getting sick."

Carponti pouted. "Seriously?"

Nicole wrapped her arms around him and nestled closer, a laugh shaking through her body and into his. Laughing with him was almost as good as sex. Okay, not really, but it felt so damn *normal*. "Not until the docs give you the green light."

Carponti angled his body and pushed the nurse's button before Nicole could stop him. "Can I help you?" The nurse's voice was scratchy over the speaker.

"Yeah, I need a note from the doctor so I can have sex with my wife."

"Vic!" She tried to snatch the handset.

"Um, I'm sorry, sir. Can you repeat that?"

"Sorry, ma'am." Nicole grabbed the button. "Ignore him. He's high. We're sorry, ma'am."

She put the button out of reach, then snuggled up to his side. "That poor nurse," she said, laughing quietly.

"I'm serious." He rolled toward her and cupped her face. "I missed you." He swept his hand down her side. "All of you."

"I missed you, too. But no sex until the doctor says so."

Carponti sighed dramatically. "You're no fun."

"It's only a little longer."

"I have to be careful for the first few weeks so the wound can heal. Are you honestly telling me we're going to wait *weeks*?" Carponti pouted for a second and then blurted, "Oh shit."

"What?" Nicole was instantly alert. "What's wrong?"

Carponti lifted his bandaged hand. "This was my right hand."

"Yeah?"

"I, ah...pursue certain pleasurable activities with my right hand. Now I've got to learn to do it with my left."

Nicole buried her face in his shoulder and laughed. "There's something so wrong with you." But her voice broke and a shudder ran through her.

The emotions snapped inside him as her tears wet the hospital gown. He held her close and let her cry, so goddamned grateful that he was there to hold her. The thought of her crying on his grave threatened to choke him. "I'm okay, babe. I'm okay."

"I know." She leaned up and sniffed, wiping her eyes. "I just... I'm just glad you're here. I don't care about anything else. You're here. You're okay."

"I mean, I'd rather be elsewhere—"

She slapped his chest gently. "You know what I mean."

He smiled. "Yeah. I know what you mean."

He held her for a while. The noise from outside the hospital room faded away and he fell into sleep, holding the one person in the world who mattered most to him.

11

He woke up to a gentle kiss on the side of his mouth. He turned and nuzzled his wife. The doctors didn't like her sleeping in the bed with him but he didn't actually care. For every night over the last week, she'd waited until the late night nurse had completed her rounds and then she'd crawled into bed with him, careful not to bump his arm.

He slept better when she was with him. Her weight against his side was comforting and solid and real.

She'd stayed with him and he counted his blessings every single morning when he woke up and she was there. "Good morning," she whispered, nestling closer.

"Morning." He kissed the top of her forehead, savoring the quiet warmth of her body against his.

As hospitals went, Landstuhl Medical Center was pretty good. Food wasn't bad, nurses were nice when they weren't irritated with Carponti's antics.

The door opened and Nicole tensed. Carponti's arm tightened around her to keep her from leaving the hospital bed.

"You're going to get in trouble," she whispered.

"Don't care."

The doctor walked in. Carponti grinned. "Good morning, Doctor Kevorkian."

The doctor's face flushed red beneath his white hair. He did not look amused. "My name is Doctor Goldstein, sergeant. I've told you that about six times."

"Well, yeah, I heard you the first five times. But Doctor Kevorkian has such a nice ring to it."

Nicole was crying in hysterics next to him, trying to catch a breath to talk.

His wife's hand shot up to cover his lips. He kept talking but it was muffled beneath her palm. "Just ignore him," she said. She looked up at him. "Stop before you give the man a heart attack."

Carponti turned his wide-eyed expression on his wife. "What?"

Nicole's face was lit up with a brilliant smile. "The doctor does not share your sense of humor. What can we do for you, sir?"

The doctor's flush retreated a little bit with the knowledge that at least one person in the room wasn't clinically insane. "Looks like we're going to release you."

Carponti stilled. Nicole dropped her hand from his mouth and slipped from his embrace.

"Okay." She climbed out of the bed and pulled on a sweater and paid close attention to what the doctor said. She asked questions Carponti didn't hear over the loud buzzing in his ears.

Somehow, things had reached stasis in the hospital room. He felt safe here. He'd learned to get his pants down with one hand. Started getting used to the idea that he was suddenly left-handed. But now? Now this was like jumping out of the airplane without a parachute. Being released? He wasn't ready to face the world. Not like this. Would people stare? Yeah, they'd stare. Hell, he'd stared every time he saw someone with a missing limb. He'd felt like an ass doing it but it was just so...different.

And now he was about to be released into the wild? He wasn't ready for that.

The doctor left and Nicole turned, a stack of papers in her hands. "They're going to bring all your medication up so we don't have to wait in the pharmacy," she said softly. Concern was written all over her face and he loved her for it.

But Carponti couldn't find a single thing to say.

SHE WASN'T USED to her husband being quiet. Before, when her normal had included mundane tasks like getting groceries and paying bills, she'd always assumed her husband's silence meant he was getting into something. Mischief and all that. Now? Now a new silence emanated from him and she was not used to it at all.

She read over the discharge paperwork, watching him out of the corner of her eye. He sat on the edge of the bed, his back to her. His head was down, his shoulders slumped.

She didn't think he was getting ready for a joke.

She set the paperwork down and climbed over the bed. She slipped behind him and dropped her legs around his hips then wrapped her arms around his waist. She simply sat there, leaned against him, and said nothing. Hoping that her actions were enough because she wasn't sure she could say anything without the tears breaking through again.

After a long moment, he leaned back against her, his hand sliding over her forearm.

"It's going to be okay," she whispered when she was sure her voice wouldn't crack.

"I know."

"But?"

He paused for a long time, his thumb rubbing along her skin. "I don't have any pants. I am positive that if I go strolling around the medical center in my gown, I will give at least six sergeant majors a heart attack."

She laughed then and, this time, tears didn't come. She laughed and simply held on to her husband because he was okay. He was a little shaken up, a little unsteady but he was okay. If she kept telling herself that often enough, maybe she'd start to believe it.

"I can go to the PX and buy you some clothes."

"Just pick me up some sweatpants, okay? Nothing fancy with buttons or anything?"

She crawled around and stood in front of him, her arms draped around his neck. "What's that supposed to mean?"

"It means you always dress like a million bucks and you'll probably find some very uncomfortable, starchy clothes that will make me itchy."

"You're always itchy in real clothes. It's like you have an aversion to them."

He grinned. "I do. Dress pants are a lot harder to get off when we're getting ready to do the horizontal tango." He held up his bandaged arm. He slid his hand down her side, resting it on her hip, and urged her close to nibble on her lips. "You have no idea how turned on I am," he murmured against her mouth.

Her throat went dry. She wanted very badly to kiss him. To feel his mouth on hers, his tongue slide against hers. But she was terrified that if she did, she wouldn't be able to stop.

And there was a fear, nestled deep inside her, that he wasn't as okay as he was pretending to be. And she'd be damned if she was going to do anything that would risk getting him hurt or sick or keep him in the hospital any longer than he'd already been here.

"Me, too," she whispered. "But doctor's orders."

He made a growling sound deep in his throat. "I'm going to

find someone with the first name Doctor to write me a note." He stroked his hand over her hip and tiny bolts of electricity hummed through her. God, but she missed him.

"I'm going to go buy you some clothes before I do something stupid," she said, slipping out of his arms.

"Define 'something stupid'?" he asked, his eyes glittering in the fluorescent light.

"Stupid as in lifting up that all too sexy hospital gown and riding you off into the sunset."

"Oh, I definitely think we should do something stupid." She scooted off the bed before he could grab her. "Not funny," he said.

"It's a little funny."

He lifted said hospital gown, revealing a very healthy erection. Nicole's body ached for him. She released a shuddering breath. "We can't, honey."

"First I lose a limb and now you're going to leave me like this? What kind of wife are you?"

She laughed and finished getting dressed. She palmed her wallet and her phone and paused. "So do you, ah, want to go home right away?" She looked up at him, watching his expression carefully.

"Do you?"

He glanced down at his bandaged arm. "I don't know. I mean, we're already here and we always talked about coming to Europe. I suppose we could travel a little bit before going home?"

She tipped her head and studied him. "Are you up for that?"

"I mean, I'm not skiing the Matterhorn any time soon but there's no reason why we can't ride the trains around Germany for the holidays, right?"

There was something in his voice, something that whispered to her that he wasn't cracking any jokes. She leaned in quickly and kissed him lightly. "I'll be back in a little bit."

"I'll be here. Learning a new skill."

She paused by the door. "Huh?"

"Learning how to masturbate with my left hand."

She laughed and ducked out of the hospital room before he lured her back to that far-too- tempting bed. He was making jokes.

It was a good sign.

CARPONTI STOOD in the middle of the hospital room in fuzzy new blue sweatpants and a t- shirt. The new shoes were rigid on his feet but they'd break in easily enough. It felt strange, being in real clothes again. Even stranger when he forgot to reach for something with his left hand because he kept forgetting that his right was no longer there.

There was a tingling in his phantom limb but he could manage it. He wasn't due for his medication for a while longer. But the pitch in his stomach had nothing to do with the medication or lack of food.

He was fucking scared. Scared of facing the world and the staring eyes and the stolen glances full of unspoken relief that it wasn't them.

His wife's arms came around him from behind and he covered her hands with his one.

"You okay?" she asked. Her voice vibrated through his back.

"Yeah," he said lightly, hiding the panic twisting inside him. "So it looks like I'm on convalescent leave for oh, the rest of the year." He turned and pulled her close. "When do you have to be back at work?"

She tipped her head up and wrapped her arms around his waist. "I've got the greatest boss in the world. She told me to take my time."

He held her close, loving the feel of her body against his.

He brushed his lips against her hair, hoping this celibacy was going to end soon. But it was enough, for now, that she was here and things were as normal as they would ever be again. "So I was serious about going sightseeing around Germany for the holidays. There's a little town down south called Rothenberg Ob Der Tauber one of the nurses told me about. Supposedly it's like this little Christmas village and stuff." He shrugged. "Since—well, I kind of didn't make it home for Christmas—maybe this will make up for it."

She slipped her arms around his neck, brushing her lips against his. "You made it home just fine."

"Just not in one piece."

She shook her head, her lips curled in a faint smile. "None of that matters. You're home. You're safe. There's no better gift for Christmas." She kissed him then and he thought to hell with the doctor's orders and kissed her back.

He lost himself in the feel and taste of his wife. The beauty of her faith in him and the solid feel of her love.

He had her.

Nothing else mattered.

She eased back.

"I swear to God I'm going to kill the doctor," Carponti growled, lowering his forehead to hers.

His wife laughed and brushed her nose against his. "You ready to face the world?"

"Not really," he said honestly. "I've already got two strikes against me and now I'm missing a hand. I'll never be in the cool kids club again."

She frowned. "I have no idea what you're talking about."

"I'm already a ginger kid with a smart mouth. Now I'm short one appendage? Oh yeah, I'm going to be the life of the party," he mumbled.

She kissed him gently. "You'll always be the life of the party with me."

"Hopefully that will be a private party really soon," he grumbled.

She laughed against his mouth then rested her cheek against his.

Carponti held on to the relief that sighed against his heart.

12

The Bavarian countryside sped by as the train rolled through the evening. There hadn't been snow when they'd been further north in Frankfurt, but as they traveled south in Bavaria, snow capped the roofs in traditional German villages and bright Christmas lights illuminated houses against the darkness that fell as they traveled.

Nicole watched the hills roll by, amazed by the pockets of villages and hamlets that dotted the countryside. And trees. There were so many trees. Not miles and miles of suburbs or highways. Just beautiful countryside lit up like a Christmas card. It was nothing like where they lived in the States, with thousands of strip malls that looked exactly the same on every corner.

Beside her, Vic's head bobbed and he yanked it up.

"Hey," she whispered.

"Hmm?"

"Lay your head in my lap," she whispered. "Sleep."

He didn't argue. They shifted around so he could keep his bandaged arm elevated and then he rested his head on her thigh. It was a comfortable weight and she ran her fingers over his hair and rested them on his neck. His pulse beat steady and strong beneath her fingertips, in time with the rumbling of the train over the tracks. The rhythm was steady. Comforting.

His hair had grown. It was longer and thicker than she'd ever seen it. He still hadn't shaved. She'd thought about offering to shave him but hadn't. She was worried about how to handle his new normal. Did she offer to help? Leave him be? She didn't know. But she'd gotten slowly used to the idea of her husband and his new beard. He looked rugged and sexy, but she couldn't tell him that.

He'd try to seduce her in the rail car and while she was always up for an adventure, she didn't really feel like getting arrested by the *polizei*. Spending Christmas in a German jail was not on her bucket list.

She'd fired off a few e-mails before they'd left the hospital wifi, but otherwise her phone was currently useless unless she wanted to pay ridiculously high overseas charges.

Besides, she didn't really need to know what was going on in the outside world. Not really.

She brushed her fingers over Vic's hair. His breathing was steady and low. He'd fallen into a deep sleep.

He was trying so hard to act like everything was normal. And a large part of things *were* normal. She hadn't expected that. Not after something like this.

But it was still a shock, getting used to the missing space where his hand used to be. She'd catch him looking at it every so often, and then he'd make some kind of joke and deflect her concern away. But she knew. She wouldn't call him on it but she was going to watch him carefully.

He was okay. Mostly. But that didn't mean she wasn't still worried.

He shifted against her thigh. She rested her head back against the seat and closed her eyes against the tears that threatened.

He was okay.
It was all that mattered.

THE VILLAGE of Rothenberg was something out of a Christmas filmmaker's dream, nestled inside an old walled city. It glowed against the starlit sky, full of beautiful gold and silver Christmas lights. Massive Christmas trees, decorated with classic German ornaments, stood in the central squares and brightly lit, festive shops were overflowing with shoppers. The cobblestone walkways glistened with ice as the heat from the day's sunlight faded, and the moisture on them started to freeze after the sun disappeared into the west.

They walked through the gates and into the walled city down the main *strasse*. The air was crisp, biting at their exposed skin. His arm was starting to throb but he took another pill and buried the pain. It was bad enough he'd landed in the hospital without a hand, but he didn't even have a Christmas present for his wife. He wasn't going to ruin their pseudo vacation by being a wuss about the pain.

It was just a missing limb. He still had three other ones.

Carponti walked with his wife down the narrow streets, past the ancient buildings and clock shops. Christmas was everywhere. Christmas trees—*tannenbaums*—and Santa Claus figurines were stacked on tables as people wandered by. Everything was slower here. People didn't rush, even though it was Christmas Eve.

They stopped by a tent and bought *gluhwein* and bratwursts.

"How are you feeling?" she asked as she squirted dark brown mustard on the bratwurst for him.

"Can you take the napkin off?" he asked. "Don't feel like eating paper and wrestling with it."

He glanced over at a little kid poking his head out behind his mother's wide hips. The kid couldn't have been more than seven or eight. His eyes were glued to Carponti's bandaged arm.

Slowly, the child lifted a finger. "*Was is das?*" His mother looked down, then followed the direction of her son's gaze. Horror spread across her face rapidly and she yanked her son's hand down. "*Entschuldigen.*"

Carponti looked at his wife as the mother hurried off with her child, scolding him in sharp German. "Well, parental mortification looks the same in any language," he said dryly.

"I suppose that's going to take some getting used to," she said quietly.

"What, getting stared at?" Carponti said. He stroked his hand over his beard. "Why wouldn't people stare at a sexy beast like me?" he asked with a grin.

Nicole smiled but his joke fell flat. "I think it'll get easier," she said, her hand on his chest.

"Yeah." He brushed his lips against her forehead. "I'm sure it will." But he didn't sound convinced. "Maybe I should get a puppet for it or something."

They ate quietly for a few minutes. Nicole didn't say anything and he watched her as she ate her brat.

It was a damn good brat. First real food he'd had since before he'd left for Iraq. The chow halls over there were pretty good, all things considered, but there was nothing like a freshly grilled bratwurst.

Carponti set his brat down and tugged her napkin from her. He ran it slowly over her cheek, catching the tiny spot she'd missed. He loved the way her lips parted, her breath freezing in a huff. "Think we should try to find the *gasthaus?*" he asked.

A huge Christmas tree lit up the square behind her. She was framed in soft light. There was moisture on her eyelashes.

He loved that he could still touch her. She nuzzled her cheek against his palm. "I think that sounds good," she whispered. "I want to run into one of these shops and try to find a restroom."

He didn't move. Neither did she. He stroked his thumb over her flushed cheek. Standing in the fading winter night, Carponti kissed her. A gentle kiss. Conscious of his beard hurting her, he parted her lips with his. He felt her quick intake of breath, her palm on his chest to steady herself.

This. Oh God, but he'd missed this. Her tongue slid against his, reminding him of everything he'd missed, everything he'd longed for while he'd been gone.

Everything he'd been terrified he'd never feel again.

Nicole opened herself to the hesitant caress of his gentle touch. She sighed and swayed against him, bracing herself as a floodgate opened wide and unleashed a torrent of desire.

Their lips broke apart with a gentle suction. He lowered his forehead to hers. "I've missed you so much," she whispered.

He closed his eyes, unable to speak, unwilling to break the moment with something crass. With one single kiss, she'd nearly dropped him to his knees.

"I really need to find a guy named Doctor," he muttered against her lips.

There was nothing sweeter than the sound of her laughter. In front of that tree, he wrapped his arms around her and simply held her.

THE SUN CREPT into their tiny room at the *gasthaus* early the next morning. The window was covered with frost, sending soft rays of light into the room.

Carponti shifted and pulled Nicole tighter against him, rolling until she was entwined with him. Her thighs were tangled in his; his good arm wrapped around her shoulders. He rested his bandaged arm on her hip, keeping it elevated and away from being bumped. At some point, he was supposed to start toughening up the tissue to start prepping for a prosthetic but he wasn't there yet.

Nicole made a sleepy sound in her throat and nestled closer. He lay there, on Christmas morning and was simply...still.

It took a lot for him to be still. He closed his eyes and breathed in the smell of her shampoo, the scent of her skin. His eyes burned and he blinked hard a few times, not believing that this was real.

Never in his life had he thought this day would come. A day where he held on to his wife with one arm because a piece of the other one had been sacrificed to the gods of war. He thought about Garrison. He needed to get an update on him asap. It dawned on him that he had no clue what had happened to his boss. Maybe Nicole would know. He'd have to remember to ask her later.

He wondered how the platoon was doing without him. Captain Davila hadn't been doing well before that last explosion. He was worried about him but there wasn't a damn thing he could do about that now.

Nicole shifted in his arms and he realized she was awake. He brushed his lips across her forehead and she lifted her mouth to his. "Merry Christmas," she whispered.

"I got you something," he said. He untangled himself from her and sat up, reaching under the bed for a small bag.

"When did you have time to do that?"

"When you ducked into that shop to find a bathroom." He was proud of the fact that despite everything that had happened, he'd still managed to get her a gift. It was small but he kind of thought she'd like it. He twisted, bending one knee in front of him before he handed it to her. "Didn't have time to wrap it, though. You didn't take nearly enough time in the bathroom."

She smiled and shook her head before taking the bag from him. "I wasn't in the bathroom. I got you something, too."

"Sneaky woman."

"Well, you can't use it for a while." She handed him a small box.

He fussed with the bag until he got the box out of it, then managed to get the top of the box open. It was slightly smaller than a shoebox. "What the heck is it?"

He pushed back the tissue paper and pulled out a German beer *stein*. It was a large mug with a pewter lid, decorated with a scene from the village in Rothenberg in a wild splash of reds and blues and creams. A thick lump rose in his throat when he saw the date scrawled on the largest building. December 25, 2007. He looked up at his wife.

"So we'll always remember this Christmas," she said quietly.

Carponti sniffed and said nothing for a long moment, simply staring at the mug in his hand. Nicole shifted closer, sliding one hand onto his knee and tipping his face to meet hers.

"You made it home," she whispered. "I know it's not how we thought it would happen but you're here. And I will always cherish this Christmas as the one when you came home to me."

Carponti swallowed the lump in his throat and blinked back the burn behind his eyes. "Damn it, there's something in my eyes." He swiped at them, stuffing down the storm of emotions inside. He handed her the small bag he'd hidden beneath the bed. "Open it?"

It was a silly thing he'd bought her. It had been on a whim but he thought she'd laugh. Now, after the stein, he wasn't so sure. The morning felt more somber. More real. Hell, this vacation wouldn't have happened if not for the explosion.

He watched her intently as she opened the first of two boxes. She pulled out the small globe and held it up in front of her face. Inside the globe was a space for a photo. "I figured you could put a picture of your dad in it," he said quietly.

She offered a watery smile as she leaned in and pressed her lips to his. "It's beautiful. I love it."

"Open the next one."

She narrowed her eyes. Damn it, she'd heard the funny note in his voice. He had to get better at hiding things from her. Or maybe not.

She set the next box on her lap and lifted the lid. "What is it?"

"Look closely."

"Oh my god, Vic, you didn't."

It was a tiny piece of cloth. Nicole covered her mouth with her hand and laughed hysterically. "Is this what I think it is?"

"That depends on what you think it is," he said carefully.

"Man dress?" Tears welled in her eyes and spilled down her cheeks as she laughed. She was still laughing as she crawled into his lap and kissed him.

"I take it you like it," he said.

"You have a sick sense of humor but yes, I like it." She kissed him until he was breathless and the sadness he'd felt a moment before dissipated in the love of her touch. "I love it. Did you actually make it yourself?"

He smiled, loving the fact that his wife was in his lap.

"Merry Christmas?" he said.

Her laugh bubbled up, warming his heart and so much more. She wrapped one arm around his neck while she slipped her hand down the front of his pants. "Cute. How long did that take you? And when can we try it on you?"

She slid her hand down the length of him and a shudder tore through him. "Jesus, that feels good," he whispered.

Arousal, hot and needy, pulsed through him as she stroked him.

She kissed him, her hand sliding up and down his length slowly. "I don't want to wait anymore," she whispered.

"Thank God."

He started to lift her shirt. "Let me," she said.

She pulled her long-sleeved t-shirt over her head, gently easing it up, teasing him with every inch of exposed flesh before pushing his pants down over his hips.

He tugged at her bra and she reached behind her to unhook it. His hand on her breast felt so good. Like a piece of her had been missing until that very moment, that single touch that lit her entire body on fire.

She moaned when he gently took one nipple between his teeth. "Oh god, I missed you," she murmured, holding his mouth to her.

She rocked against him, felt his erection rubbing against the seam of her pants. "You're wearing far too many clothes," he said.

"I can fix that." She stripped off the rest of her clothes then crawled back into his lap, pushing him down onto the bed.

His body was hot beneath hers, his hair crisp against her inner thighs. She loved the rough feel of him beneath her. She rocked against his erection, savoring the feel of that first touch.

"Honey, I hate to tell you this but I'm not going to last long."

"I don't care." She kissed him then and angled his erection to just there at the entrance of her body. She rocked gently and he hissed between clenched teeth. She bit his bottom lip.

Then she slid down his length, taking him deep.

Taking him home.

Her throat closed off. She buried her face in his neck for a moment, unable to process the intense emotion of having him there, inside her, around her.

With her.

His arms wrapped tightly around her. The bandage on his arm was rough against her back. She didn't care. She didn't care because everything else was real and hot and good. So goddamned good.

She started to move, to rock gently over him. His expression tightened. His body tensed.

And then she felt him coming, deep, deep inside her. Touching the last reserve of her soul.

Reminding her that happiness—her happiness—was with this man.

"Sorry," he mumbled against her neck.

"Oh, I'm sure you'll take proper care of me later," she whispered, still rocking against him, her own pleasure there, just there.

He slipped his hand between their bodies, finding her swollen and aching. He fumbled with his touch. His face flushed but she leaned back, giving him space, letting him learn how to touch her body all over again.

He touched his wife, their bodies still connected. He stroked her just right and she clenched around him, rocked against him. Made the tiny sexy sounds that he'd missed so goddamned much while he'd been gone.

She rocked hard against him, her pleasure exploding, squeezing his still hard body deep inside her. She buried her face in his neck as it rocketed over her and sent them both tumbling into the abyss.

He held his wife close and fought back tears that burned behind his eyes. Her arms were tight around him, her breath hot against his bare skin.

Now, he was finally home.

It didn't matter where they were.

He'd made it. Maybe not all of him, but he'd made it. Safe and warm in his wife's arms, he'd made it.

He was home.

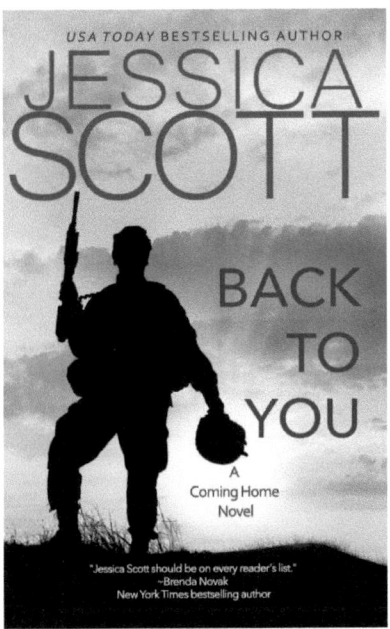

Thank you for reading **I'LL BE HOME FOR CHRISTMAS**. I hope you enjoyed Carponti and Nicole and their Christmas homecoming.

Keep reading to find out what a broken hero will do win back the woman he loves. Find out what happens in **BACK TO YOU**.

Trent has given his life to the Army. When he faces his darkest challenge, it will take the love of a strong woman to get him on his feet again and dare him to love again. Can Laura forgive him for leaving her alone for so many years

One click BACK TO YOU, a sensual second chance romance now!

EXCERPT FROM BACK TO YOU

Prologue

Fort Hood
2007

"I put your checkbook in the front pocket of your ruck sack. Did you find the sleep medication? You'll need to sleep on the plane so that you're rested when you land. And I put your calling card—"

Captain Trent Davila looked up from where he sat on the edge of their bathtub. He held a tiny folded flag in his hands. For a moment, he'd been somewhere else. Sulfur scorched the inside of his nose. The thunder of the fifty cal reverberated off his breastbone.

"What's that?" she asked softly, watching him from the bathroom door.

He held out his palm so she could see the little flag. "Good luck charm. I can't deploy without it."

A thousand questions flickered over her face as her gaze fell onto that tiny flag. She bit her lip and turned away, but not before he saw the naked fear looking back at him.

He moved, stepping in front of his wife and capturing her face in his palms. Her skin was smooth and soft and achingly familiar, and a deep part of his soul missed her already.

But that part of his soul wasn't in control right now. The moment she touched him, his soul recoiled, refusing to let him take even the simplest pleasure in her touch.

He'd cheated death and he knew, *knew* he didn't deserve to be there with his wife when so many of his men had died.

That's why he had to leave. Again. It didn't matter to where. It didn't matter if it was the war in Iraq or a transition team somewhere in the mountains of Afghanistan. He needed to get away. To get back into the fight.

And pray that his wife would understand why he had to go.

"Laura." He whispered her name, capturing her attention.

She tried to look away, to pretend that today was just another day. But Trent knew her too well. He saw the doubt and the fear that she tried to hide. Her eyes, though, her eyes always gave her away. He stroked an errant strand of copper hair away from her forehead, meeting her golden eyes, unable to speak any words of comfort. He knew they'd just be more empty lies.

She offered a watery smile. "I'm terrified of losing you again," she whispered.

"I've deployed since I got hurt. This time is no different."

"You didn't get hurt." She refused to meet his gaze. "You died. Your heart actually stopped beating. And this time is worse. This is the Surge." Her voice broke. "I can't lose you again," she whispered. Her voice cracked as the tears tumbled down her cheeks.

He hated to see her cry. Worse, he knew he could prevent those tears.

He pulled her close and simply held her, wishing he could

feel as alive with his wife and family as he did when he was at war. Maybe someday, when the war was over, he could figure out what had broken inside him and how to fix it.

He stroked his thumbs over her cheeks as the kids shrieked in Ethan's bedroom. The sound sent a spike of anxiety through Trent's heart, but he smiled, hoping to cheer her up. "Sounds like someone just lost a Lego."

"Daddy!"

"He's probably going to beg you for a hamster again," she said. Laura swiped at her eyes, blinking rapidly. "Can't let them see me like this."

He slid from her embrace, regret sealing the walls that four deployments had erected around his heart. Trent tried not to notice how intently Laura watched him, her gaze sweeping over the scars on his body as he finished getting dressed. His dog tags banged against his ribs as he dragged his t-shirt over his head and pulled on the rest of his uniform and then his boots.

"Well, you could get one," Trent said, needing the distraction of simple conversation.

"Or," Laura said with a smile that didn't reach her eyes, "you could promise him one when you get home. It'll give him something to look forward to."

Trent frowned at the odd note in Laura's voice and focused on tying his boots and tucking the laces beneath the cuff of his pants. "He won't even notice I'm gone. They're both too little."

Trent straightened as Laura approached, placing her palm over the scar on his heart. It burned where she touched him. It took everything he had not to flinch away from the gentleness in that touch. "Keep telling yourself that," she said with a soft kiss. "They miss you when you're gone. We all do."

He sighed quietly and glanced at her, resting his hands gently on her hips. "Laura, you know I have to go."

He couldn't explain it. Didn't have the words to explain the emptiness inside him that consumed every waking moment when he wasn't over there. And worse, he didn't ever want her to see the emptiness he tried so hard to hide from her.

She believed he'd come home. As long as she continued to believe that, his world would continue to exist.

She brushed her thumb over his bottom lip. She blinked rapidly and the sight of her tears almost penetrated the cold empty space where his heart had been. "I just wish it got a little easier waiting for you, that's all." Her fingers wrapped around his dog tags, her thumb sliding along the chain. "But we'll be here when you get back. We always are."

He ran his fingers lightly over her face. The lie he'd told his wife so often sat like a concrete wall between them. She didn't know that he'd volunteered for this deployment, for so many others, and he had no way of killing the lie without killing their marriage. "Don't go getting a deployment boyfriend while I'm gone."

"I don't think you have to worry about that." Laura wrapped her arms around him, nuzzling his neck. They stood for a long moment before Laura eased away.

Trent swallowed and let her go. Again.

FIVE HOURS LATER, Trent kissed his wife good-bye for the fourth time in six years. His four- year-old son and two-year-old daughter were getting antsy, climbing up and down the bleachers non-stop. As he walked away from the gym where he and the rest of his unit had checked in for the deployment, he glanced up at her in the stands. She was steady. Stoic. Trying valiantly not to join the ranks of the wives and children who were crying as their soldiers left them, assault packs and weapons in hand. God but he wished he didn't have to go. That he was man enough to stay home and fix whatever was broken inside him. Wished that he were man enough to need her more than the heady, uncertain terror of war.

"You ready, sir?"

Trent glanced over at First Sarn't Roy Story, a man who'd taught Trent the right way to kick in doors and the difference between knowing when to wipe a nose or whip an ass. The war was lined into Story's leathery face. Fifteen years as an infantryman that had started in Mogadishu and continued with the long slog through Iraq.

"Are we ever really ready for this?" Trent asked, taking one more long look at his wife and kids. And then he turned away, needing to harden his heart for the battles to come.

Outside, Trent climbed aboard the bus that would take them to the airfield. Spouses filed out from the gym along the sidewalk. In the seat behind him, Sergeant Vic Carponti was harassing one of Trent's platoon sergeants, Sergeant First Class Shane Garrison. He almost smiled. With those two around, things would never be dull.

He scanned the crowd, searching for his wife amongst the blurry faces of other people's spouses lining the sidewalk. There. She held her vigil in front of a light pole, a tiny hand in each of hers. Beside her, Ethan stood bravely, tears streaming down his face. He held a tiny salute, his mouth pressed into a flat line as he tried to be a tough little man. Emma waved brightly at the bus, still too little to fully understand that Daddy was leaving for longer than a trip to the grocery store.

He looked away but it was far, far too late. When he closed his eyes, the image of his small family was seared onto his retinas as the bus pulled out of the parking lot and headed for the airfield.

"Never gets any easier, does it?" Story asked quietly, sucking on the end of an unlit cigar while he fiddled with a light on his helmet. There was little love left between Story and his wife. Story deployed to avoid his wife.

But Trent deployed to avoid his *life*. Because life back in the rear was too complicated, too loud, too chaotic. War was simpler.

The scar on his chest ached and he rubbed it, wishing he could forget the way his family looked as the bus pulled away.

He closed his eyes, trying to put them out of his mind. He didn't want to remember his wife with her cheeks streaked with tears or the raw grief in her eyes. He wanted to remember her face as she slept curled into his side. Or laughing with their kids. He needed to carry those memories into war with him. Because that was all that would steel him against the long hours and bone-crushing fatigue to come.

He had soldiers to command. His family would be there when he came home.

He hoped.

Chapter One

*Fort Irwin,
California 2008
One year later...*

Trent walked out of the ops tent, needing a few minutes to himself. They'd just sent word that the wife of a kid in one of the companies was in the hospital. She was going into labor while her husband was enjoying the fun and sun of the National Training Center.

At least the kid wasn't deployed. He'd be able to get home quickly. Sure, not as quickly as if he was back at Fort Hood, but still. It beat the hell out of trying to get home from Iraq.

The notification was something simple, and yet it had struck Trent that yet another soldier was going to miss the birth of his child because of the Army.

He knew exactly how that felt and right then, a thousand

bitter memories rose up, reminding him of everything he'd willingly squandered. The resurrected hurt was so raw, the regret so powerful, he nearly choked on it.

He should be used to the hurt by now, but lately it seemed to be getting worse. It overwhelmed the dead space inside him, forcing him to feel things he didn't want—and wasn't ready to feel.

He didn't know *how* to feel them, how to deal with them. So for the moment, he sat outside the ops tent and let the raging emotions storm inside him. Until he could get them under control. Until he could function again.

It had been happening more and more this year. The things he'd stuffed away had started having a nasty habit of reappearing when he least expected them.

He was starting to get comfortable with the crazy, but at least now he was starting to recognize the warning signs. Which was why he was sitting outside the ops tent.

"So your BFF Marshall is looking for you." Story walked out of the ops tent, a smirk on his face that only meant bad things for Trent. It was so strange calling him "master sergeant" instead of "first sergeant" but Story wasn't a first sergeant anymore. Just like Trent was no longer a commander.

Trent sat on the hood of a Humvee, smoking a cigar and contemplating his sixth cup of coffee since he'd come on shift twelve hours ago. He pushed his glasses up higher on his nose then glanced over as Story hopped up next to him.

Since they'd both been fired more than a year ago, they'd been hanging out on the staff together, responsible for nothing but PowerPoint slides. Funny how getting fired meant giving up the hard jobs in the Army. You still got to stay in the Army, but you just weren't trusted with taking care of soldiers anymore. It was a punishment, being put in the easy jobs. Trent would have given anything to get his old job as a company commander back, but that wasn't going to happen so he and Story and

Iaconelli kept each other sane and avoided the new commander. Captain James T. Marshall the Third drove everyone fucking crazy.

"Should I be worried?" Trent asked dryly, adjusting his glasses again. He'd long ago given up getting upset when Marshall attempted to piss in his corn flakes. Marshall had been tapped to take over Trent's company when he'd gotten himself fired and Marshall took great pleasure in reminding everyone that he was fixing all the things that Trent had screwed up. It grated on Trent's last nerve every time the words, "Well, sir, I'm still fixing the mess I was left when I took over" came out of Marshall's mouth at staff meetings, but what could Trent say? He *had* gotten fired. It didn't matter why. He supposed part of his penance for being a shitty commander was having to listen to Marshall without knocking his teeth out. He'd leave that for Story and a few of the captains, like Ben Teague, who were leading the insurgency on the staff. Trent had other things on his mind.

Like his wife. His two kids. The house that was no longer his.

He cleared his throat and tried to listen to Story.

"I don't know," Story said. "Marshall wasn't screaming so I think maybe you should be okay?"

Sergeant First Class Reza Iaconelli, one of Trent's former platoon sergeants, stepped out of the ops tent. "No, you should definitely hide," he said, interrupting the conversation. "He's bitching about having to transport you back to the rear early and he's pretty cranky."

Iaconelli was a big man: broad shoulders and built like an ox. He was steadfast and solid downrange but when they got home? Yeah, that's when things went to shit for Iaconelli. He'd never met a bottle of alcohol that he didn't like. He was lucky he still had a career but the sergeant major liked him. Trent respected his ability in combat enough to overlook any personal failings. Trent was the last one to judge someone's personal failings.

He reined his thoughts back to the present and the feeling that flittered in the dead space around his heart. "I'm getting sent back?"

Iaconelli shrugged. "Maybe they're finally going to court-martial your sorry ass," he said

lightly.

Trent flipped him off. "That would be nice, actually. If they'd at least get the damn thing

over with. If I never see Lieutenant Jason Randall ever again, it will be too soon.

"He is a special little fuckstick, that is for certain," Iaconelli said, staring at the end of his cigar for a moment.

Iaconelli may or may not have threatened to kill LT Randall downrange. Twice. But all of Randall's interpersonal hostility had been a sideshow, a distraction to keep Trent or anyone else from figuring out that he had been selling sensitive items and funneling the money to bribe the Iraqis to stop blowing their boys up. Randall had finally gotten caught and now was determined to take down Trent and anyone else he could with him. Iaconelli chopped the tip off his cigar and sucked on the end while he tried to light it.

"Too bad I won't be around for his court-martial," Story said.

"Did you get reassigned?" Iaconelli asked Story.

"Yeah. I'm deploying again in about two weeks. As soon as we get back from here," he said.

"Your wife isn't going to be happy," Trent said quietly.

"Actually, she's going to be thrilled. It'll give her a chance to find her some twenty-year- old boy toy to keep her busy while I'm gone." Story spat into the dust.

"So you're still married because...?" Iaconelli sucked on the end of his cigar.

"Because it's too fucking expensive to get divorced," Story said. "I'll take care of it after this next deployment. I'll save up some money first, though."

"Sure you will," Trent said. "You've been saying that since '04."

It was Story's turn to flip Trent off. "At least I'm willing to accept my marriage is over."

Trent rubbed his heart, knowing his first sergeant hadn't meant to score such a direct hit. At least, not with malice. "Yeah well, my divorce is complicated."

"These things always are." Iaconelli leaned against the truck. "Which is why I've never gotten married."

Trent snorted and was going to make a crack but Marshall took that opportunity to step into the darkness outside the ops tent. "Davila, you're going back to Fort Hood."

Trent glanced at his watch. "It's four thirty in the morning."

"And you're going to be on a plane in three hours. Pack your shit." Marshall turned to stalk off, mumbling about pain in the ass captains and not having enough time for this shit.

Iaconelli blew a smoke ring into the darkness. "God but he is such a charmer."

Trent sat there long after Story and Iaconelli went back into the ops tent.

He wanted to go home. But now that it was happening, fear slithered down his spine.

It had started slow. One day, he'd wake up, dreaming about Laura. Other times, he'd be in the mess tent and he'd think he heard her laugh. He'd hear a kid giggling on the TV and he'd look up, expecting to see Ethan or Emma.

Always, though, he was alone. He'd wanted it that way for so long. He'd wanted quiet when they'd been running around his feet, shrieking and bickering like kids did. He'd craved silence at the end of the day when someone would get out of bed for a glass of water.

He'd certainly gotten the silence and the solitude.

And the oppressive emptiness of it all ate away at him. He'd thrown himself into work here in the California desert. He'd pulled eighteen hour days gladly. The longer he spent away from the war, the less he felt its siren call, luring him back. And somehow, work wasn't enough anymore. Nothing he did pushed away the aching need to get to the one place he simply didn't belong: home.

He was back in the States but he couldn't go home. Not with an investigation hanging over his head and the potential for a very long jail sentence standing in front of him. And the worst part about the entire court-martial was that his brigade commander was changing command soon. If Colonel Richter left before the case was resolved, Trent would be at the mercy of the new commander—a new man with no loyalty to the soldiers he'd put in leadership positions.

It was not a comfortable place to be. The power plays between the senior officers never ended well for junior officers, and Trent? Trent was caught right now. He had to trust that Colonel Richter would take care of this before he left.

But a year after Trent had been sent home, Trent was running low on trust and patience.

Patience had never been his strong suit. Every other time he'd been home, he'd been prepping to go back to war. This time, the year had stretched in front of him like an unending slog.

It was the longest time he'd spent in the States since he'd gotten shot. It had taken him almost that long to realize just how badly he'd fucked up everything in his life that was supposed to be important.

His marriage. His kids. His family.

If there was a grade lower than an F at being a husband or a dad, he'd earned it. He'd come home from Iraq nearly a year ago—pending a court-martial and a divorce. And since then, nothing had happened. The case had been stuck in investigation mode forever. And the divorce? He just wasn't able to sign the papers. His life had been frozen in carbonite on all counts.

The investigation had moved slower than molasses in winter. And he was glad.

Because standing out here in the California desert, he'd come to a conclusion. He wanted his family back. He wanted his *wife* back. When she'd slapped him with divorce papers last year, he'd refused to sign them, hoping that the investigation would go away and that he could fix things with her. But that hope had proved futile. The distance between them was too much. The warmth he remembered was gone, but still, he'd been unable to let her go. He couldn't. Sure, they spoke on the phone or when he saw her at the office, but they were a few stolen minutes here, a quick chat about the kids. There was nothing there to give him hope that he could fix things with her.

He'd volunteered to train soldiers anywhere he could so that he didn't have to face the cold emptiness of the reality that he was no longer welcome in his own home. And if he volunteered, someone else wouldn't have to.

Now? Now he sat in the middle of the California desert and thought about the new dad who wouldn't be there for the birth of his child. He looked down at his wedding ring and thought of all the time he'd willingly given up.

He was a goddamned fool. He wanted her back. Damn it, he wanted his *life* back. The life with this woman who had once smiled and laughed with him and wrapped herself around him while she slept. Who was as beautiful changing Emma's diaper as she was dressed up in an evening gown for the Cav ball. This woman who used to ask about his day when he called home at two in the morning, even after she'd been up half the night with one of the kids.

He sobered, his hands trembling at the thought of his children and the tiny family that had grown while he'd been away. The tiny family that overwhelmed him and terrified him and dropped him to his knees with a need so strong, it crushed his lungs until he could not breathe.

He didn't know how to feel good, but he knew he'd never figure it out without them.

He had no clue where to start. He had no idea how to be a father to his kids. Or a husband

to a wife who could barely look at him.

Trent hopped off the top of the truck. He had a phone call to make.

Because it looked like he was getting exactly what he wanted.

And it was time to figure out how to be the man his family needed him to be.

Fort Hood

"Son of a bi-iscuit!"

"Bad Mommy!"

Laura Davila wrapped her scraped and bleeding knuckles in a paper towel and prayed to the patron saint of Army wives for patience. Her six-year-old dishwasher was currently spread in carefully laid out pieces across the kitchen floor and counters. And now the cavernous white interior was splattered with her blood. Awesome.

Her son Ethan looked up at her with disapproval in his dark brown eyes, and Laura flinched. "Sorry, honey. Mommy just hurt herself."

"You said a bad word." This from her daughter, Emma. "Agent Chaos said you're not allowed to say those words."

Laura glared at the fat brown hamster that was clutched in her daughter's hands. Agent Chaos looked up at her with disapproving beady brown eyes. Sitting there, silently judging her.

She had joked with Trent that he should buy the kids a hamster when he returned from his latest deployment. By the time he came back, things between them had already crumbled but he still remembered the damn hamster. He'd bought not one, but two of the stinking, smelly creatures. The hamster cuteness factor did not override the pain in the ass factor of having to clean their cages every other day to keep the smell from overpowering the entire house.

Maybe if Trent had been around more over the last year, she wouldn't have minded them so much. But instead of sitting at Fort Hood and working in an office like any other officer who was under investigation, he'd volunteered for several rotations at the National Training Center in Fort Irwin. He'd spent more time there than at Fort Hood over the last year. He might as well have just moved there.

She took a deep breath and pressed on her throbbing knuckles, focusing on the pain so that she wouldn't feel the tension that squeezed her heart every time she thought about her husband. She regretted sending him the divorce papers. She could admit that now, but she'd done the only thing she could at the time.

She could still remember that stupid flare of hope when he'd stood in her office that day. Hope that maybe, finally, he had come home to her.

But he hadn't.

And as time had ticked by and he'd refused to sign the papers and let her go, she'd moved beyond regret. Now, she wanted to move on with her life. Maybe someday she'd be able to think of Trent without the hurt and frustration that kept reminding her of everything she'd lost.

"You have to pay us each a quarter," Ethan said, stroking the fat orange hamster in his hands. Laura was seriously thinking about buying a cat—that would solve the hamster problem quickly enough. But it would be just one more thing to clean up after.

And she wasn't really up for the trauma of finding a dead hamster under the bed.

She could only imagine the therapy bills.

She pursed her lips and counted to ten...thousand. "Okay, guys, why don't you go play in the garage or something? Mommy has too many parts in here, and I don't want you to get hurt."

Or move anything. But she didn't say that out loud, because that would only encourage them to run off with some vital component that it would take her three days to identify and two more days to find online and order. A new dishwasher was not in the budget at the moment. Besides, she wanted to see if she could actually fix the thing herself.

She shooed the kids and their accompanying hamsters out of the kitchen and made her way through the master bedroom to the cache of Band-Aids she hid in her bathroom. The kids were all too eager to use every bandage in the house if she let them, which always meant that she couldn't find a Band-Aid when she really needed one. She'd resorted to hiding them like they were some kind of precious commodity. In her house, they were.

Laura pulled down the shoebox that held the first aid kit. She held her breath as she cleaned the cuts on her knuckles with iodine, then wrapped gauze halfway down her fingers, covering the empty space where her wedding and engagement ring had once been.

She paused, staring at her ring finger. Blood pooled on the pale band of skin there, as if her finger refused to forget the rings that had been there since forever.

Her finger might not forget the rings but that didn't mean it was a marriage worth waiting for. No amount of waiting or wishful thinking was going to change that. Trent had seen to that. And broken her heart all over again.

She knew in her heart that they were finished. He had lied to her so many times about his deployments. That alone had destroyed her trust in him. And then there was the rest of it...

She was ready for the pain to stop. Ready for her heart to stop waiting for the phone to ring. Waiting, so desperately, for her heart to stop beating for a man who was never coming home.

A spike of melancholy pressed on her lungs. Damn it, what was wrong with her today? She was past mourning the death of her marriage. At least, she kept telling herself that. So when was it going to stop hurting?

She briefly considered a shot of vodka to numb the pain, but that wasn't really a good idea since she was alone with the kids. She barely ever had a drink these days. She sighed and glanced wistfully at the discreet box on the top shelf in the bathroom closet. Droughts were not limited to alcohol.

She had gotten used to it, this new normal. While the kids were vibrant chaos, full of life and joy, the married part of her life was... well, it simply was. There was nothing there anymore. No joy. No hatred. Just silence and cold detachment overlying a dull aching sadness.

She simply wanted it to be over. And damn Trent to hell for dragging it out when he wasn't even willing to fight for them. And the silence between them? Between her and the man she'd thought she'd love for the rest of her life?

She sat on the edge of their bed, one finger rubbing absently over the bruised knuckles and her empty ring finger. She could hear the kids shrieking in the garage. One of the hamsters had gotten away. She smiled. She really didn't mind them, not when the kids loved the judgmental little beasts so much. It was a gesture of kindness from a man who couldn't be a father. She knew that.

It didn't make it hurt any less. She'd married him knowing what she was getting into, thinking her love for him was strong enough to withstand whatever the Army could throw at them. Knowing that the Army was a demanding job, that he'd be gone a lot. But that first deployment had done something to him, something deeper than just the visible scars on his body.

Once, she never would have thought the silence would grow too loud or that his empty side of the bed would become too heavy to bear. Once, she would have waited forever for him to come home to her.

But forever was a long time.

And her faith in their love had died long ago on some distant battlefield.

ONE CLICK BACK TO YOU NOW!

ACKNOWLEDGMENTS

This book was probably the most fun I've had writing in a long, long time, and first and foremost I have to thank my readers for clamoring for Carponti ever since the scruffy sergeant first hit the page. I hope you enjoy his story as much as I enjoyed writing it.

As with all my projects, it takes a village. First, I have to thank my agent extraordinaire Donna Bagdasarian for believing in me and being there when the poo and the fan were making babies. You don't know how much your support and faith means to me. To Amy Pierpont, thank you for proving there is still loyalty in the world. Paula Robinson, thank you for keeping me straight on series continuity! Finally to my talented editor Michele Bidelspach, thank you for seeing the potential in these stories and helping me write them the way they needed to be written.

And to my family. We're off on a new adventure but most importantly, we're off on it together. I'm so eternally grateful that Mommy and Daddy are home for Christmas.

USA TODAY BESTSELLING AUTHOR

JESSICA SCOTT

COME HOME TO ME

A Coming Home Novella

"This is an emotional and heart felt story, it makes you stop for a little while and think about all the things that you are grateful for, especially at this time of the year." ~ Claire, Goodreads Reviewer

From USA Today Bestselling author Jessica Scott comes an all new novella about a woman who came back from war changed and the man who loves her enough not to let her go in this emotional, snowed in second chance romance.

All Major Patrick MacLean wanted was Christmas with the woman and child who were his family in everything but name. But Captain Samantha Egan has come back from the war a different woman than the one who left - and she doesn't know if she can love him anymore.

But neither of them counted on the determination of a little girl

they both call daughter and if Natalie has her wish, her parents may have no idea what's coming for them. It's going to take Christmas miracle to bring these two scarred heroes back from the edge of a broken heart.

Previously published as
ALL I WANT FOR CHRISTMAS IS YOU

THE COMING HOME SERIES
Because of You
I'll Be Home for Christmas: A Coming Home Novella
Anything For You: A Coming Home Short Story
Back to You
Come Home to Me: A Coming Home Novella*
Carry Me Home*
A Place Called Home*
Take Me Home*
Homefront
After The War
Last One Home*

Note – these books are fiction. Any resemblance to real people or events is purely coincidence

Author's Note
The Coming Home series and Homefront series were originally published as separate series. I have rebranded them to get things organized as they were originally intended.

Come Home to Me: A Coming Home Novella* was originally published as part of the Homefront series

Carry Me Home* was originally published as Until There Was You as part of the Coming Home series

A Place Called Home* was originally published as All for You as part of the Coming Home series

Take Me Home* was originally published as It's Always Been You as part of the Coming Home series

Last One Home* was originally published as Find My Way Home as part of the Homefront series

1

It was hell getting your heart ripped out right before Christmas.

And no matter how much scotch he threw at the problem, Major Patrick MacLean couldn't make the bleeding stop.

Sam was gone. And she'd taken Natalie with her.

Patrick knew all the stages of grief—at least a few of them. The anger. The denial. Maybe not in that order, but he knew how to deal with Seriously Bad Shit.

Except that he hadn't moved—not from the couch or from the bottom of the bottle that he'd crawled into at the start of the holiday half-day schedule.

On the coffee table in front of him, his cell phone vibrated violently.

He blinked rapidly a couple of times. The angry gadget was blurry and out of focus. He was on leave. He didn't have to answer the damn phone if he didn't want to.

At least, he didn't think he did. He *was* on leave, right? He'd signed out, right? He rubbed his temples, trying to think if he'd called the staff duty. Hell, he couldn't remember. He groped in the dark for the bottle as the phone went silent.

Except the damn thing started vibrating again.

Someone didn't know how to take a hint.

He snatched the phone off the table, too irritated to look at the number. "Yeah?"

"Daddy?"

He froze, the haze burning from his brain instantly. The wound Sam had left on his soul ripped open again at the sound of Natalie's voice. He closed his eyes, fighting to breathe against the tightness in his throat. Losing his family was worse, so much worse, than anything Iraq had thrown at him.

"Hey, sugar bear." He cradled his head in his hands, his heart breaking at the sound of her voice.

Natalie wasn't his daughter. Not by blood or legal paperwork.

But he was still her daddy. The only daddy she'd ever known, and in his heart, she was his.

She was his family. Sam was his family.

And they were gone. Just. Gone.

He cleared his throat.

"You're up late," he managed, hoping she didn't hear how bad he sounded to his own ears. "Shouldn't you be sleeping?"

"Something's wrong with Mommy."

Hello, Captain Obvious. He didn't say that, though. He wasn't sure the eight-year-old would appreciate the sarcasm. "Is she hurt?" he asked instead.

"She's crying all the time. And she doesn't talk to me." Her little voice broke. "I don't know how to make her okay."

"Are you okay?"

"No." A tiny, hitched breath. "I want to come home. I want to see you. Mommy... Something is wrong." A sniff, followed by a muffled sob. "Can you come get me?"

"Honey, you're all the way in Maine."

Silence for what felt like an eternity. "Isn't this why they have airplanes?"

He smiled at the deadpan voice. Nat had been working on her repertoire of smartass skills. Any other time, he would have been so proud. Except that his heart hurt at the sound of her voice.

"I—" His voice locked in his throat.

"Daddy, I'm scared." Another quiet sniff. "Please come. This was supposed to be our first Christmas together since you and Mommy came home from Iraq."

Damn. The kid was good at getting what she wanted. He'd told himself that she was too little to remember when he'd kissed her good-bye and gotten on that plane. That she wouldn't remember the phone calls when she'd cried that she wanted him to come home. That she *misted* him when she couldn't say *missed* right.

That maybe she was too little to notice that her mother had packed them off without so much as saying good-bye.

At some level, he'd rationalized that letting Sam go was the right thing to do. That if she wasn't happy anymore, it was better that she left before they started hating each other. That things had changed between them, and he should remember the good times.

It was obvious since she'd come home that something was wrong, but he hadn't pushed. He'd given her space, thinking she needed it to get things sorted in her head.

Except that space, apparently, had been the wrong thing to give.

"Please, Daddy."

He closed his eyes. And made a decision that was either going to damn him to hell or save the little girl and the family that he loved with all his heart.

It was still dark, the moonlight frozen on the path in front of her. The cold penetrated her bones and seeped into her soul. The only sound on the wooded path was the crunch of her boots on the frozen crust. The air froze in her nose and seared her throat, biting at her cheeks as she walked.

Captain Samantha Egan walked through the Maine woods where she'd grown up and felt like she didn't belong there anymore. She didn't belong anywhere. Not at Fort Hood. Not back home.

Everything felt wrong.

And she was cold. But it was more than cold from the temperature. No, it was the cold of something dead in the space where her heart had been. She was more used to the Iraqi heat—even in the dead of what passed for winter there—than the frigid central Maine subarctic temps.

She'd hoped that coming home to Saber Falls might jolt the dead space in her chest back to life. That the darkness would burn away in the bright sunlight sparkling off the frozen trees.

But it hadn't. She'd been home for a few days, back from the war in Iraq for less than a month, and nothing she did felt right. Not being around Natalie. Not being around her mother or her old friends from high school. Especially not being around friends from high school. She'd tried to stop in and see her friends Garrett and Finn Rierson but her lungs had stopped working before she'd even pulled into the police station where Garrett worked. She'd kept driving, avoiding the reality of seeing them. Avoiding the reality of the loss of her best friend that threatened to cut off her air every time she thought about her. She breathed out as she rounded a bend in the snowmobile trail, turning back toward her mother's house, trying to ease the automatic tightness in her chest when she thought about Mel.

The hole in her heart was matched by the hole left in their lives from the war.

Nothing felt right but work. Work and being around the soldiers she'd deployed with were the only things that didn't feel wrong.

Even then, being around the guys from work wasn't the same now that they were all home. She was the odd woman out as the men went home to their wives and the women went home to their husbands and kids.

She pulled her hat down over her ears, trying to keep out the penetrating cold.

Sam had gone home to her daughter. To the man who'd been a part of her life for the last nine years.

And she'd felt nothing.

No joy at seeing Natalie. No happiness at being with Patrick.

Oh, she'd smiled and said all the right things. But inside, something special was broken. There were no words for the utter lack of any feeling. Everything was mechanical and stilted. Off.

Especially with Patrick.

He was a good man. A man she'd loved with everything she was.

But things weren't the same anymore. Something had changed during her deployment. She'd stopped calling as much, unable to bear hearing her daughter's voice on the phone. The pain in her heart when her daughter cried for her ripped out her soul, made her question everything she was doing in the war, in the Army.

But it was different with Patrick. She'd stopped calling him, too; not just Natalie. She hadn't been able to deal with hearing about the homework or dinner or all the other normal things he did while she was deployed. He managed her being gone so much better than she'd done without him.

It wasn't like he hadn't deployed, too. She'd been the worried other half on the other side of the world before.

Maybe the war had taken her ability to feel any happiness

at all ever again. The deployment …the deployment had broken her ability to feel anything for him, and she couldn't say why, only that now she looked at him and felt…nothing. She'd hoped, prayed, that seeing him would make her feel again, would breathe life back into the dead spot in her chest.

But that first night home, when he'd slid into the bed next to her, she'd feigned sleep and denied them both. She sucked in a deep breath, letting the cold burn in her lungs until her eyes watered.

He was no warrior saint. What she'd done—or rather what she hadn't done—had hurt them both. She'd seen his hurt and the anger and frustration just there beneath the surface.

But it hadn't cracked the frozen glass encasing her heart.

She couldn't say what had happened to the love she'd felt for him. But after a week of pretending, she'd broken the news.

"I'm going home for Christmas," she'd said as he'd stripped in the bathroom after PT.

He'd turned slowly, his dark brown eyes filled with expectation and a thousand questions. "Okay?" he'd said cautiously.

"I'm not coming back," she'd said, her voice as flat as the emotions in her chest.

The veins in his neck had bunched, standing out against his skin. "Back to me or back to the Army?"

She looked away from the penetrating concern in his eyes. Patrick was a good man. A strong man. A man who had loved her daughter and who had loved her.

And she wasn't capable of loving him back anymore.

It was better to end it now. Cauterize the wound before it festered and grew in hatred and anger. Maybe they could figure out how to be friends.

Maybe someday, when things weren't all wilted and frayed inside her.

"I'm sorry," was all she had managed.

Walking through the woods now, she couldn't say when

things had gone wrong. She couldn't put a mark on the calendar that she could pinpoint and say *here's when things went to shit* in her life.

She'd hoped coming home would fix things. That the fog would clear away and she'd feel *something* again. But the fog was still there.

And it still felt like she was looking at life from very far away.

So she walked. Through the woods as the sun slid higher over the frozen Maine trees and hills, hoping that something would snap her out of it.

There was no reason for her to feel this way.

She'd made it home from the war when others hadn't. She had a daughter who was healthy and a man who'd taken care of their lives while she was deployed. A career that she was damn good at.

She'd come home.

She just didn't know what that actually felt like.

She didn't know if she'd ever feel again.

But she had to keep going. Had to put one foot in front of the other. She just needed to suck it up and snap herself out of it.

Because she had a daughter to raise. And the war was far from over.

For her, it would never be over. The ghosts would be with her, no matter how far she walked or how hard she tried to pretend they weren't.

Her toes burned from the cold. She needed to get warm. Maybe Mom and Natalie wouldn't be up yet so she could sit by the fire and just let the heat seep into her bones.

Natalie was an early bird, though. All those mornings of getting up for daycare since she was a baby had set the little bugger's internal clock for the ass-crack of dawn. Maybe, though, maybe today she'd sleep in.

It was Christmas, right? Miracles could happen.

Sam had promised her a trip to see Santa. Damn, but she didn't want to drive the hour to Bangor to the mall. She used to love coming home to Central Maine for a visit, but she damn sure hated the thirty-minute drive for the nearest real grocery store or the hour plus to Bangor.

But she'd promised and, well, a promise was a promise.

So if the weather held, she'd bundle her little bear up and head to the mall.

But first she needed to get warm. Badly.

She opened the sliders to her mother's back door. She'd always loved her mom's house. The back of the house faced away from the road and civilization in general. It was peaceful.

She kicked the snow off her boots and slid the door shut behind her.

There was movement in the kitchen. The light was on now. Probably Mom. Guess Natalie's early riser tendencies were genetic. "Mom?"

Silence greeted her question.

She frowned.

Then froze as the shadows near the kitchen sink moved and morphed into the man she'd abandoned.

Patrick stepped into the pale morning light.

"Hi, Sam."

2

She wasn't sleeping.

Damn it, she looked good. Her cheeks were flushed, her lips red from the cold. Her dark hair stuck out from beneath the cap she'd worn. He almost smiled. It was her PT cap.

You could take the soldier out of Fort Hood and all that...

He didn't want to notice how seeing her made his guts tighten and his heart race. He focused on the tired lines around her mouth, rather than how seeing her made the anger and the hurt and the longing surface all at once. It was all churning together, twisting around inside him and making him wish for things that he couldn't have.

Her lips parted but no sound came out.

"Natalie called me," he said quietly.

"No one told me you were coming." Her voice was quiet and cold. Brittle.

Like she was one step away from the edge of a cliff.

"I didn't tell anyone." He stuffed his hands in his pockets because he couldn't think of what to do with them.

"You should have called."

"Would it have mattered?" He wasn't going to apologize for coming to Maine to see his daughter. Damn it, he wasn't going to let Sam take that away from him while she sorted out whatever the hell was going on with her.

She closed her eyes, and he could see the strain on her lips, in the tired lines of her neck. "Where are you staying?"

"At the bed and breakfast next to Finn's place." Finn Rierson had become a friend of Patrick's over the years.

"They're not booked this time of year?"

This polite conversation was strained, like something that happened between strangers.

"Guess not."

She said nothing, and just like that the conversation petered out. She stood there for a moment, still and cold.

She shivered and turned to strip off her coat. He watched her move, part of him so fucking grateful that she'd made it home from the war.

A man wasn't supposed to send his lover off while he stayed home with the kids. No matter how liberated he was, no matter how much he knew she loved her life in the Army, he'd worried about not being there to protect her. To keep her safe.

Guess he'd gotten familiar with how Army wives had felt. The year he'd had with Natalie when Sam had been gone had given him new respect for what she'd gone through when he'd deployed and a newfound respect for life on the home front. He'd counted down the days until she came home.

But the woman who stood before him now, shivering in the doorway, stripping off her coat and boots, wasn't the same woman he'd kissed good-bye all those months ago.

There had been distance on this deployment. Too much time between phone calls, short stuttered e-mails. No response to the notes he'd sent her telling her that he missed her. He'd been so busy with Natalie that he'd held out hope it was all his imagination. But when she'd come home, his fears had been manifested in reality.

The floor above his head creaked, followed by small, muffled footsteps. A moment later, a sleepy Natalie shuffled down the stairs. Patrick's heart melted as she rubbed her eyes. She hadn't seen him yet. She was tired and rumpled and adorable. Her hair was a twisted mess. She must have gone to sleep with her hair wet.

That had been a fun lesson to learn when he'd stepped into the role of primary parent. Sam had always taken care of putting Natalie to bed but when she'd gone, Patrick had gotten a crash course in little girl hygiene requirements. Put the kid to bed with wet hair, wake up with a rat's nest to comb through.

Which was always so much fun when trying to get out the door at five-thirty in the morning.

She stopped at the bottom step. Paused and blinked slowly.

Then her face lit up, and with a burst of energy, she shot across the small space, a happy cry of "Daddy!" filling the void in his heart.

He scooped her up, holding her close and breathing in the scent of her. She was clean and safe and warm.

She was his little girl.

"You came." She nestled close with a happy sound.

He caught Sam's eyes over Natalie's shoulder. Her expression was blank, but in her eyes was a hint, the barest hint of something beyond the dead, listless stare he'd seen since she'd come home from Iraq.

He wanted to shake her, to push her to snap out of it. To bring back the woman he'd fallen for all those years ago when she'd let him into her home and her life. A life that had included a baby girl that he'd fallen hopelessly in love with the moment she'd entered the world.

He didn't know how to fix things. He didn't know how to fix her.

And because of that, he was losing everything that mattered in this life.

Natalie leaned back. "Will you come with us to see Santa today?"

His gaze collided with Sam's. He saw her open her mouth. Braced for the denial. Braced for her to ask him to leave.

To ask him to stop being a father to the little girl in his arms.

"Honey, I'm sure Daddy's tired. It's a long flight from Texas to Maine."

Patrick stilled, analyzing her response. Her words bounced around his brain, seeking some point of reference before he recognized that she hadn't said no.

"What time are you going?" he asked when he could find his voice without risking embarrassing himself.

That feeling, that choking, uncertain feeling was hope modulated by pure terror.

"I was thinking about noon," she said quietly. "You could get settled first. Maybe take a nap if you wanted."

He tried to keep the surprise off his face and was pretty sure he failed.

Natalie bounced down and rushed to her mother. "Thank you! This way Grammy can go visit Mr. Thomas and have Grammy and Thomas time."

Patrick choked. He didn't want to know if "Grammy and Thomas time" meant what he thought it meant. He'd known Nancy and Thomas were close since the first time he'd come home with Sam. Natalie raced back up the stairs, yelling for Grammy. If Nancy had been trying to go back to sleep, she definitely wasn't now.

He'd always liked Samantha's mother. Nancy Egan hadn't approved of her daughter's choices, but she'd never breathed a rude word toward Patrick. When he'd shown up on her doorstep that morning, the only thing she'd done other than let him in the house was make coffee and then go back to bed.

Patrick watched Sam closely at the mention of her best friend's father. Had she seen Thomas since she'd been home? Sam may have lost her best friend but Thomas had lost a daughter.

How on earth was Sam coping with her death? He looked at her then, seeing the too-familiar grief looking back at him. He wanted to ask, to say something that would make the pain easier to bear.

But nothing, not even time would do that. It would sneak up on her, again and again over the years.

It was something no one told you about going to war. That it never really leaves you when you come home.

"I'm sorry, Sammy," he whispered.

She turned away, but not before he saw the tears glittering in her eyes, and his heart broke for her all over again.

HER LUNGS HURT. It felt like a massive sucking chest wound that ripped open all at once with the mention of Mel.

She thought she'd made her peace with her best friend's death on that convoy.

But standing there in her mother's kitchen beneath the sparkling white Christmas lights, her chest felt tight, her lungs compressed.

She couldn't breathe.

All she could do was feel.

And it fucking hurt.

She swiped at her cheeks, blinking and trying desperately to shove the emotion back down where she could pretend it wasn't a live thing, choking off her air.

That her heart wasn't shattering into a thousand pieces in

her chest.

She felt rather than heard him move. One minute, she was standing alone at her mother's sliding glass doors, her reflection staring back at her through the frozen glass.

The next, a shadow stood behind her.

His hands were strong on her shoulders, the heat from his palms radiating through the chill in her bones.

He was solid and steady behind her. A thousand emotions surged inside her, storming toward the gates, threatening to drop her to her knees.

It was too much. The sympathy in his touch, the ragged pain in her chest, the burning behind her eyes.

She sucked in hard, deep breaths, wrestling everything back into the box that she locked then threw into the darkest corner of the abyss where she could safely ignore it.

She'd deal with the emotions in that box some other day.

It was only when she was certain she wouldn't shatter that she turned to face him.

And felt the loss immediately as his hands slipped from her shoulders.

"Natalie is glad you're here," she finally said carefully as tiny feet pounded on the ceiling above them.

A neutral topic. One she could handle.

She hoped.

"She was pretty upset when she called me," he said. He didn't move, but he didn't crowd her either. He was simply there. Right there. All she had to do was reach for him. A single touch to cross the chasm between them.

It wouldn't fix things, wouldn't fix them. Because it wasn't their relationship that needed to be fixed. It was her. And she had no idea how to say the three hardest words in the English language. *I need help.*

"What did she say?" Sam asked, steering her thoughts away from the emptiness inside her.

His eyes reflected the frozen landscape in the glass behind her. Dark and whip-smart and so often filled with laughter.

Today they were filled with worry.

"That something was wrong." His voice was thick, filled with recrimination.

"She's not wrong." It hurt to admit that.

"I can't help if you don't tell me what's wrong, Sam."

She retreated a single step, her back colliding with the slider behind her. The cold seeped through her fleece. "You can't fix this, Patrick." *You can't fix me.*

"So that's it? You're just going to walk away and take my daughter and leave, and I don't even get an explanation as to why?"

"She's not—"

"Don't." He held up one hand, shutting down the words she'd been about to speak. His eyes flashed violently. "Don't tell me she's not mine. We never got around to the paperwork, but I've raised that little girl like she was my own. Don't you dare say she's not mine."

Sam swallowed the lump in her throat. "Patrick."

He shook his head and stepped away, out of her space. "I can't do this right now. Do you want to meet here or at the place I'm staying for the trip to go see Santa?"

"You don't have to go. You look exhausted."

He pinned her with a deadpan look. "That's what happens when you catch a red-eye to the middle of nowhere because your daughter says she's scared."

She wasn't prepared to deal with his anger. She supposed that was why she'd told him and then left the following day.

She hadn't wanted a confrontation. She'd been hoping things could just... dissolve quietly. Without any nastiness.

He hadn't fought her when she'd said she was leaving. She'd assumed that meant he was relieved. That he was going to just let her go.

But he was here now.

"You didn't have to come. You could have just called me."

"Phone calls didn't seem to be the right way to discuss things," he said quietly.

Hell, she'd run away to Maine in order to put some distance between them. Because obviously the distance between them for the last year hadn't been enough.

She could see his reflection in the glass behind her. The worry in his eyes. The hurt.

It was her fault. He was a good man. He didn't deserve this.

And yet she couldn't find any feelings in her heart for him. There was simply nothing there. She hadn't wanted to hurt him. She hadn't meant to. She'd only wanted to stop hurting him, to stop feeling like nothing mattered. To stop feeling afraid that if she said those three little words, he would turn away from her in disgust at her weakness that she hadn't been able to go to war after all. That she would lose her lover because she'd lost her ability to feel and she was ashamed to admit it.

She'd thought she'd been hiding what was wrong with her. One look at Patrick told her otherwise.

And she'd lost him anyway because she could no longer remember what loving him felt like.

But she couldn't be around him and remember that once upon a time, she'd felt something for him. Standing there now, facing him, was just a reminder of something else she'd lost along the way home from war.

And she hated it. Hated the war. Hated the pointlessness of it.

So why did she stay in the Army? Wasn't that the hundred-thousand-dollar question?

"I don't want to do this right now, Patrick." Words filled with sadness and regret. "We can talk about how to split things up after Christmas."

The patient, steadfast Patrick she'd fallen in love with all those years ago was there but he was angry now. And hurt. He stepped into her space.

His hands were rough where they slid over her cheeks. He didn't stop his advance until she was pressed between the cold glass behind her and the raw heat of the man in front of her.

"You act like things are already over," he said fiercely. "They're not."

And then he kissed her.

HE DIDN'T KNOW what pushed him to invade her space. He couldn't say what happened between the moment the idea formed in his head and moving. But part of him needed to feel, to touch her and remind himself that she was real, not simply a shadow of the woman who had left him.

He had to know.

But then her skin was cool and soft beneath his palms. Her body was hard and warm against his, her lips soft and warm and *Sam*.

They parted with a gasp. It was a shock to them both as he took, demanding access to her secrets and her pain and everything she was holding back from him.

From them.

Because this distance—this wasn't just about physical distance.

She was his best friend.

And he kissed her like he was dying without her.

Because he was.

He wanted his Samantha back. The warrior goddess who'd laughed when they'd been at the range and she'd outshot him. The fierce lover who took her own pleasure while driving him wild.

The woman who didn't take shit from anyone.

He kissed her like it was his first taste of pleasure in months.

Because it was.

Her response was a deep, shuddering thing between them. One hand curled around his forearm as he claimed them both, held nothing back. Poured everything he was into that kiss and told her without words that he wasn't giving up on her without a fight.

The briefest flare of passion and then it was over.

But it wasn't. She was still in there. His Sam was there. Damaged and afraid, but there. He'd felt her in that kiss, the echo of the love they'd felt for each other.

He stepped back, knowing he was leaving her off-kilter and unbalanced and knowing there was nothing else he could do.

"I'll meet you here in an hour."

And he was gone before she could protest.

Because in that kiss, Patrick had made a decision.

That kiss wasn't a kiss that said they were over. She'd responded to his touch, she'd swayed against him. He knew in his bones that had they been alone, he might have been able to press his advantage and find a way into the dark where she was trapped.

If there ever was a time for a Christmas miracle, now would be the time, he thought as he drove out of the snow-packed drive and turned onto Route 16, heading into the tiny little town of Saber Falls.

He didn't have a plan. He didn't have a fairy godmother to tell him what was wrong so he could figure out how to fix it.

But if the war had taught him anything, it was that time was so very precious.

He was going to figure this out.

Because if he lost her and Natalie, he'd have truly lost everything.

3

"Why are you being so quiet, peanut?"

Patrick glanced in the rearview mirror at Natalie. Her little brown head was bowed, and she was scribbling on a piece of paper.

There was no kicking the seat, no whining about having to pee five minutes after leaving the gas station.

There was just silence.

And silence plus kids always equaled trouble.

He'd learned that the hard way when Sam had first deployed, too. He'd thought he'd have a nice Sunday afternoon watching football while Natalie played in her room. He'd dozed off, only to wake up in a panic when he realized he hadn't heard a peep from her in who knew how long.

She'd been painting the bathroom floor. With nail polish. Which had been much harder to get off porcelain tile than he'd been prepared for. He'd also learned the difference that day between acetone and non-acetone nail polish remover. And hadn't that been a fun conversation to have in the middle of Wal-Mart with a little old lady who looked ready to call Child

Protective Services because Natalie was out in public in pajamas, a bath robe, and bunny slippers. At three in the afternoon.

He smiled at the memory.

"Nat?"

She looked up. "Nothing, Daddy. Just writing a letter to Santa."

He glanced over at Sam, who shrugged and remained quiet.

"What are you going to ask him for?"

She looked up at him, and he saw her mother looking back at him from those somber blue eyes. "I can't tell you that. It's a secret."

"Baby, it's a secret when you blow out your birthday candles and make a wish. It's not a secret to tell us what you're going to ask Santa for."

She shook her head. "Nope. Not telling."

He saw Sam's lips curl in a faint smile before turning his attention back to the logging truck in front of him.

That kiss stood between them like a live thing, demanding attention and unwilling to be ignored.

And yet, Sam was doing her best to pretend nothing had happened. That he hadn't seen the spark in her eyes when he'd stepped away. That she wasn't gone forever.

But she was still there. Hiding. Deep in the shadows.

All he had to do was figure out a way to draw her out, back into the light.

He sighed quietly and focused on the road. A better man might have let her go. Might have cut his losses with a woman who was, even after nine years together, still skittish. Still didn't trust that he wouldn't cut and run.

That he was not her father or the man who'd left her high and dry.

"How was your flight up?" he asked, trying to fill the silence.

"Fine."

"Well, let's not waste too much air on conversation, now shall we?"

She shot him a bland look. "I'd rather not do this with little ears in the car, if it's all the same to you."

A tiny voice chirped up from the back seat. "Are you two getting divorced?"

Patrick glanced over at Sam, who looked just this side of horrified.

"No, honey, we're not getting divorced," Sam said quietly. "Why do you know what divorce even is?"

"My friend Elsa's parents are getting divorced. She said her mommy called her daddy a two-timing pig. What's a two-timing pig?"

Patrick rubbed his hand over his mouth to keep from smiling. Sam was less than impressed.

"It means that her parents aren't going to live together anymore," Sam said gently.

Patrick glanced at Natalie. She tapped the pencil against her cheek. "So if you and me move to Maine and Daddy stays in Texas, how is that not divorce?"

Patrick felt slightly ill. He sighed quietly. "It means Elsa's parents aren't going to be married anymore. Your mommy and I aren't married, so we can't get divorced."

And holy hell, he did not want to do this right now. Talk about making it difficult to pay attention to the truck in front of him.

"Why aren't you married?"

"It's a long story, honey," Sam said. "It hasn't mattered before."

Except that it damn sure mattered now. Patrick tried not to be bitter.

Patrick cleared his throat. "Why don't you work on your letter to Santa some more?" he said, hoping, praying that she would drop it and knowing that she probably wouldn't. She was usually incessant with questions.

So the silence that came out of the back seat ended up being quite a surprise. After a while he looked back in the rearview to see she was still busy writing.

"What the heck could an eight-year-old be writing that takes so long?" he asked Sam beneath his breath.

"She's always had an active imagination."

There was nothing more to say, because Sam was right. The things that needed to be said couldn't be said in front of Natalie.

Instead, there was only silence as the drive continued.

∽

SAM TOOK a deep breath as they stepped out of the cold and into the cavernous mall entrance.

It hadn't changed much since she'd worked there as a teen. She'd been so excited when she'd gotten a job at Chess King. It had been so cool to have a job in the mall.

The Chess King was gone now, replaced by some place that sold purses and Maine kitsch. She wasn't sure who at the mall would buy the refrigerator magnets or bumper stickers. Probably for folks who lived out of state now or had friends who visited.

She'd braced for the overwhelming sense of the familiar.

She did not count on the anxiety that slithered around her chest, squeezing like a wet wool blanket.

She looked back for Natalie. "Nat, honey, hold my hand."

Patrick looked over at her, a question in his eyes.

"I don't want her to wander off," Sam said.

The fear was relentless, a pressure on the back of her neck that made her want to keep turning around. She rubbed Natalie's hand, trying to focus on anything other than the sensation of being unable to breathe.

Patrick's hand on her shoulder startled her. Her breath lodged in her throat.

"Sam." His voice was gentle, his touch strong. "We can go," he said quietly. "We don't have to do this right now."

She blinked rapidly. There was no judgment in his voice, no condemnation.

Simply understanding.

She smiled sadly. "We just drove an hour."

"Are you okay?"

"I have to be, don't I?"

He slipped his hand over her neck, cradling her. "Not all the time. No."

She bit her bottom lip and looked away. Wishing she could explain the pressing fear on her heart. Wishing she could make the insurgent trepidation go away and leave her alone.

Wishing she could have a normal day at the mall with her daughter to go see Santa. But she couldn't. Because she had decided that going to war was going to be a day at the damned beach. She hadn't counted on the fear of getting blown up in a convoy grafting itself violently onto the fear of losing her daughter in a mall. They were not even remotely related and yet she knew that one had led to the other. There was simply no other source.

She'd done this before—gone to the mall and gone shopping like a normal person. Before the deployment. Before she'd spent days on the roads with her battalion commander.

She'd been fine before the war.

Now? Now she was just this side of a paranoid basket case. And wasn't that a fun way to spend the day?

She was *not* going to ruin her daughter's trip to see Santa.

She sucked in a deep breath. "Thank you for saying that, Patrick," she said softly.

She met his gaze then. Saw the worry and the concern.

But it was the hurt that struck at her. The hurt that lashed out and resurrected the guilt she'd been trying to ignore. Because leaving him had not been an easy choice.

It had simply felt like the only choice. Cut him free from the dead weight. Let him be with someone else. Someone not broken by the war. Someone who could admit there was something broken and get help and get better. Not her, who was terrified of those three little words.

A full-blown person rather than a shadow.

Maybe someday, she'd finally feel normal again. Maybe then, she could start unpacking everything that had happened. But for right now, she needed to lock things down. Needed to keep the box sealed tight.

Because the darkness within was just itching to get out.

And she was not prepared to deal with that emotional tidal wave.

Better to walk away. To leave sleeping things where they lay.

"Mommy, let's gooo."

She let herself be tugged away. Felt his hand slip from her neck and the cool kiss of air where the heat from his touch had been.

He stayed with her, though. He walked by her side, keeping an eye on her, she knew.

He was good like that.

The war hadn't broken him like it had broken her. She wondered why. What was it about her that hadn't been able to handle the boring days, the long hours, the relentless stress? He'd lost friends. Good friends. He'd deployed three times to her one tour.

Why was he okay and she wasn't?

They found their place in line. Sam tried not to scan the crowds. Tried to enjoy listening to Natalie chatter on about Santa and Rudolph and the elves.

Instead, all she could focus on was Patrick standing behind her. Warm and solid and silent. Not trying to argue with her. Not shaming her or demanding what the hell was wrong with her that she couldn't relax.

It should be easy, to turn to him. To say *something is wrong. I want to get help. But I'm afraid.* But it wasn't easy. Even with him there, solid and steady behind her. Guarding her back.

Just like always.

4

"Who knew seeing Santa was that exhausting?" Sam murmured. "She's out cold."

Patrick glanced in the rearview, confirming Sam's assessment that Natalie was indeed asleep in the back seat, laid out across the bench seat, the seatbelt tucked around her chest and hips. He glanced over at Sam, trying to gauge how she was coping with everything. He'd seen her skittishness at the mall, remembered it well. The panicked feeling of too many people, of no easy access to cover. It wasn't a rational fear but that didn't mean it wasn't real.

It had taken him a long time to put those instinctive reactions behind him and even then, they were still there, a latent energy that sometimes snuck up on him.

"She's not the only one who needs a nap," Patrick said quietly.

"You didn't sleep when you left earlier?"

"No. Dropped off my stuff, got some coffee, and met you at the house." He was more relaxed than he'd been earlier. Less tense once they'd left the mall.

He'd watched her trying so hard to be normal. Trying so

hard to pretend that she was just another parent at the holidays, trying to squeeze in a visit with Santa in the chaos of last minute shopping.

But she wasn't a normal parent. She was a mother who'd deployed to Iraq.

It had dawned on him when they'd first stepped into the mall and he'd seen the fear etched into the lines around her mouth, the panic in her eyes.

This was more than having a hard time adjusting to being home. There was a very real thing going on with her, and he figured out in that moment that she was trying to ignore all of it.

She was trying to do what so many soldiers did: stuff down the uncomfortable and unsettling thoughts and emotions. Lock them away and pretend that nothing about the war was out of the ordinary.

Pretend that deployment was just another day at the office, except that the office was now half a world away. Ignore the fact that sometimes, you needed help in coming home.

When you were deployed, there were no trips home to reset the mind. To release the tension and the stress until the next day.

No, whether you were out walking the streets or working at a desk, the stress was constant. The fear of a mortar didn't only haunt the infantrymen or the maneuver forces. Patrick knew that all too well.

And until she dealt with everything that'd happened to her downrange, she would never come home. Not fully. He wondered if she'd even considered seeing Doc back at the unit. Doc could point her in the right direction. Keep things quiet for her.

"There's a Dunkin' Donuts off Broadway on the way home," she suggested.

"That is a brilliant idea."

They drove in silence for a little bit before they stopped to order coffee, being careful not to wake Natalie. She'd normally sleep through a train wreck, but that didn't mean he wanted to test that theory.

There was so much he couldn't say with Natalie in the car. But there were other things he could.

"When I came home from that first tour, I hated leaving the house." He kept his voice neutral, his words soft. Not some big revelation of a tragic homecoming. Just a statement of what had been. "I couldn't stand going to the grocery store and listening to people complain about the lines or about Wal-Mart being out of their favorite toilet paper."

She cracked the barest smile. "I was so happy when we got to the FOB that we had a real toilet. And showers. We were always out of toilet paper, though. I carried a roll in one of my cargo pockets."

"I can see where that would be a problem." This was such a simple conversation. Like they were talking about the weather instead of latrine conditions in a war zone. "You know, if I ever deploy again, I'm going to take pictures of all the Porta-Potty graffiti. Maybe write a book about it."

"Valuable history, huh?" she said dryly.

"Some of it was pretty good. 'Course, I can't imagine hanging out in a Porta-Potty long enough to draw some of it."

She snorted softly. "That's some dedication right there."

"Well, there wasn't much else to do."

"You have a very limited imagination if drawing on latrine walls is all you can think of to pass the time in Iraq." Her voice thickened a little at the mention. Just a hint of emotion but enough that he noticed it, now that he was looking for it.

"Well, I didn't exactly have free time. I worked pretty much round the clock. Except Sundays. Sundays were the big sleep days."

"We did that too. There was always a movie playing at the chow hall after evening chow."

Silence stretched between them. He wanted to ask her what she was thinking about. Were there other memories that haunted her beyond losing Melanie?

"It's funny the things I remember. Like I remember how the gravel felt beneath my boots and the mural on the T-wall outside the chow hall. But all the days? Most of them blended together." His throat tightened as memories circled, just out of reach. Sensations, really.

"Except for the ones that stand out." She looked out into the cold Maine afternoon.

He reached for her then, daring to cross the chasm between them and rest his hand on her shoulder. A tentative gesture. One meant to offer comfort. Solace.

Understanding.

His breath lodged in his throat when she covered his hand with hers.

"Yeah, there were a few of those." He twined his fingers with hers. "More than a few I wish I could forget."

She didn't look at him, keeping her focus at the hazy winter sky. "I haven't slept well. Not since about halfway through my tour."

A quiet admission. He could guess how much it cost her to admit but it was an opening too precious to ignore.

"Did you ask Doc for some Ambien? Maybe talk to someone about not sleeping?"

"No." That single word was laced with fear. She unthreaded their fingers, slipping away from him once more with that quiet admission.

He swallowed, tapping his thumb on the lid of his coffee mug before taking a sip, buying himself some time. He wanted to push her, to ask her why she was trying so hard to be so tough when she clearly needed to talk to someone. Hell, it didn't have to be him, but someone. Anyone.

Instead, he took a deep breath and chose a different tactic. "My first tour, I worked eighteen-hour days. Nonstop. I remember curling up under my desk to catch a nap, then I'd get back up and keep going." A deep breath. "I hit the wall about eight months in. Punched my ops sergeant major for taking my last RipIt."

She looked at him, a single eyebrow arched. "You punched someone over a RipIt?"

"And some copier toner. It was already a tense relationship. Then he used the last of the toner for no smoking signs around the TOC when I had a packet to prepare for the brigade commander. I missed my briefing and got my ass handed to me. Then he took my last RipIt, and it was all over." He smiled flatly. "I don't actually remember doing it. My boss at the time was less than impressed that his brand new captain socked his senior NCO. Sent me to the doc, and ordered me to get some sleep." He shrugged. "So I kind of appreciate what a good night's sleep can do for the soul."

A long moment stretched between them. "I don't even remember what that feels like."

He hesitated, unsure how far he could push this relative truce.

"Maybe when we get back to Texas, talk to Doc. Can't hurt, right?"

CAN'T HURT, *right?* She let his words sink in, turned them over in her mind. He wanted her to talk to Doc. For sleep meds. She'd thought about it, so many times. Had even gone so far as to make an appointment with Doc only to cancel it at the last minute. Because fear was such a powerful thing.

Can't hurt, right?

Except that yeah, it could hurt. A lot. Because what if it didn't work? What if she was well and truly broken and nothing would ever help put her back together again?

She sighed softly. "I tried an Ambien once. Terrible nightmares and woke up feeling like hell the next day." She badly needed to turn the subject into something safer. Something that involved less soul-baring intensity.

She wasn't ready to unpack everything that happened in Iraq. Yet somehow, they'd just carried on a completely normal conversation without dredging up bad memories or worse.

And he wanted her to talk to Doc.

It was a completely normal conversation between two people pretending to be normal about a situation that was everything but normal.

He took a sip of his coffee. "I had a sergeant major who chewed them like they were Tic Tacs. Said it took five of them to knock him out every night."

She looked over at him. "The RipIt sergeant major?"

"Nah, this was my second tour. He'd stayed in and volunteered to do back-to-back tours to put his kid through Johns Hopkins Medical School."

"Why do I feel like you're not making that up?"

He covered his heart with one hand. "Swear to God. Sarn't Major Megholtz. Meanest SOB you ever met. Daughters had him wrapped around their little fingers."

"Sounds like someone else I know," she said quietly.

He glanced back at Natalie. "She's a good kid." His words were suddenly thick.

Her heart ached at the love in that simple sentence. "You're a good dad."

He said nothing for a long moment. The muscles in his neck bunched, his knuckles tensed on the steering wheel. "Whatever happens between us, Sam, please don't take my daughter." His voice cracked a little in the fading afternoon light.

She closed her eyes at the pain in those words. Pain she'd caused. She folded her arms over her chest and sank into the seat, struggling to hold in the wave of sadness his words sent surging.

There was nothing she could say to make things right. Nothing to take back the hurt she'd inflicted on him.

Nothing to make her feel the happiness that she should feel when he was around her daughter. The joy and the gladness that her daughter would grow up with a father who would be there for her. Who wouldn't leave her.

But Patrick was a soldier. And soldiers who went to war sometimes didn't come home. She knew that now. Up close and personal. And the thought of him at war again while she waited at home…

The sadness was back. Seeping out of the box. Threatening to destroy the latches and the hinges and send everything crashing over her.

She couldn't do it. It was easier not to feel. Easier to pretend she didn't care. Easier to pretend she didn't need help, that she'd snap out of it if she just tried harder to feel normal.

If she told herself she didn't care often enough, maybe it would be true. Because not caring was the only way to survive his next deployment.

Or hers.

God, how was she going to get on that plane again and leave Natalie? What if she didn't come home?

What if she was like Mel? There one day, gone the next.

Who would Natalie have left? Her biological father? That scumbag had no claim on Natalie. His name wasn't on her birth certificate. He could never come back and hurt her if anything ever happened to Sam.

Patrick was the only father she'd ever known. And he was a good father. A good man.

She trusted him with Natalie.

She just didn't trust herself with him anymore.

"Where'd you go just then, Sam?" he asked quietly.

"Nowhere." She sniffed. "You can't fix this."

"Maybe not." A cautious pause. "But we won't know unless we try. We haven't even tried. You...you just left."

She couldn't answer for the longest time. Her throat closed off and her eyes burned. She swiped at her cheeks, trying to keep the tears at bay.

Her voice broke when she finally managed the words. "I don't want to take Natalie from you."

"This isn't just about Natalie, Sam. This is about you. This is about us."

They rolled to a stop at a random light in the middle of nowhere. He turned to face her. "This isn't over yet. And the sooner you accept that, the better off all of us will be."

"Maybe it's been over a long time...we've just both been gone too much to see it."

"And maybe we've just been gone too much to remember how to be us," he snapped. There was steel in those words. Resolve that she was so intimately familiar with. "We haven't had that. There's been no you and me. We've both been working our asses off since the war started. We don't know how long this damn thing is going to go on. We don't know when it's going to end, when we'll finally get to be a normal family again. But we damn sure won't get that chance if we just cut sling load because the first time we're together again after almost two years, things don't fall magically back into place."

She shifted in her seat, his words hitting her at center mass, dead in the heart.

"I wish I had a better answer for you." Shame and fear laced those words. "But I don't. I'm sorry. But that's the best I've got to give."

He shook his head, the muscle in his jaw tensing. He looked at her then, his eyes furious and dark. "That's not good enough, Sam. Our family deserves better."

PATRICK STOPPED at the gas station in Saber Falls, needing to fill up the rental car and a badly needed jolt of a ridiculously good cup of coffee to warm his blood. He'd come home with Sam in the past and the best cup of coffee north of Bangor was clearly the Green Mountain Coffee served there.

He always forgot to order some to take with him.

Maybe he'd remember this time, especially if this was going to be his last time here.

He sighed heavily, needing to clear space in his lungs for... oh, oxygen. Breathing was fundamental, but he couldn't do that with this elephant of sadness sitting on his chest.

He was not going to spend this entire trip sulking like a kicked puppy.

He knew Sam. He could figure this out, right? They'd been through rougher things before.

"Hey, Patrick, how's it going?"

He turned from the coffee to see Finn Rierson step into the gas station, followed by his cousin Garrett, the local sheriff. Sam always made it a point to see the Rierson boys every time they came home. The first time, Patrick had been mildly jealous, curious about these men that Sam had insisted on meeting at the Whistling River Pub.

But then he'd met them, and they were both damn hard to be jealous of.

They were good dudes. Friends from high school that Sam

had refused to let go of even as life and the war and the Army kept her away from home for longer and longer periods.

And over time, they'd become his friends, too, so that he no longer felt like an awkward third wheel but part of the memories they shared every time they got together.

"I didn't know you were coming home," Garrett said. As though Saber Falls was as much his home as Sam's.

He supposed it was.

"It was an unexpected trip. Sam...really needed to come home after the year she's had."

"Yeah. The whole town was devastated when we lost Mel." Finn's voice was edgy and raw, the grief still sharp. A shadow crossed Finn's face and Patrick knew he was looking at a sadness that would never leave the other man. Mel and Finn... they'd been a thing, despite the war, despite the distance. And now she was gone, like so many others.

Finn took a step toward the coffee. Patrick only knew the fear of waiting for a lover to return from war, not the loss.

"I can't imagine what he's gone through," Garrett said quietly. "It was bad enough when I had to bury my parents and Derrick didn't come home."

Patrick frowned. "When did your folks die?"

"Last year. Right after Fourth of July."

"Ah hell, man, I'm really sorry." He'd only met Garrett's parents in passing but Joan and Ken Rierson had struck him as good people. "Derrick didn't come home?"

He'd never met Garrett's brother but had heard enough stories to know the prodigal son was missed.

"Said he couldn't get leave out of Iraq. Something about his unit not letting him go. That doesn't sound right."

"It happens. It all depends on the commander and what's going on at the time and how many people are already gone."

Finn sipped his coffee as he rejoined them. "I've got to get going. I've got a meeting over in Dover," Finn said. "It's good to see you, Patrick."

Patrick cleared his throat roughly. "You, too." He waited until Finn stepped out of the gas station and into the cold, the door shutting with a jingle behind him. "How's he holding up?"

"As good as he can, I guess. He stays busy." Garrett shrugged, and that was the end of the conversation. "Anyway, you and Sam should come out to the house. I've got some ice cleared off. You guys can skate on the pond."

"I'll ask her." He dumped cream—real cream—into his coffee. "She's been having a rough time of things since she's been home."

Garrett twisted the lid off his stainless steel thermos and reached for the darkest blend. "That doesn't sound like Sam. She's always so damn...fierce."

"Tell me about it." It felt strange to talk about this. He hadn't told anyone at work about things going to shit after Sam had gotten home. The couple of guys he'd been close to had their own *stuff* going on.

He'd just tried to muscle through. Until Sam had left him.

He looked up from his coffee to find Garrett watching him. "Something you want to talk about?"

Patrick tested his coffee, buying time. "Sam left me."

Garrett said nothing for a moment, focusing on twisting the lid back on his thermos. "So is this the last Christmas home or is this the surprise 'I'm here to fight for my woman' visit."

Patrick laughed bitterly. "You have been watching too many Lifetime movies, my friend."

Garrett grinned. "I have to go check on Mrs. Poole once a week. We sit for an hour, and I have to watch whatever's on while she tells me the entire plot, backstory, and spoilers."

"Dude, are you like even a real person? You sit with old ladies? Next thing you'll tell me you brake for squirrels or something."

"So? What's wrong with that?"

Patrick smiled. "Nothing. Nothing at all. And to answer your question, this is the 'I'm not letting her go without a fight' visit."

"She didn't know you were coming, did she?"

"Nope."

"And?"

"And we made it about six minutes before she tried to tell me that Natalie wasn't mine, and that we were over." They paid for their coffee and stepped out into the bitter cold morning. "Dear god, how do you people live in this kind of cold?"

"Where are you from originally?"

"Florida."

"Meh, you'd get used to it if you were here long enough."

Patrick shrugged. It wasn't like he was going to get a chance to get used to it. Not if Sam had her way and they were really over.

"She's not, you know," Garrett said after a moment. "Legally, Natalie isn't yours."

Patrick looked over at Garrett. "I've known you for a long time, and that is the single most fucked up thing I've ever heard you say."

"I'm a cop, Patrick. I deal with this shit all the time. It doesn't matter that you were there from the beginning. It doesn't matter that Nat calls you Daddy. Legally, you don't have a leg to stand on."

"I've got powers of attorney naming me her guardian when Sam deployed." But he felt his certainty slip away. He knew the law. Hell, he was a damn lawyer.

But *Only a foolish lawyer has himself as a client* wasn't a cliché for nothing.

"Damn it, Sam," he muttered.

Garrett gripped his shoulder. "You're going to try to fight a custody case for a little girl that has neither your name nor your blood in a region of the country that notoriously does not consider taking children away from their mothers for even the worst transgressions."

Patrick's mouth fell open. "I don't want to take her away from Sam. I just want to be part of her life. Sam's a good mom. She's just..."

"What?"

Patrick paused. "I wish I knew. It's like only part of her came home from the war." He sipped his coffee. The shock of heat burned against his partially frozen lips. "She's there, but she's not. It's like she's a shadow."

Garrett scoffed quietly. "I wish I didn't get that. The one time I've seen Derrick since the war started, he was definitely not in the moment."

"How is he?"

"I don't know. He's gone into complete radio silence since last year. I kind of went off on him for not coming home for the funeral, and well, we haven't talked since."

"I'm sorry."

Garrett shrugged. "I can't live my brother's life for him."

There was more there, but now wasn't the time or the place.

Patrick sighed after a long moment. "The war's fucked up everyone's life, hasn't it?"

Garrett snorted quietly. "Wars tend to do that, don't they?"

Patrick said nothing for a long moment. "Yeah, I guess they do."

5

Sam wasn't sure how long she'd sat, alone in the sunroom, sorting through the myriad emotions riding roughshod through the landscape of her soul, listening to Natalie and her mom make cookies.

It was morning. She should have been finishing up last minute Christmas shopping but she couldn't summon the energy.

The wind slapped against the plastic her mom had used to insulate the sunroom. Sam curled up in the chair, cradling her mug of coffee, savoring the warmth.

Wishing the taste on her lips was still Patrick's.

It would be so easy for her to drive to the bed and breakfast where he was staying. To open his door and slide into bed with him.

She could go back to pretending that everything was fine, that the smile on her lips was real. She could drive down Route 16 and ask him to forgive her. She could put their family back together again.

So why didn't she?

She closed her eyes. Because she would be lying. To her

daughter. To her lover.

To herself.

She looked up at the sound of a car pulling into her mom's driveway. Her pulse beat a little faster at the thought of it being Patrick. She supposed that was a good sign—her body remembered how to feel even if the rest of her didn't.

But it wasn't Patrick. All the air left her lungs and she swallowed, trying to squelch the rising emotions that swelled at the sight of her second dad.

Thomas Carreau.

Melanie's dad and the man who'd helped raise her after her father had hightailed it to Idaho when she'd been about six.

She wanted to run out into his arms. She wanted to hear him laugh and call her Samsquatch or one of the other terrible nicknames he was forever coming up with for her and Melanie.

But instead, she sat unmoving as he climbed the front porch and walked into her mother's house without knocking.

Because he and Nancy had long ago become close friends—enough that her daughter noticed and knew about "Grammy and Thomas time".

Sam was happy for her mom. She deserved someone to make her happy.

But Sam had been avoiding seeing Thomas since she'd come home. Had left the house the moment her mom mentioned he might come by. Had avoided any chance of running into him.

Because she wasn't ready yet. She didn't know if she'd ever be.

Except that he was here now and there was no more running.

"Hey, Nattie Bear."

"Hi, Mr. Thomas," came Natalie's response.

"Where's Grammy?"

"In the bathroom. She had a sour tummy from all the

cookie dough."

Sam smiled. Leave it to Natalie to share information that she was reasonably certain—no matter how close Nan and Thomas were—her mom would not want shared.

"Whatcha making?"

The exchange was normal. Completely ordinary. The kind of conversation that a grandfather would have with a granddaughter.

Except that Thomas would never have grandkids now.

"When my Melanie and your mommy were little, they used to bake chocolate chip cookies every Friday night and watch *Mystery Science Theater 3000*."

"What's that?"

"A show about a guy trapped on a space station with two robots forced to watch bad B movies for the rest of his life."

Natalie laughed. "That sounds awful. TV in the old days must have really sucked."

It was Thomas's turn to laugh quietly. "Don't underestimate it. There were some quality shows back in the dark ages of the 1980s."

"Did you have electricity when mommy was growing up?"

"Of course we did. It was twenty some odd years ago, not last century. Well, I suppose it was last century. Anyway, yes, we had power and television and phones. Life wasn't so different then."

"But you didn't have iTunes. You had to walk to the store for music."

"Yes, and don't forget about barefoot, uphill in winter. Sheesh, kiddo, you make a man feel his years."

"Natalie, stop making Mr. Thomas feel old." Nan had finally returned. Sam caught a reflection of her kissing Thomas quickly in greeting.

Why didn't they just get married? Her mom was so damn weird.

"You can just call me Thomas," he said to Natalie.

"My mommy says I have to call adults Mr. or Ms. because I'm a kid," Natalie said.

"Then how about we just let it be our secret?"

"Nuh-uh. Mommy knows when I'm keeping secrets."

"Yeah, well, Mommy doesn't know everything."

Sam took a deep breath and stepped into the kitchen. "It's a Southern thing," she said when she was sure her voice wouldn't break. It did anyway. "Kids down south don't call adults by their first names. At least not the ones I've been around."

She braced for it, that shockwave of emotion crashing over Thomas's face.

It rose violently, tearing at her insides, ripping open the chest wound that ached and bled for the sister she'd lost and the daughter he'd buried.

"Hi, Samwise." His words were choked and thick.

She blinked rapidly, trying to keep the tears from cascading down her cheeks.

She failed.

And when his arms came around her, she surrendered to the wave of crushing sadness that dragged her under.

NATALIE and her mom were making another batch of cookies. Gingerbread men this time, apparently. Sam and Thomas sat out in the sunroom. Sam was curled in one of her mom's old wicker chairs, nursing a sad cup of coffee that was neither warm nor energizing. It didn't matter. She couldn't swallow past the block in her throat.

"We were just north of Baghdad," Sam said quietly. "There hadn't been any attacks in days. We were on patrol, meeting with a local sheik, trying to see what services they needed, what we could provide."

"Did you leave the base often?" Thomas asked.

"We did. Mel was on the battalion commander's personal security detachment, and I was with public affairs." She shrugged. "We were always together. It was just like camp. Except for the explosions and all that."

Thomas smiled. "You two were always into something. You and the damn Rierson boys and the McLaurin girls."

Sam swallowed at the mention of Cass and Ashley McLaurin. She needed to go see Cass, but she hadn't really thought through everything she was going to say.

Ashley—Cass's sister—was still in Afghanistan. She didn't know how to mourn one friend while worrying for others. It was too much, too overwhelming.

Still, seeing Thomas... For a moment, the floodgates had opened and released a cascade of grief and ragged anger. And for a moment, just a moment, it had felt good to release some of the pressure hiding in that black box she tried to ignore.

"Yeah. We had some good times," she said. Because they had.

Before the war.

"She used to write home every night." A long pause as he sipped his coffee. "I would always worry when I didn't have a note. She tried to explain to me that sometimes, the phones and Internet were shut off because someone had gotten hurt or..."

"Yeah, we'd cut the communications when someone died because we don't need families finding out about things on Facebook."

He nodded, then reached for and squeezed her hand. "Thank you for telling me before the Army showed up on my doorstep."

Sam's throat closed off, and her eyes burned again. She'd violated the rules that day.

She hadn't even given it a second thought. She'd been

numb, dead inside when she'd picked up the phone in the signal officer's office that was on the exemption list and placed the call.

"Your mom stayed with me the whole time." His voice cracked a little. "It was the hardest day of my life. But couldn't you have gotten into trouble?"

Her throat was tight, locked shut, making it difficult to speak, to breathe. "Sometimes, breaking the rules is the right thing to do."

"Yeah, well, don't go breaking any more rules for me. Melanie wouldn't want you to get in trouble for her."

Sam smiled. "No, she'd be mad at me for getting into trouble without her."

"Yeah, she would, wouldn't she." Thomas chuckled. "I wonder where Nan and Natalie went off to?"

She frowned. "Mom said she was running into town for ice cream. Who eats ice cream in December in Maine?"

"Ah, everyone that I know. Ice cream isn't seasonal. Except for peppermint stick."

"You know you can't find that down in Texas. Not the good stuff anyway. Just some crappy brand made with corn syrup. It's so nasty."

"Weren't you going to take Natalie to finish Christmas shopping today?"

She glanced at the old clock on the beam above them. "I was thinking about it…"

"Well if you go, keep an eye on the weather. There's a nasty storm coming in. Lake effect snow."

"That's what I'm hearing. We might wait until tomorrow, honestly." She looked up, daring to meet his eyes. "How have you been? With everything?"

He scrubbed his hand over his scruffy grey beard, then leaned forward, folding his hands together. "When I lost Mel's mom, I thought it was the worst thing I'd ever go through. I was wrong." He looked up at her. "There's a word for when a man loses his wife. Or a wife loses a husband. There's no word for what I am now. Orphan parent is the closest thing I can come up with." He shifted a little. "But I'll get through it. You just try to keep going, try not to think about it too much because the sadness... Man, the sadness is like quicksand. It'll suck you down before you even realize you're sinking."

Sam looked away. "Yeah." It was all she could manage.

Thomas sighed heavily. "So what are you and your mom doing this week? And where's your other half?"

Sam bit her lips, wishing at that moment that Thomas wasn't as close with her mother as he was. But he knew Patrick. Knew that he'd been there from the start and raised Natalie like his own.

Knew that he was currently missing from the picture.

And Sam didn't have a good explanation for it. She couldn't put a name to the lack inside her. To the emptiness that was so deep and so dark that it felt like no light would ever penetrate it.

Someone told her that shadows were a good thing because it proved the light existed, that it was as real as whatever lurked in the shadows.

But when there was no light, there was nothing to push back the darkness. It just kept coming and coming until it overwhelmed its prey, dragging it down, further from the light.

"We're taking some time off," she said after a moment, when she realized she hadn't answered him.

Thomas said nothing for so long, Sam dared to finally look up. "You know, when I came home from Vietnam, I thought I was going to be so happy. I was alive. I'd made it. I had a wife to come home to." He paused, his gaze going to a memory decades in the past. "But that didn't happen. It was... Things didn't feel right. At the time, I thought it was because of all the bullshit we had to endure. People calling us baby killers and murderers."

He rubbed his eyes behind his coke-bottle glasses. "But after a while I realized that it wasn't the public's problem. It was mine."

Sam listened intently. There was no public antiwar sentiment to make her feel like this. No, the problem was strictly hers. A problem that defied explanation.

"What did you do?"

"Self-medicated for a long time. Melanie's mother left me for a while. Was hooked on heroin for a while."

Sam frowned. "Heroin is some pretty heavy stuff." She never would have guessed that Thomas had been an addict.

"Started smoking opium while I was in Vietnam. Bunch of us did. And let me tell you, that is a habit that you never quit. Every day I wake up and have to remind myself why I'm not chasing the dragon today." He paused for a long moment. "And then I woke up one day, no idea where I was or what I'd been doing for the last year. Checked myself into a VA rehab center."

"Mel's mom took you back?"

"After a while. Took me a long time to unpack all my shit from the war." He leaned back in his chair. "So whatever is going on with you or with him, give it time. You just got home. Don't make any decisions right now because you think things are going to be this way forever." He hesitated a moment. "If you're not talking to someone, you should."

She closed her eyes, unable to find the words she needed. How to explain the fear that threatened to choke her when she even thought about what to say, how to say it?

He shifted, pointing his finger at her. "It feels like it will but it won't be. This, I promise you." He stood. "But pretending that everything will get better if you just try harder isn't the answer, Sammy. Believe me, I tried it. Sometimes, the hardest thing in the world to do is admit that your stuff is too much for you to deal with on your own."

6

It was almost noon when he woke up.

His heart slammed against his ribs, his blood pounded in his ears as the panic receded, leaving him in a cold sweat.

The nightmare slipped through his fingers, leaving nothing but the echo of fear and terror. He frowned, tracing his thoughts, trying to remember what he'd been dreaming about and finding nothing but empty grey trails that led to dead ends.

He didn't have nightmares often. He couldn't say what triggered them.

But waking up in a strange bed in a strange room that felt a hell of a lot colder than it had when he'd crashed earlier was a way to do it.

He picked up his phone, about to call Sam when he saw her text:

Big storm coming in. Not going Christmas shopping.

From two hours ago.

Damn, he must have been tired. He never slept during the day. At least not for more than a few minutes at his desk before he got up and started slogging through the caseload yet again.

He dropped his booted feet to the floor and cradled his head in his hands. He had the start of a massive headache. That always happened when he pulled twenty-four hour duty, too.

Except he'd slept on the plane up. He shouldn't be this tired.

He palmed the phone and tapped out a message on the touch screen. *What are you doing for dinner?*

He supposed he could drive back out to Nancy's house. Not give Sam the chance to avoid him. Maybe if he hadn't given her space in the first place, they wouldn't be in this situation.

He snorted. Yeah, he should have gone all eight-hundred-pound gorilla on her. Because women totally thought cavemen were sexy.

He shook his head. He'd backed off when she'd clearly needed him to.

He remembered feeling off-kilter the first time he'd come home from war. But that was three tours ago. Now, he was used to it—and those strange feelings were nothing but a distant memory.

Still. He'd thought giving her space had been the right thing to do.

What the hell was he doing? He hadn't flown all the way to Maine to sit in a rented room with his daughter and the woman he still loved a few miles away.

"Now, that's a good use of airline miles," he muttered.

He stripped off his clothes and stepped into the tiny shower. He wasn't sure it was actually big enough for a hobbit, but he managed to get everything reasonably clean before damn near busting his ass on the bare floor.

Clearly, someone was new at the bed and breakfast thing because there was one hand towel and a tiny bath towel. He supposed it could be worse. He could be drying off with a washcloth.

He scrubbed his hands over his face then dug through his overnight bag for clothes.

And discovered that he had nothing to wear. Literally.

He sighed heavily. "And this is what packing while drunk gets you."

"Do you always talk to yourself?"

The door to his room eased open, and he spun around. Sam stood in the doorway, arms folded over her chest. Her chestnut hair was pinned to the top of her head, her cheeks flushed.

But it was her eyes that he noticed. In the deep blue eyes, he saw a spark of life that he hadn't seen in…since before she deployed. The emptiness was still there, the darkness still filling them.

It was a spark. A small one.

But it was there.

He dragged the tiny towel over his hips. "Doesn't this place have locks?"

She shrugged. "Why are you naked?"

"Isn't that a question normally reserved for Natalie?"

Sam's eyes sparkled. "You're the one standing there in a towel."

He ran his tongue over his teeth. "So I didn't really pack the right clothes for the trip."

Her lips almost twitched. "Did you forget underwear, too?"

A flush crawled up his neck. "Maybe."

"Were you drunk when you packed?"

The flush got a little hotter. "Maybe."

She shook her head slowly. "So what do you have?"

He laid everything out on the bed. "A grand total of one sock, one pair of long john bottoms, a T-shirt and a toothbrush. No toothpaste." He finally looked up at her. "Why are you here, Sam?"

The wariness was instantly back, her eyes shuttering closed. "You didn't answer my text," she said quietly.

"The phone still works."

She looked down at her booted feet. "I figured it was easier to talk to you in person. You flew all the way here and all that."

He looked at her for a long moment. A thousand ideas and harebrained schemes raced through his brain. She was here. They were alone.

Hell, he was already naked.

And hello, didn't his body like the scenic detour his brain had decided to take.

He swallowed and grabbed his pants off the floor.

He met her gaze just as the fan kicked on in the small heater.

He dropped the towel.

And refused to look away as her gaze dropped down his body and back up again. He stood there, naked and exposed and completely at her mercy.

He wondered if she knew that she could ask him anything at that moment and he'd probably do it.

Her nostrils flared ever so slightly. Her eyes darkened. Just a little.

It was the only sign that him standing there naked sparked any kind of reaction in her. But she didn't move. And wasn't that hell on the ego?

"I've got to go buy some clothes," he said, dragging his pants over his hips.

"Going commando?"

"Does that get you horny, baby?" Her lips twitched at the cheesy line from *Austin Powers*. A thousand small reactions but they added up to convincing him that he had a chance to fix this. A chance to reach her in whatever darkness had pulled her away from him and drag her back to him. Back to them. "I don't really have many options right now, do I? Not with the storm coming in. And I have no earthly idea where a laundromat is around here." He frowned. "I should probably know this but I'm drawing a complete blank. Where the hell can I get clothes?"

"There's a small trading post down the road in Greenville or you can ride to Wal-Mart in Newport."

"Isn't Newport like an hour from here?" He usually let her drive when they came home. Their visits hadn't been so long that he'd learned his way around without GPS.

"Forty minutes."

"Seems like I should get what I need closer to home tonight. Or I could just wait until the storm passes."

She shook her head slowly. "You don't want to be riding around without underwear or socks. If you go off the road, you'll freeze off some of your bits and pieces."

He lifted one brow. "Sounds like you might be concerned with my bits and pieces."

She lifted one shoulder. "They're nice bits and pieces."

He grinned and said nothing for a moment, not pressing his advantage in the opening she'd just left him.

He wanted her. He'd love nothing more than to lay her down in that bed and feel her body surround him. He wanted to savor the heat from her skin, the soft, silken wetness between her thighs. He wanted to feel her gasp as he slid inside her. Wanted to feel her breath on his ear, her nails in his back.

He wanted that and so much more.

But looking at her standing near the door, seeing the faint hints of awareness sparking in her eyes, he had an idea.

It was a terrible, terrible idea.

It was dark and wicked and would either work beautifully or ruin everything.

7

He'd asked if she'd go with him. To keep him from getting lost and dying in a snow bank on the side of the road.

She'd thought about saying no. About heading back to her mother's house and finishing decorating the Christmas cookies with Natalie and her mom.

But Natalie was being strangely clingy with her grandmother, so Sam let her be when she'd told her mom she was going to go talk to Patrick.

"Good," she'd said simply. "Natalie and I will stay out of trouble. Promise."

She'd frowned. "What does that mean, Mom?"

"It means that she'll wear a helmet if we go out on Thomas's snowmobile later today."

Sam had glanced at her watch. "It's already one. It'll be dark soon."

Darkness came early up in the great north woods. It had taken her a day to remember that when she'd gone into the grocery store in broad daylight and come out in pitch darkness. At four p.m.

"Snowmobiles have headlights."

So her mother was making cookies, her daughter was being exceptionally cooperative, and Sam was shopping for clothes with a man she was leaving. She'd sent her mom a text to let her know she was going to be late.

She'd gotten no response, which meant that Natalie and her mom were probably passed out from sugar overdose.

Now, she meandered around the men's department, looking at sweaters, turtlenecks, and other articles of clothing suitable for surviving the Maine winter.

"I can't believe how much flannel is still being sold in this state."

She turned to see him standing behind her. He wore a charcoal grey turtleneck beneath a red-checkered flannel shirt.

"You look like an L.L. Bean commercial."

"I feel like an escapee from a Pearl Jam concert circa 1994."

"Pearl Jam concert goers did not wear turtlenecks with their flannel, and they damn sure didn't tuck them in." She tipped her chin at him. For the first time since she'd come home, she smiled and it felt normal. "Flannel is an incredibly functional fabric, especially at ten below."

"Yes, but it went out of style in the rest of the country somewhere around 1996."

"So did mom jeans, but you still see those up here, too."

He glanced around. "Really? There are pleated jeans for sale?"

"Why do you know that pleated jeans are mom jeans?" She held up one hand. "Never mind, don't answer that." She paused, taking in the entire selection of clothing he'd picked out. "If flannel is so nineties why are you wearing it?"

"Because this is the warmest thing I've tried on. Nerdy turtleneck included."

She shot him a baleful look. "You realize that men are

supposed to run hot. It's the women folk who are supposed to be cold."

"Are you calling me a woman? Because I might have to take offense to that." He took a single step closer, blocking her from the view of the rest of the store. "I assure you, flannel or not"— he leaned closer, until his breath slid across her ear—"I'm all man, baby."

The corniness of his line did nothing to undermine the heat of his touch. She closed her eyes as his lips barely brushed the outside of her ear. A sliver of pleasure shivered over her skin. Her breath caught in her throat as she waited for the sensation of his lips against her skin in the place he loved to touch her.

And then he was gone, his warmth replaced by the cool circulating air.

He untucked the shirt. "I'll be in the changing room." He plucked a blue and grey sweater from a table.

And left her there.

She stood for a moment, watching his retreating back before he disappeared behind the curtain.

She narrowed her eyes. He'd done that on purpose. He'd stepped too close, teased her with one of the things he knew drove her crazy.

And then he'd simply stopped.

She breathed deeply, wishing for a moment that things were normal. That the feelings he'd just sparked inside her weren't fleeting.

That the flash of desire hadn't already faded, dissipating into the darkness inside her.

She wanted to feel it again.

Because in that single instance, she'd felt real. She'd felt whole.

She'd felt like her again.

She stuffed her hands inside her jacket pockets and walked toward the dressing room.

"Hey, Sam?"

"Yeah?"

"Can you come check something out for me?"

She paused. "Is this going to get us arrested?" Silence greeted her question. "Are you done trying things on?"

More silence.

"Patrick?"

Nothing.

She reached for the curtain.

At the same time he stepped out.

Wearing nothing but silkies—white ones that clung to his skin like some kind of superhero leotard, outlining every hard line and yes, every part of his body. He'd pulled them up high so the waist was up to his chest.

"What do you think?"

She covered her mouth and tried not to laugh. "That looks painful," she said when she was sure she wouldn't choke.

"Well, it's not like I've got any future kids to worry about."

The minute the words were out of his mouth, they both sobered. It was instant and simultaneous.

She hesitated, only a moment, turning his words over and inspecting them and coming up with no easy answers. "What are you talking about?"

"Nothing. Never mind. It was a bad joke."

He disappeared into the changing room, leaving her feeling completely alone. He was two feet away and he might as well have been on the other side of the world.

"Patrick?"

He didn't answer. She didn't expect him to.

She stood on the other side of the curtain. It would be so easy to step inside. To cross that threshold and wrap her arms around him and ask him to help her.

I'm sorry. But the words wouldn't form in her throat.

Because there was so much for her to be sorry for, and she didn't know where to start.

But she was tired. So tired of feeling like a dead thing going through the motions.

She stood there, on the other side of the curtain, unable to move, unwilling to leave.

Stuck. Just like always.

And she was so damn tired of being stuck.

He felt the air move across his bare back a moment before she stepped into the changing room.

His pants hung open. His shirt was in his hands.

Her coat was unzipped, revealing the red fleece vest she wore over god only knew how many layers of clothing.

"Sam." Her name was a whisper. A plea.

A moment before he would have loved for her to step into this dressing room with him. Would have enjoyed standing a little too close. Running his lips down the edge of her ear the way he knew she liked.

But right then, he needed some space. He wasn't ready to have the conversation she probably expected the moment she stepped into that changing room.

"I'm finished," he said. "I'll get dressed and we can go."

Her eyes betrayed her. He saw the unasked question looking back at him.

It was his own fault. He shouldn't have opened his damn mouth.

But he'd been teasing her, and she'd been responding. Slowly, like a flower first stretching in springtime, he'd seen her, really her, not the shadow that had been masquerading as her.

Then he'd slipped up.

He hadn't meant to tell her he couldn't have kids.

But there was no taking those words back now.

And she wasn't about to let it go. "What did you mean?" A hushed question.

He closed his eyes. Dropped his hands to his sides. "Last deployment. There was a mortar attack."

"You never told me."

He swallowed hard. "Since we weren't married, they didn't notify you." He looked away. "I didn't know how to tell you. I didn't want you to worry." He paused, searching for the words to explain what happened. It was hard, so damn hard to put something like that into words. "I got hit. Some things didn't make it out okay."

She said nothing for a long moment. "I never noticed."

He smiled sadly. "It's not like you spend a lot of time inspecting my bits and pieces these days."

The truth. Not meant to be unkind. It was a painful truth. Then again, weren't all truths painful? Things had started changing between them long before her deployment. After his last tour, he'd just been happy to be home.

He hadn't noticed the distance growing between them. Not until she'd deployed two weeks after he'd come back.

They'd literally done a battle hand-off with Natalie's schoolwork and contact information, and she'd been gone.

They'd spent almost two years apart between their two back-to-back deployments.

He swallowed. It was too much time lost, too many hours spent working and not nearly enough time tending to the thing that had drawn them together to begin with. They'd simply grown apart, and now? Now here they were, trying to figure out who these two strangers in a room were.

Strangers who shared the only daughter Patrick would ever have.

"You could have told me," she said quietly.

He shrugged and the gesture felt empty. "It never really

came up. Hard to fit 'oh, by the way I got blown up and my balls got rewired' with 'where's your spaghetti recipe,' you know?"

Her response was not what he expected.

She laughed. She covered her mouth and laughed until she doubled over.

Patrick stood there, not sure what to do or what he'd said that was so damn funny.

"I guess my emergency neutering is funny. Okay then."

She straightened, tears running down her cheeks. "I'm sorry. It's not funny. It's just the way you said it and..." She doubled over again, laughing until she slid down the wall and covered her face with both hands.

He watched her, amazed at the sound of her laughter. In that moment, he realized that she hadn't really laughed in... He couldn't remember the last time she'd laughed like this. Slowly a matching smile spread over his lips, and he stood there and simply savored the moment.

It was something he'd forgotten. Something that had slipped away as the distance between them had grown wider and deeper.

He'd enjoyed making her laugh once upon a time. A thousand memories surfaced and tormented him with the pleasure of her laugh. God but he loved the way she used to smile.

She swiped at her eyes, looking up at him from the changing room floor. "I'm sorry."

"For laughing at my neutering or my being neutered?" he asked lightly, holding his hand out to help her up.

"Both." Her palm slid against his.

He gave a gentle tug and she was on her feet, close enough that he could see the moisture sparkling in her eyes. "It's been so long since I heard you laugh," he murmured.

Her mouth was a breath from his. Warm air brushed against his skin. He could almost taste the laugh on her lips.

She smiled ruefully. "There hasn't been a lot to laugh about lately."

Her hands came up, braced against his skin. Her palms were cool on his bare shoulders, sending a shiver through his veins. It had been so long since he'd touched her. Since she'd touched him. This. This was opportunity.

In a perfect world, he could kiss her then. Rock her world and remind her of all the things that had once been right between them.

But this wasn't a perfect world. This was a flawed and damaged world.

But it wasn't hopeless. No, he hadn't given up hope yet.

He stood there for a moment, his eyes locked with hers. Her lips were parted, the slightest space. He wanted to nibble on her there, to suck gently until she sighed.

Instead he lifted his hand. Ran his thumb gently, so gently over her bottom lip. She was soft and smooth and warm. It was meant to tease them both. It was meant to control the situation, to keep himself from deviating from his game plan of trying to lure her out of the darkness and shadows where she'd been for too long.

Instead, Sam took over.

She'd never been a passive lover. Her tongue slid over the bottom of his thumb. A gentle rasp of heat on heat. It was warm and wet against the roughness of his skin.

So long. So fucking long since he'd touched her. That single gesture drove his resolve away, turning his plan on its head and sending him headlong into the abyss of sensation. She slipped her tongue around the tip, swirling a teasing pattern, her eyes never leaving his. She sucked him further into the warmth of her mouth and he gave himself over to the sensation.

This. This was always good between them. This was always right.

He backed her up against the wall, his thumb slipping out

of her mouth with a soft pop. It was just them, alone in the bright lights of the changing room. Their breath mixing as they stood, his bare skin pressing against her clothed form.

He lowered his forehead to hers. Stroked her cheek gently with his thumb.

"I miss you."

8

Sam waited outside for him to finish checking out. Snow was already falling, big fat flakes that stuck to everything. A gust of wind from Moosehead Lake sent it swirling around her. She huddled deeper in her jacket.

In the end, he'd decided on a couple of pairs of heavy socks, a couple of wool sweaters, and two pairs of jeans, along with, yes, a flannel shirt. And somehow, damn it, Patrick made flannel look sexy.

He wasn't exactly a flannel kind of guy. He wore expensive button-down shirts and loafers. He drank aged scotch and listened to classical music and pretended to be a cultural omnivore when he was in public. She knew his secrets, though, knew he listened to heavy metal when he was at the gym.

And she remembered how to make him beg when they were alone.

But the flannel shirt he wore now beneath the heavy Patagonia jacket made him look more rugged. Less polished.

Less like Patrick the soldier and more like someone else.

Someone else who had just pinned her to the wall in a changing room and sent her blood spiking.

It was that Patrick that she was drawn to now. That Patrick who instead of kissing her had simply stood for a moment, his heat and warmth surrounding her, urging her closer, urging her to *feel* for the first time in forever.

She didn't know what to do with all the feelings he'd aroused in her. There was an ache deep in her belly that made her crave more. An ache she'd once not hesitated to satiate with him.

So why was she hesitating now? Why hadn't she leaned forward and kissed him when he'd been so close? God, but she'd loved seeing his eyes go dark when she'd run her tongue over his thumb. She'd pushed him closer to the edge. Closer to taking.

But he was too much of a good man to do that.

She knew that.

And yet, standing there in the swirling snow, waiting for him to step outside, she felt the darkness stalking her. The numbing sensation was wrapping around her, chasing away the awareness and arousal he'd sparked in her and leaving her with nothing but the memory.

She was clawing her way toward the surface at the bottom of a long dark well. She could see the light. She wanted to be in the light.

But it was so far away.

The bell on the door behind her jingled as he stepped into the cold.

"Hey." His voice was thick. His breath froze on the air in front of him. He looked up at the darkening sky. "Looks like we didn't miss the storm."

She nodded toward the rental car. "Does that thing have four-wheel drive? It's about to get nasty."

He looked at the sedan. "I have no idea. Do cars come with four-wheel drive up here? Are they specially made for living in the great north woods?"

She shook her head. "We should get going before the roads get worse."

"We'll be able to get home, right?"

She smiled. "The road crews up here are pretty busy in the winter. The main roads are usually fine."

"I hear a but in there."

"But we probably don't want to tempt fate. We'll end up sleeping in the parking lot 'til morning if there's an accident."

He stepped closer to her, his coat rustling in the falling darkness. "I'd keep you warm."

She lowered her eyes from the temptation in his. "I have no doubt."

They walked in silence to the car.

"I cannot get over how cold it is up here. How on earth did you grow up and not freeze to death?"

"Listen, Florida boy, not all of us are used to sunny weather and sandy beaches all the time."

It felt good, teasing him. To have such a normal conversation that felt like things weren't so irreparably damaged between them. Like maybe there was a chance she wasn't completely broken.

Maybe she could hold on to this normalcy. Maybe she could claim this moment and cherish it.

Maybe she could hold on long enough to climb out of the well.

The snow was falling faster now, looking like the streaks of stars when the *Millennium Falcon* jumped to light speed. Visibility sucked and was likely to get worse. "So, want to tell me about when you got hurt?"

"There's not much to tell. Shrapnel in a very special place, the docs said things were probably destroyed, and wow, isn't this a fun and entertaining conversation."

"Probably destroyed?"

His knuckles whitened where he gripped the steering

wheel. "I could have gone back to Germany and had surgery to try and save the boys." He released a deep breath.

It was not an easy conversation to have.

It was even harder now.

She should have let it go. She should walk away from the edge of the argument teetering just in front of them. But she couldn't. "Why didn't you?"

"Because it felt wrong to try and keep my balls in good working order when other guys were losing arms and legs and eyesight." He ground his teeth. "And I had Natalie," he whispered. "It sounds fucked up, but I wasn't overly worried about it. I didn't die, the important thing still works, and it just seemed more important to stay in the fight."

She watched him while he spoke. Watched the tension crank higher and higher until his hands looked like they were going to break the steering wheel.

"I thought I was okay when I made it home. But I wasn't." He swallowed hard. "Spent some time talking to a counselor off post," he said cautiously.

She looked down at her hands. "You never mentioned that."

"It's a hard thing to admit that you're not okay. Everyone pretends that everything is fine when it fucking isn't." He rubbed his hand over his mouth. "I got my head straight and, well, it never came up. Maybe it should have. Maybe if I'd been honest with you about what I'd gone through..." He stopped suddenly.

"What?" A broken whisper.

"Maybe you wouldn't have felt so alone. Like you were the only one who'd ever had trouble coming home." He brought their vehicle to a stop as the taillights of the tanker truck in front of him lit up. Finally, he glanced over at her. "Maybe you wouldn't have felt like leaving was the only option."

The admission hurt: it was staring at the reality of his own failure. He'd tried to be strong, tried to keep from laying his own burdens on her. In doing so, he'd left her alone when she needed someone, anyone to lean on.

He'd never thought that she'd leave him. Maybe it was his own naiveté that they'd get through the war and figure things out on the other side. He'd always respected what she stood for, what she needed. He'd never pressured her to get married. He knew how important it was to her to keep her name, to feel like she could do things on her own. She was stubborn like that.

She'd been burned badly by Natalie's biological father. He remembered the first time he met her. He'd been at BookPeople in Austin, one of his favorite haunts when he wasn't working.

He'd seen her standing in the politics section. She'd looked adorable in a pale blue and white sundress. It had taken him a minute to recognize her from work. A lot of military women looked completely different out of uniform, and Sam was no different. Her hair had been down, spilling down her back and brushing over her shoulders.

Then she'd glanced toward him, and he'd seen the tears streaming down her face.

Before he'd seen those tears, he'd been on the fence about approaching. About saying hi. But those tears had punched him in the gut. She was always so strong at work. So confident.

In that moment, he'd made a decision that had changed the course of both their lives.

He'd approached cautiously. "Whoever it is, I'm sure it's nothing a good kick in the balls can't solve."

She'd been embarrassed. She'd tried to shrug off his concern.

But he'd convinced her to cross the street with him and let him buy her lunch.

She'd confided in him that day. Told him about the boyfriend who hadn't just run out on her, but had emptied her bank accounts and run up her credit cards first. He'd left her broke and betrayed everything Sam thought that she'd had with him.

They'd been dating for a month when she'd dropped a land mine on both of them.

She was pregnant. And since they hadn't yet made love, she hadn't had to tell him that it wasn't his.

God, he could still see her face when she'd told him the news. She'd braced for him to walk out on her.

But he hadn't. And over the years, he'd gotten used to the careful balancing of her independence with her relationship with him.

"I never pushed you on the paperwork for Natalie because I never thought I'd have to," he said now, sitting on a snow-covered road behind a stopped tractor-trailer in the middle of central Maine. "And we managed to make this stuff work without being married." He looked at her then, and crossed the boundary he'd never broken with them before. "I get that you have your stuff. We all do. But I never thought you'd take her away from me. I never thought through what would happen the day you decided you'd had enough. I loved you—I still love you—and I always thought that was enough."

"You make it sound so simple." A ragged whisper. "It's not."

"Yes, actually it is." He forced his voice to remain level. To stay calm and not shout at her that she was destroying everything he loved in this world. "That this isn't just about Natalie, but about the life we've built together. This is about you and it's about me and about us. And things are a little fucked up right now but you're doing exactly what you've always been afraid I would do to you. You're running away."

Her mouth opened, then closed again. He wanted her to fight, to deny what he said. To tell him he was imagining things. But she didn't. She simply bit her lips together and looked away, avoiding his eyes.

It was an old familiar story in the military. Too many soldiers deployed to return home to find their spouses shacked up with someone else. Too many soldiers strayed while they were deployed, figuring deployment meant they didn't have to honor their marriage vows.

He'd done neither. He'd always believed she would do the same.

But now the ugly suspicion settled around his heart, and he had to ask. Had to know. "Is there someone else?" he asked flatly.

Better to excise the wound than to let it fester.

"No." She turned away, looking out into the swirling snow. "There's no one else."

He dropped his head back against the headrest, lashing at his temper that was fraying at the edge. "Then explain to me what happened, Sam. Because if you're going to destroy everything we built together, I deserve to know why."

She flinched when he spoke. His deceptively calm words hurt. He knew that. Could see the evidence on her face.

She didn't answer. Not right away. He waited patiently, let the silence stand between them, growing until it was a live thing, crackling with energy that snapped and hissed.

"Because I don't feel anything anymore." Words like shattered glass. "Because nothing between us feels alive. It feels like we're going through the motions, waiting for bedtime when we can both roll over and pretend to be asleep." She finally dared to look at him. "I can't pretend to feel something that isn't there anymore. I can't do that to Natalie." She looked away again. "And you deserve someone who can make you laugh. Someone who isn't broken." Her voice cracked on the last sentence.

He glanced at the truck in front of them. Let her words sink in. Weighed them against the woman he knew. The woman he loved.

She was lost, utterly and completely lost. He remembered

feeling that way, feeling the need to hide it from the world. Being unable to see his way out of the darkness that surrounded him.

And he'd missed the signs in her. For a thousand pointless reasons, he'd missed them. He'd left her alone in the dark.

Because he could do nothing less, he reached for her then. Cradled her cheek until she turned to face him. "You're not broken, Sam." He gave up on his plan. Abandoned it in the nearest snow bank, needing only to be there for her. To hold her and let her know he was there. At that moment and forever. He'd never leave her alone again. He brushed his lips against hers. "You went to war. You lost people you care about." A gentle nudge. "You're not broken. You're just different. We're all different when we come home."

She closed her eyes, avoiding his.

It was a long moment before she nuzzled his hand with her cheek. "I don't want to be different." Tired words filled with sadness. She leaned in, resting her forehead against his. "I want to feel normal again." She pressed her lips to his. Slid her tongue against his. A hesitant touch. "Make me feel again, Patrick."

And he was lost.

9

It started as something gentle. Something hesitant.
And then it wasn't. Not gentle. It was not tame or timid or questioning.

It burned her down to the roots of her soul. It touched something deep and dark and hidden.

Something she'd thought was long since dead and buried and gone.

His tongue slid against hers, stroking to life the very sensations she thought she'd never feel again.

It was electric, the feel of his mouth against hers. The scrape of stubble against her chin, the taste of him. The smell of his skin.

He nipped her. Pinched her bottom lip between his teeth and sucked it. And she sighed at the pleasure, at the raw ache his taste and touch aroused in her, pushing aside the darkness that haunted her.

She felt him. Felt everything. The heat of his skin. The warmth that drew her closer. That made her want to crawl into his lap and unzip his pants and push up that damned flannel shirt until they were skin to skin and there was nothing between them but sweat and heat.

One hand slid down her side. Tugged at her fleece and...

"Dear lord," he muttered against her lips. "How many layers of clothing do you have on under this thing?"

She smiled. "You weren't wondering why I wasn't cold?"

"Well, you'd be a champ at strip poker right about now," he said dryly.

Then his fingers found her skin, and she was no longer thinking.

He traced the very tips of his fingers over her belly. Light, feathery strokes that made her skin quiver. She gasped when he slipped them higher, finding the swell of her breast. Every cell in her body was alert to his touch, anticipating the next stroke of his fingers.

He lifted his mouth from hers. Pressed his tongue to the corner of her lips before nipping her there.

Then he paused, pressing his cheek to hers. Just for a moment, the world fell away, and he was there, holding her, cradling her, reminding her of everything that was still good between them.

It was a moment before she felt it. His breath teasing the sensitive flesh around her ear. A quiet huff of air against her skin. Her body tensed, waiting for his touch, his tongue.

A delicious torment. An old familiar heat slid through her veins, warming her, pulling her out of the darkness at the bottom of the well.

In the silence of heated desire, of hushed passion, she heard it.

Someone gently rapping on the driver's side window.

She pulled back, seeing the wanting smile on Patrick's lips. "Someone's timing sucks."

He released her and her skin protested the loss of his touch. She shivered as he rolled the window down.

"Well," Garrett said, leaning down on the side of the car, "it's certainly awkward meeting you like this."

Sam offered a guilty half smile. "I was going to call."

"Sure. I get that all the time. Anyway, you two probably need to turn around. Bad accident up ahead, and the road is going to be closed until we get it cleaned up. With the storm coming in, you're not getting by any time soon."

"Where are we supposed to go?" Sam asked. "I don't think this thing has four-wheel drive."

"Well, maybe if you two weren't making out like a couple of horny teenagers, you'd have paid better attention to the roads." He pulled a single key off his loop. "My parents' house is about a half a mile that way." He pointed back the way they'd come.

She swallowed the resurgent lump in her throat. Her mom had told her about Garrett's parents last year when it happened. She'd been deployed.

She'd sent flowers from Iraq because it was the only thing she could think to do from half a world away.

Patrick accepted the key.

"I'll find you tomorrow with the key."

"Sure." He stepped back away from the car, using his flashlight to guide them as they turned around. "Now get your asses out of the storm before I have to dig you out in the spring."

It was easy enough to find the Rierson's house. Set back in an old field, the driveway that led up to the old log cabin had recently been plowed.

The silence between them was quiet. Comfortable.

And filled with needy tension.

They walked into the old house and Sam felt an aching sense of the familiar twisted now with age and experience. It was the same and not the same. It felt smaller, somehow, from the house she remembered as a teen.

She paused in the entryway as Patrick closed the door behind them. For a moment, the world fell away, taking the darkness and the sadness and the emptiness with it. Leaving a warmth, a sense of being home in its place. Funny. She hadn't spent time in this house in years but it felt...good.

She glanced over at Patrick. Saw him watching her. Standing close, too close and not close enough. She met his gaze and in that moment, realized with aching clarity that they were alone.

Really alone.

Her mouth went dry.

He waited. In the shadows and the snow by the door, he waited.

She wanted him to move into her space and kiss her and make her feel alive again.

But she knew this man. Despite the chasm that had grown between them, she knew him.

And she knew that he would wait. Would stand quietly by until she made that first choice.

She would never be alone.

But that first hesitant step, she had to make by herself.

He wouldn't force her.

It was one of the things she loved about him. He was steadfast and loyal and good.

And she was losing him through her own inaction.

She stood there then, taking in the sight of the man who'd stood by her the day she'd told him she was pregnant with someone else's child.

The day he'd held her hand and told her he'd always be there for her.

The day he'd gone with her into the hospital and went through labor and delivery to bring their daughter into the world.

He'd never left her alone.

Not even now when she'd left him alone in the cold and the dark.

It was a long moment. The storm whipped against the outside storm door, slamming it open, then shut and startling them both.

Shattering the moment and leaving a chill between them. She shivered at the suddenness of the feeling.

He stepped to her then, running his hands down her arms. "I'll start a fire."

She let him go because she was a coward. Because she was afraid. Afraid of what he made her feel.

Of what her life would feel like without him.

Of what her life would feel like if all the emotions she'd locked away came tumbling out.

The fire was warm on his face. It penetrated the flannel and the wool and heated his skin.

But it didn't heat the fear in the seat of his soul that said he was losing her. That she was slipping further away.

He'd hoped she would make that step. That after the car and the changing room, she would trust him enough to let him help with whatever was eating at her.

But she hadn't moved, and it had *hurt*.

He hadn't been prepared for the hurt. He should have expected it. He knew she didn't do impulsive or rash. She always looked before she leaped.

He was asking her to leap. Without saying the words, asking her to take that step, out of the darkness and back into the light.

And so to avoid the hurt, to avoid saying something that would set his campaign back a dozen lifetimes, he let her be.

He made the fire instead and hoped that maybe this storm was a blessing in disguise. That maybe this time alone was something they'd both needed and hadn't realized it.

Because maybe they'd gotten so caught up with being

Captain Samantha Egan and Major Patrick MacLean and Mommy and Daddy that they'd forgotten how to be Sam and Patrick.

She walked up behind him. "Beer?" She held out a dark glass bottle.

"Thanks."

"I figure we'll replace it tomorrow when we find Garrett and give him the key." She sank down on the floor next to him, leaning back on the old worn couch.

"Sounds like a good plan. Did you call your mom?"

"Yeah. Natalie's being funny. She didn't even ask where we'd be."

He twisted off the cap, turning it over in his fingers before taking a long pull. "You know she called me, right?"

"Yeah, you mentioned that."

"I'm pretty sure she's conspiring to get us together," he said quietly.

"I fail to see how an eight-year-old can do that."

He shrugged. "I won't go so far as to say she's got a direct line to God, but I'll definitely give her some credit in this whole scheme. I mean we wouldn't be snowed in if she hadn't called me." He glanced over at her. The firelight danced over her skin, teasing him with orange and red and glowing shadows and light. "She's a pretty perceptive little bugger."

"You know she hasn't said a word about why we were here without you." She twisted the cap off her own beer, nestling the bottle between her bent knees. "And I wasn't ready to explain."

"What did you tell her when you left?" Because he needed to know.

"That you had to work." She lifted her gaze to his. "A convenient lie."

It was Patrick's turn to look away. To avoid the hurt that rose sudden and sharp inside him.

"She figured it out anyway," he said when he could speak.

"Yeah. She did."

They sat in silence, the fire crackling and snapping in front of them. She shifted after a bit until their shoulders were touching. Until her thighs pressed against his.

He didn't move. Didn't take advantage of her closeness.

He just savored it. Savored the fact that she was there. That she'd moved closer.

That she hadn't run away.

He'd expected her to.

"I remember the day you told me you were pregnant with her." His voice was hushed, now. Calm.

"I thought you'd leave. Any other guy would have." She looked into her beer, rubbing her thumb over the condensation. "Not my proudest moment."

"It was a pretty rough day for a month-old relationship, I'll give you that."

She glanced at him, the fire reflecting in her eyes. "Why are you so damn patient? And calm. I've never seen you not calm."

He took a long pull off his beer. "You didn't see me the day you left."

Quiet words. Filled with hurt and pain and grief.

"I spent two days at the bottom of a bottle."

"I don't think I've ever seen you drunk."

He raised his beer in mock salute. "I save getting plastered for special occasions." She snorted quietly. He looked over at her once again.

"When I came home after that last tour, I couldn't wait to see you. I was so goddamned happy to be alive." He rubbed his thumb along the edge of the label. "Part of me, though, whispered that you wouldn't stay if you knew about my accident. I was ashamed of that voice, those whispers. They weren't me. They lied." He swallowed hard. "I couldn't shut them down, though, until I recognized what they were."

She closed her eyes, letting his words sink in. Turning them over, inspecting them. Weighing them against the truth of her life for the last few months. "I couldn't—I can't—believe that I won't always feel this way." An admission laced with guilt. With fear.

He shifted then, resting his hand on the back of the sofa where they leaned against it on the floor in front of the fireplace. He brushed her hair gently away from her neck. "You can get better. This stuff—it's just post deployment stuff. You went through an incredibly dangerous experience. This—what you went through, what I went through—it took me a while to learn that it's a completely normal reaction to a completely abnormal situation."

"What if it's not?" Fear, dark and powerful, laced those words. "What if it doesn't get better? What if talking to Doc and taking meds and getting sleep—what if nothing helps?"

"What if it does?" He leaned closer then, brushing his lips against her forehead. "I'm so sorry I didn't see how hard this was for you," he whispered.

She couldn't speak. Her throat was tight, her heart pounding violently in her chest. The voice in her head told her he wouldn't—he couldn't still love her after this. But it was wrong. He was there, standing strong and steady with her, just like he always was. She just had to trust. To ignore the whispers that told her she was a broken, useless thing. That he would be better off without her.

After a moment she set her beer on the edge of the hearth. Pale golden light danced in the glass.

And then she moved. Urged his knees down and slid into his lap until she straddled him.

He froze. Unwilling to move or unable, she wasn't sure.

He set his beer down and lowered his hands to the floor. Just near her hips.

And waited.

For an explanation. For answers. For any sign that she heard what he said and believed he'd meant every word.

Neither of them were perfect. Neither of them was without sin in the decay of their relationship.

* * *

SITTING THERE, the woman he loved straddling his hips, her hair surrounding her face in a chestnut halo, he waited. It was the longest wait of his life but he couldn't move. Couldn't risk screwing up and shattering the tentative bridge spanning the distance between them.

Until she was ready.

And prayed that she would make the leap.

10

She slid her hands over his shoulders. The flannel was soft beneath her touch, the man under her palms solid and rock steady.

She ran her hands down his chest. Felt the strength and the stillness.

The anticipation.

It was a delicious thing, touching him again.

A feeling that brought things to life inside her, that terrified her.

She was afraid. Afraid of the feelings she couldn't control. Afraid that if she opened the box, she'd never get it closed again.

Afraid that if she let him in and showed him all the broken things that were left of her life from before the war, he would walk away. That he'd finally leave her alone.

To face the world without him.

She leaned closer. Inhaled the warm, spicy scent of his skin. Smelled the fire and the heat as she pressed her lips to the edge of his mouth. Flicked her tongue out to press against the seam of his lips. Felt the shudder run through him as she explored.

Knew that he wouldn't move until she was ready.

Each touch of her lips to his skin ignited a fire in her. Flicked the latch off the box and weakened her hold on the darkness inside her. It was a gamble, a risk.

She could do this. She could give in to the need, to the desire without completely losing control over everything she'd struggled to keep locked away.

A rasp of teeth against his earlobe. His hands gripped her thighs then, kneading gently. A gentle movement beneath her in the ever so slight rocking of his hips.

She wanted this. Wanted him.

Her fingers danced down his chest, flicking the buttons open on that flannel shirt. The turtleneck came untucked easily.

"I love your chest." A throaty whisper, her voice thick. She leaned down, pressing her lips to the soft hair on his stomach. He was still but the quiver beneath her lips gave away the tension he struggled to control.

She looked up at him. Loved the sight of him watching her, his eyes heavy lidded and dark. His breath came in short huffs.

Heat flooded her. She loved the idea that he was watching her. That she could use her lips and her tongue and her fingers to tease him, to touch him.

To tell him with her body what she could not speak.

She couldn't explain why she'd left. She couldn't explain to him the lack in her or find the words to describe it. Losing her best friend shouldn't have destroyed her like this. She should have been stronger, should have fought harder to keep the depression from consuming everything. Going to war should not have utterly dismantled everything she'd thought she was.

But it had. And her denial, her stubborn denial had compounded everything.

She stroked her thumb over the soft hair just above the waistband of his pants. He licked his bottom lip, his body tense.

"Sam." A plea. A prayer. Maybe both.

She nipped him there, just above his jeans. Scraped her teeth over his skin and felt his stomach jump beneath her lips. Felt the answering heat deep in her own belly.

She'd missed this. Missed touching him. Missed feeling him beneath her. Missed the pleasure of sliding her body against his.

Missed *feeling*.

She opened the button on his jeans, her eyes locked on his. Slowly, so slowly opened the zipper.

His lips parted. Anticipation. Arousal. Maybe both.

She narrowed her eyes at the slow smile that spread across his mouth. "What are you thinking?" She pressed her lips to his belly.

His lips quivered. "It's been a long time since you inspected my bits and pieces."

She swallowed hard and pushed his pants open. The tip of his erection rested against his groin. Teasing her.

It had been so long since she'd done this with him. Since she'd taken him in her mouth and tasted him.

Brought them both so much pleasure with something so simple.

She urged his pants down. He lifted his hips, and she slid them down farther, exposing the thick length of him. She hesitated, curious now that he'd brought it up.

"Here," he said. He slid her finger over the soft skin at the bottom of his sac near a rough, ragged scar.

"I wouldn't have found that," she whispered.

He shrugged. "Now you know."

There was more there. Unsaid things that could wait.

Because he was right in front of her. And she wanted to lose herself in the sensation of touching him. Of feeling his body tense when she used her mouth on him.

She watched him carefully. Lowered her lips to press a soft

kiss on the tip of him where he was moist and smooth. Savored the warm smell that was uniquely and completely his.

She took him in her mouth. Sucked on him gently. Heard his shuddering sigh of relief or pleasure or both.

She cradled him where he was soft as she swirled her tongue over his length. Felt his gasp when she dragged her teeth gently over his tip before kissing him gently there once more.

He reached for her then. He urged her up until she was in his lap once more, his mouth feasting on hers. There was no restraint in his kiss now. No patience.

Only hunger. Raw and powerful and filled with needful things.

"Why am I always naked and you always have clothes on?" His words were a murmur against her mouth a moment before he feasted on her again. One hand gripped her hip as he rocked against her. Sparks simmering in her belly exploded in full-blown, wild pleasure.

Tighter. Higher. Harder. Until she thought she would snap from the pressure. "Patrick, please."

He stilled then. Cupped her cheeks and sipped at her lips. Bringing them both back from the edge of mindlessness.

Her body protested at the edge of the cliff, needing, craving the release he'd brought her so close to.

She arched against him. "Please." Her words were almost a sob. "I need you," she whispered.

HE TOOK his time stripping her naked. One piece of clothing at a time, inch by inch.

Felt her shiver beneath his touch as he traced the pad of his index finger over the smooth skin of her belly.

Her skin glowed in the firelight. The flames and the heat licked at her even as he used his tongue to follow his fingers. Her body was tense, her muscles tight with a lithe tension. He slipped his palms over her ribs, urging her arms up, over her head. She parted her thighs, urging him home as he leaned over her. He nuzzled her nose before lifting his hips away from the contact they both craved.

She scowled at him. "You know, for a man who hasn't been with a woman in a long, long time, you've got remarkable staying power." She arched beneath him, a beautiful, fire-licked goddess.

He smiled, trailing his fingers down the underside of her arms. Tracing the edge of her breasts. Her nipples puckered beneath his touch.

He ignored her taunt. "You're so beautiful, Samantha." He'd waited for this. Hoped for it. Hoped that it would be the miracle they needed to put their relationship back together again. This alone time, this precious moment when it could be just him and just her. The storm outside was far away.

She narrowed her eyes at him. "I may stop speaking to you if you don't get your damn pants completely off and..."

He covered her mouth with his, cutting off her words with a kiss meant to drive them both closer to the edge. "I want to go slow. I want to remember every detail."

"Can we do the remember-every-detail thing in a few minutes?"

He splayed his palm over her belly when she moved to sit up. He shook his head. "My turn," he whispered before placing a kiss at the soft center of her belly.

She bowed her back off the blanket with a quiet gasp.

It was good, so damned good to see her like this.

The fact that he'd almost lost her made it all the more sweet.

He nuzzled her belly for a moment, then traced his fingers beneath the edge of her panties.

She made a sexy sound deep in her throat.

She wasn't used to lying back. She was not a submissive, passive lover. She took as much as she received. He knew that, and he damn sure was going to enjoy this for as long as it lasted. Tonight, though, was for her. For them.

He slipped her panties over her hips, exposing her to the heat of the fire. She was beautiful and swollen and glistening wet.

He wanted to feast on her. To use his mouth on her and tease her in all the ways he'd learned she liked.

He could suckle her where she was swollen. He could stroke her gently and feel her arch beneath his touch. He wanted to do everything and nothing all at once. He was content for a moment just to see her spread out before him, evidence of her pleasure glistening on her thighs.

He slipped the pad of his thumb along the seam of her body. A caress that was barely there. Her heat radiated against his skin. His thumb came away slick and warm.

"Tease." A choked whisper.

He licked his bottom lip, finally daring to meet her gaze. His eyes locked with hers as he slid his thumb into her heat, circling her where she was so, so swollen. She didn't look away as he stroked her softly. Her lips parted, though, and her breath came in quick, quiet gasps. She tensed as he continued to slide his fingers over her body. Gently, so gently. Driving them both wild with the simplest touch.

He leaned down, blowing against her skin where she was exposed to him. Felt her frustrated gasp. He smiled at her. Kept stroking her until she met his gaze again.

Then he took her in his mouth. Suckled her where she was swollen and sweet and...

Dear lord, she almost came right then. The pressure spiraled wide the moment his tongue connected with her, and he felt the tension wind up beneath his touch. He ached for this woman.

Her fingers were fists in his hair the moment she created the wave and started to come. She arched beneath his touch, offering herself completely, surrendering to the pleasure of his touch. It was beautiful, watching her body bow off the floor, to feel her shudder in her release.

The orgasm still shivered through her body as she urged him up until his erection was poised at the edge of her heat. "Now. I need you." She kissed him, hard and fierce. "I need you now."

He was there, just there, her silken wetness surrounding him. No barriers. No fear. Nothing but the tight, wet heat of her body surrounding him, urging him deeper. He gripped her hands, dragging them over her head as he slid inside her, inch by inch. Her body engulfed him, clenching around him tightly in that first touch of being home, really home.

He moved then, slowly finding the rhythm that pleasured them both. Moved when her fingers tightened in his. Drove them both closer to the edge until her body tensed and the wave cascaded over them both. Until her pleasure burst again, crashing over him, sending him spiraling out into the darkness beyond the storm.

And in the aftermath of it all, he held her close. Because there was nothing else he'd wanted more.

11

They lay in silence, their bodies twined together in the glow from the fire. Quiet strokes. Soft whispers of breath on skin. She tried to hide the emotions burning behind her eyes, waiting to break free. To spill. They were there, just there.

She closed her eyes and waited, hoping, praying that she would be okay. That the crash would not destroy her.

The crash always came when you tried to ignore it. Sometimes it was within days, weeks, months.

Other times it took years. Decades away from the war before things finally burst out of the place where they'd been stuffed and ignored.

She lay cradled in his arms. She couldn't remember the last time she'd simply sat, comfortable and wrung out all at once.

Her heart was heavy and full, echoing every beat of his against her back.

She waited for the numbness to circle back up, to rise out of the darkness and drag away the echoes of sensation. To steal the pleasure at the warmth of his touch and leave her empty once more.

It didn't come.

Instead, sleep drifted over her and she stayed, feeling his arms around her, feeling safe and secure and *loved*.

God, how she loved this man. Loved him so much her heart ached with it. He shifted, nuzzling the top of her head with his cheek.

How could she have walked away from this? From everything that he meant to her? He was still here, still alive. Still warm and solid and steady.

"I remember the first time you deployed," she whispered, unsure if he was awake but needing to talk. Needing to release some of the pressure against her heart. "I was terrified you wouldn't come home."

She closed her eyes, seeing him again the day he'd walked out of the gym and toward that first deployment. She'd hated, *hated* being left behind.

She continued, needing to get the words out before she panicked and locked them down again. "I watched the news every day. First thing in the morning. Last thing at night. I was so afraid I was going to lose you." His fingers threaded with hers over her heart. Tightened just a little.

Letting her know he was there.

He was always there. He was the most steady thing in her life.

How could she have forgotten?

He shifted so her head leaned against his shoulder. "I wasn't prepared for you to go." He brushed her hair from her face. "I wanted to drag you out of that gym that day." He scoffed quietly. "I thought about converting to some religion that wouldn't let you out of the house."

She smiled in the firelight. "That probably wouldn't have gone over too well."

"I didn't say it was rational. Just that I'd considered it." His voice was deep against her back. "I don't know what I would have done if you hadn't come home, Sam," he whispered.

"It was a close thing." Her words choked off. Crushed in a wave of emotion that had been just there, just below the surface, waiting for its time to crash over her and drag her back into the emptiness of the abyss.

HE FELT the shudder escape her a moment before hot tears splashed onto his forearm. She'd been steadfast when they'd each deployed. Solid and stoic as first he'd shipped off to war, and then she'd followed. But this? This was different. This was a thousand years of emotion trapped and bottled up, finally breaking free.

Great shuddering sobs wracked her body. He shifted, pulling her closer, wishing he could lend her his strength. Wishing he could take away the pain tearing at her.

He held her while she cried. Whispered nonsense in her ear. And felt his own heart break as her sobs punished them both.

"It's going to be okay," he whispered.

She sat up then, pulling away from his warmth. "You don't know that." She swiped at her cheeks. She bit her lips together, trying to wrestle the emotion back into the vault. She placed her fist over her heart. "It hurts." A ragged, pain-filled admission. "And it feels like it's never going to stop."

He shifted, pulling her close until her head rested on his shoulder. Her tears were hot on his skin, leaving cool trails behind them as they traced down his bare chest.

"I want it to stop." She leaned back, wiping her eyes.

He cupped her cheeks, his heart breaking in his chest. "I can't tell you when it's not going to hurt anymore. I wish I could." He kissed her eyelids, her nose. Tasted the warm salt of her tears. "I wish there was some magical fucking pill that you could take to make everything feel normal again." Stroked his thumb over the dampness on her cheeks. "It's easier, when you don't feel. When you stuff it all down and pretend it's just another particularly shitty day at the office."

"I thought I could go to war and everything would be fine. I had some naive notion that the war wouldn't fucking hit home." Her voice broke. "That I would go and we'd sit on the FOB and drink coffee and do our jobs and come home at the end of the year." She wrapped her arms around her middle, holding her sides. "I was wrong. I was so fucking wrong." She finally looked up at him, and he saw staggering depths of despair looking back at him. He pulled her close until she sagged against him.

"I want out." He kissed the top of her head as her words sank in. "I want out of the Army." She leaned back to look at him. "I want to come home and be around my mom and my best friend's dad who was a better father to me than my own. I'm all they have left, and I can't take that away from either one of them." She swiped at her cheeks with the back of one hand. "And I won't ask you to give it up for me. I won't." She covered her hands with her face, the strength finally gone out of her.

"You never asked me." He cupped her cheeks. "You just ran, and assumed I'd be like everyone else in your life and let you go." Kissed her gently. "I love you, Samantha." He lowered his forehead to hers. "And if loving you means we leave the Army behind then so be it."

He held her then, cradled her in his arms as great wracking sobs tore through her.

Held her until his heart broke for her, until he couldn't tell where her tears ended and his began.

Until she was finally emptied out and still.

And even when the fire died down, he held her.

Because he was never going to let her go again.

DAWN CAME TOO EARLY. It could have come at noon, and it would have been too early.

Her face was swollen. Her eyes gritty and heavy and full.

Last night's storm still swirled inside her. Less violent now but still there.

Still making her feel every ounce of ragged pain.

Patrick's arms tightened around her waist.

"It hurts."

"It always will." A gentle kiss against the back of her neck. "But I'm here. When the pain comes. When it gets too bad." His hand slid up, covering her heart. "I'm not going to leave you, Sam."

"You can't promise me that." Denial that refused to be ignored.

"No one can. But that's not enough of a reason not to live. Not to love." His palm was warm and solid against her chest.

She closed her eyes. Took a deep, shuddering breath. Held it until her lungs burned. Released it quietly and opened her eyes once more to find him watching. Waiting. Always patient. Always calm.

"When we get back...I was thinking about making an appointment with Doc." Fear, naked and raw, in those tentative words.

He stilled. "I'll go with you. If you want."

She lowered her gaze. "I...I think I'd like that." She covered his hand with hers, threading her fingers with his, daring to meet his eyes once more. "I meant it. Last night when I said I wanted out. I'm dropping my REFRAD paperwork. I'm requesting release from active duty."

He was silent a long moment. "Looks like I'll have to study up on the Maine bar exam then."

She shifted, rolling until she could see his face. "I'm not—"

"You're going to be here. With my daughter." He brushed his lips against hers. "There's nothing the Army can give me to make giving up that time worthwhile." He lowered his forehead to hers. "I almost lost you from this last deployment. I'm not going to risk it again."

She nuzzled her nose against his. "You're going to freeze up here."

"Man, here I am offering you my undying devotion, and you're trying to get me to leave. You really know how to make a guy feel wanted."

She laughed against his lips, then turned, wrapping her arms around his neck and burying her face against his skin and simply holding on. He was steady and strong and solid and real.

The nightmare wasn't over. It was a long journey back from the darkness of the war. It would always be there, always lurking.

But last night, she'd taken a step. A single step that had started with a leap of faith. Of trusting this man who had been there for her from the very start.

She nuzzled his cheek, her heart full. For the first time in a long time, it wasn't filled with pain.

"Thank you for not giving up on me," she whispered.

And in that moment, she found something she'd feared she'd lost forever.

She found hope.

12

Sam waited until the last presents were opened. Natalie was playing quietly by herself with her Lego *Millennium Falcon* she'd been eyeballing since last year and her mother and Thomas had gone out for a mid-morning walk through the snow. Patrick had disappeared upstairs a few minutes before.

Her hands shook as she found the gift she'd saved until last and followed Patrick upstairs to the room he'd shared with her since after the snowstorm.

She found him sitting on the bed, checking his e-mail. Embarrassed, he tried to stash his Blackberry. One look at her face, though, and the phone was forgotten, dropped on to the nightstand.

"What's wrong?"

She swallowed. And held out the manila folder.

He looked from her down to the folder and back again. "What's this?" There was caution in his voice.

"Gift card for more flannel." She tried to keep things light, needing a way to ease the tension around her heart.

His smile was warm, but the wariness didn't leave his eyes. "While I like what my wearing flannel does for your libido, we're going to have to discuss alternative clothing choices when we move." He looked down at the folder once more. "Sam?"

"Remember the day Natalie was born?"

Patrick went very still. Slowly, he reached for the folder.

She folded her arms over her chest, afraid he would see her hands shaking.

"When I filled out the paperwork for her parents, I left her dad's name blank."

He said nothing for a long moment. When he spoke, his voice was thick and filled with a thousand unsaid things. "That's why you never went after him for child support."

"There was no need. He wasn't her father. He's never been her father." She took a single step toward him. "She has a daddy. This...this just makes it official." She flipped the page. "It's the paperwork to amend her birth certificate. Apparently, you can just file a form from the Internet. There won't be an adoption. She'll be your daughter." She rested her hand over his heart. "On paper and in here."

She didn't expect to see his eyes fill. He ground his teeth, trying to keep the emotion in check. Her heart swelled in her chest but this time, the ache was something good. Something special.

A gift.

"This is the second best gift you've ever given me." He wrapped his arms around her waist, burying his face in her hair. A shudder ran through him. She tightened her arms around him.

"What's the first?"

"Letting me be there when she was born."

"What's wrong, Mommy?"

Sam took a step back to see their daughter standing in the doorway. Natalie looked between the two of them. "Are you sad?"

Sam looked at Patrick. He dropped to his knees in front of her. "No, baby, I'm not sad. Your Mommy just gave me the best Christmas present ever."

Natalie frowned. "But all you got her was a sweater and some coffee."

Sam covered her mouth and laughed. "Honey, I like my sweater. And that's my favorite coffee."

Natalie looked skeptical, the way only an eight-year-old could.

Patrick held open his arms until Natalie stepped into his embrace. Buried his face in their daughter's hair. Sam's heart ached. "Baby, Mommy just made sure our family would always be a family. And nothing will ever change that."

"But you two aren't married. Don't people have to be married to be a family?"

"No, baby, people don't have to be married to be a family." She looked at Patrick. "But I think I would like to be married to your Daddy very much."

"This is the best Christmas ever." A slow smile spread across her daughter's lips. She leaned forward with a happy sound, her arms around both their necks. "I got everything on my list."

Sam rested her cheek against Patrick's shoulder.

"Me, too," he whispered. "All I ever wanted was you. Both of you. Forever."

She closed her eyes and felt. Everything. All of it. The sadness and the happiness. The joy and the sorrow. It was so much. So overwhelming.

But at the center of it all was Patrick and their daughter. Steady. Safe.

She'd almost lost him. She'd almost lost herself.

The war would never leave her.

But in that moment, she knew she had a chance to really come home. *They* had a chance. As a family.

Maybe they'd gotten their miracle after all.

Thank you for reading **COME HOME TO ME**. I hope you enjoyed Patrick and Sam. Keep reading to find out what happens when a rule breaker crashes into a man who has never broken a rule in his life. Find out what happens in **CARRY ME HOME**.

The rivalry between Claire and Evan has been building for far too long. Brought together to help a mutual friend, will they be able to put their past aside - and a risk a second chance at love?

One click CARRY ME HOME, a feisty enemies to lovers romance now!

CARRY Me Home was previously published as Until There Was You.

If you enjoyed Come Home to Me, please consider leaving a review.

EXCERPT FROM CARRY ME HOME

PROLOGUE

Fort Hood, Texas
July 2005

Captain Evan Loehr was having a bad day. Granted, it could have been worse. It could always be worse. But as he pulled his Stetson out of its carrying case and dusted it off, he contemplated the consequences for blowing off the mandatory fun of tonight's hail and farewell. He was not in the mood. Not in the least. Not when he was eight weeks out from leaving on his third deployment and was up to his neck in maintenance issues and, well, other issues that he'd never in a million years thought he'd have to deal with as a company commander.

There were things he simply did not want to know about his soldiers.

But his battalion commander said they were going to the hail and farewell, so Evan was going to the hail and farewell. The brutal Texas summer sun blazed overhead, baking the earth and melting the asphalt beneath his shoes. He hoped like hell there was air-conditioning in the bar.

More, he hoped none of his more illustrious soldiers decided to attend tonight's shindig. He'd been in command for less than a month, and so far at least one of his troopers had spent a night in jail every single weekend.

Stepping into the bar, he walked into a blanket of darkness, tinged with cigarette smoke and a bouncy country song blaring at him from all sides. The dance floor was surrounded by a low wall and illuminated with flickering strobe lights. He couldn't believe they were having a military function at a bar where there would be civilians. Normally military functions like these were in separate rooms at somewhat classier establishments, not in rowdy country bars. He wasn't entirely sure it was a good idea, but then again, he wasn't in charge of planning the event. Evan made his way to the bar, needing something a hell of a lot stronger than a beer to get him through tonight.

"You realize it looks bad for you to hang out with your old enlisted buddy, don't you?"

Claire Montoya looked up at her oldest friend, Sergeant First Class Reza Iaconelli, whom she was no longer supposed to be friends with now that she'd earned her commission two years before. "You're the only person—officer or enlisted—in this brigade I know. I don't really care what it looks like."

"Yeah, well, my commander might have something to say about that if he gets the wrong idea. The guy must have been potty trained at gunpoint."

"That uptight, huh?" Claire grinned and sipped her beer. She'd been in the Reaper Brigade Combat team for all of three weeks, and Reza was the one person she trusted to have her back. "Where is your illustrious commander, anyway?"

"Working, as always." Reza grinned, and it was pure evil. "You'll never guess on what."

Claire braced for the worst. She could only imagine. "Do I want to know?"

He tossed back the rest of his beer. "Apparently, there are eight new cases of chlamydia in our company. So the battalion commander has tasked him to find out A, where they came from, and B, what he's going to do to prevent any more outbreaks."

Claire choked on a swallow of Dos Equis that went down the wrong pipe. It was a long minute before her lungs were clear and she could breathe again, let alone talk. "That is wrong on so, so many levels," she said when she could speak.

"Speak of the devil." Reza turned and pointed his beer at someone behind Claire. She twisted on the edge of the wall that circled the dance floor, prepared to meet someone starched and rigid. "Evan Loehr, Claire Montoya. You two mingle. I'm getting another beer."

She was going to kill Reza. He was forever trying to get her to hook up the way he did: with all the discretion of a dog in heat. She stared daggers into his back as he walked off. He never quite understood why she wasn't into dating. Her track record with men sucked, and she was not about to add to that losing streak tonight. She was getting ready to deploy in less than two months with the brigade. She didn't need a one-night stand with one of the company commanders to complicate things.

Not that he didn't look like the perfect candidate for a one-night dance with the devil. If she did those sort of things. Which she didn't. But still, this man didn't look remotely the way she'd expected he would. His shoulders were wide and solid, and beneath that starched white shirt, his chest looked powerful. She could easily imagine those arms wrapped around her, holding her tight while he... *Down, girl.* She might not have moved from her spot on the low wall surrounding the dance floor, but her hormones had snapped to attention, that was for sure.

The way Reza had described him made her imagine a man who would show up in military uniform despite the Texas casual dress code.

He seemed out of place in this smoky, seedy bar. This guy seemed stiff and rigid, as if he'd rather be anywhere but here at this moment. The top button of his shirt exposed the strong line of his throat, revealing dark hair and a glimpse of smooth skin and carved shadows. Beneath the First Cav Stetson, his hair was black and cut close to the strong line of his neck. There was confidence in the way he moved, a raw power that wrapped around Claire like the smoke in the bar and drew her close.

Claire stuck out her hand, needing something to distract her from her deviant thoughts. Small talk ought to do the trick. "Nice to meet you. Evan, right?"

"Yeah." His hand was rough and strong as her fingers slid into his. "How did you get the last name Montoya with hair like that?"

"I have no idea." Oddly self-conscious, she tucked her red hair behind one ear. "So you're Reza's commander?"

"For the last two months."

"And your first order of business is dealing with sexually transmitted diseases?" His scowled fiercely and Claire laughed out loud, despite her best efforts not to.

"Glad you think it's funny." His voice rumbled over her skin, holding the promise of dark fantasies and primitive yearnings. It had been too long since she'd been with a man. Being around him made her want to do reckless things.

"I've never been a commander, but I hope I never have to deal with what you're dealing with right now." Evan looked so disgruntled, she smiled. She didn't know him. She shouldn't be amused by his discomfort, but the situation was ridiculous. Plus, the conversation came with the added bonus of locking down her hormones. Nothing said sexy like diseases, she thought dryly.

He leaned forward, bracing his elbows on the low wall next to her hips and dragging his hands over his face. "I can't believe that this is what I'm dealing with. Not weapons training. Not running patrols or shooting bad guys. Sexually transmitted diseases."

"Well, commander, what's your plan for dealing with the rash of diseased penises in your formation?"

Evan groaned and buried his face in his hands, then took a long pull off his own beer. Reza emerged from the crowd and clapped him on the shoulder. "I already took care of it. I sent Ramirez to the clinic to pick up a case of rubbers. They're sitting on the counter in the company ops."

"I should make them an inspectable item and have every soldier keep one in their wallet," Evan grumbled. Claire laughed so hard, she almost fell from her seat on the wall. Evan gave her a pointed look.

"I'm sorry," she said, trying to stop laughing before she permanently damaged his pride. "But you should see your face."

He took a pull off his beer. Claire watched his throat move, enthralled by the motion of sleek muscle and dark skin. "I feel like I should have a formation and make the platoon sergeants demonstrate how to put on a condom the correct way."

"As one of your platoon sergeants, I'll be the first to refuse that order," Reza said before taking another drink.

Finally Evan laughed and the sound twisted Claire's insides, teasing away the tension and the fatigue and the bone-crushing pressure of being the new girl. Something warm unfurled against her heart, like hot steam rising from a hidden vent.

Something that told her she needed to stay far away from the source of the warmth.

THE FORMAL PORTION of the evening was about to get started, and Evan found himself regretting that. He was enjoying himself immensely, a feeling both surprising and unexpected. Claire Montoya was proving a sexy detour for the night, and while Evan didn't do one-night stands, he was not above taking her to a quiet corner of the bar. Her mouth drew him. She had the kind of wide, full lips that were made for kissing.

He wondered how his big platoon sergeant knew her, but couldn't drum up the energy to ask. He simply hoped he wasn't spending the evening flirting with one of Reza's castoffs. It hadn't taken him long to learn that Sergeant Iaconelli spent his free time curled up with a bottle or a woman.

"So other than unprotected sex, what do you think about being a commander?" Claire asked. Her breath kissed his skin as she leaned close enough so she didn't have to shout.

Evan leaned in, fighting the urge to lift her hair away from her ear. "I love it. It's the best job I've ever had. But it's the most stressful, too."

"You don't seem like you relax very often."

He shrugged, sipping his beer. "I don't. There's not a lot of time for relaxing when you're getting ready to take a company downrange into combat."

"Guess they're getting ready to do the introductions." Claire tipped her chin toward the stage. "Guess I need to get ready to smile and wave for the crowd."

Evan frowned. "You're a soldier?"

She smiled, and her green eyes glittered in the smoky bar. "Yeah."

There was a sinking feeling in Evan's stomach. "What rank are you?"

She frowned. "Does it matter?"

"Yes."

She grinned, and it was wicked. "What, afraid you've spent the evening flirting with an enlisted woman?"

"I don't date Army women as a rule." Evan breathed out sharply. "Dirt and dust on deployments aren't exactly great conditions for love and sex."

"Pretty stiff restrictions on letting yourself relax, huh?"

"Everything in my life comes with conditions," h said softly. "Besides, you don't look like you'd be in the Army." He felt a flush creep up his neck as he heard the rudeness of his own words, but Claire didn't look offended. "Sorry. I didn't mean that how it sounded."

"Relax. I'm a captain." She looked up at him, studying him quietly. "You should see your face. You were really worried, weren't you?"

Evan couldn't get the tight knot in his chest to relax. She had stunning red hair and green eyes cast in dark, smoky shadows. A body that took Evan to a dark and primal place. Her dark red hair tumbled down her back and she looked like a woman who spent more time at the mall than on the weapons range. He couldn't picture her in uniform. Thankfully, she didn't seem to care that he had been worried about her rank.

"I'm prior service. Did a stint as enlisted before I went to Officer Candidate School down at Fort Benning."

She bumped her shoulder against his, her eyes sparkling. "You really need to relax. It's mandatory fun, and you don't look like you're having any."

He turned his attention to the dais, where the brigade commander was introducing new folks to the rest of the brigade.

Her hand on his forearm dragged his attention away from

the stage. He glanced down at her fingers, long and slim against his skin, burning him. "This is a really big deal for you, isn't it?"

"No, just a surprise."

A big surprise. One that would complicate things tremendously.

"Captain Claire Montoya." The brigade commander called Claire's name, and she hopped off the wall without a backwards glance at him. "Claire hails to us from . . ."

Evan stopped listening, lost in his own thoughts, which were a hell of a lot more than unprofessional. He waited until she was up on the stage before he melted into the dark safety of the bar, putting a stop to what would have been a very big mistake.

IT WAS BETTER THIS WAY. Claire had learned a long time ago that work relationships—hell, any relationship that involved her—never really worked out. She palmed her car keys and walked out of *Ropers* into the intense Texas heat. The sun had gone down hours ago, but the temperature was still set to broil. Sweat trickled down her neck and her hair clung to her scalp.

She rounded the corner of the bar and clicked the key fob, her car lock chirping in the sweltering heat. But that wasn't what caught her attention.

Evan Loehr was talking to Reza. Arguing, more like. Frowning, Claire hurried over, knowing she had no authority to intervene between a company commander and his subordinate and prepared to do it anyway. But before she crossed the wide gravel parking lot, Reza snatched his keys and dropped them into some cute brunette's hands, stalking off.

Evan saw Claire approaching before she could veer off and pretend she'd been walking toward her own car.

"What was that all about?" she asked, tucking her hands into the back pocket of her jeans.

"Work." She could hear the lie as it rolled off his tongue. "You always walk up to strange men in dark parking lots?"

She raised her eyebrows. "Yes, it's a regular habit of mine. How did you think I earn extra money?"

Silence, thick and sweaty, hung between them for a long moment. Then a slow smile spread across Evan's mouth, followed by an easy laugh. "You've got one hell of a way with words."

"I try." She pointed to her car over her shoulder. "Guess I'll see you at work?"

"Probably not. I don't get up to brigade very often."

"On purpose?"

"Yeah. It isn't on my top-ten list of places to hang out."

She laughed. "Yeah, all we do at brigade is come up with good ideas to screw with you down in the companies." She studied him, the dark shadows cast beneath his eyes, the tight lines around his mouth. Tension wound its way around her, radiating from him with the same power and confidence he wore like a shield. "Well, then I won't see you around."

"No. Probably not."

Hesitant, unsure of her reception, she took a step forward. Close enough that she could see the faint shadow against his jaw. "Do you ever relax?"

His only movement was a slight flare of his nostrils. "No."

She took another step. Reached up and placed her hand on the solid wall of muscle over his heart. "Never?"

His lips parted, just a hint. "No."

His scent was dark and arousing. Making this big man go still and quiet? Powerful. He was wound so tight, tension burned beneath her touch. "So you think this would be a mistake, don't you?"

"Yes." His voice was rough.

"Do you ever make mistakes, Evan?" she whispered, her mouth a breath from his.

"Mistakes get people killed." His words traced over her lips, sending a hot spike of arousal racing through her blood.

"Hmmm." It was nothing to brush her top lip against his. His chest stopped moving beneath her palm.

His mouth opened, until she could feel his breath mingling with hers. Her blood sang with thick and heavy sensual need. His tongue flicked against hers, an open, hot invitation.

EVAN HAD no idea what the hell he was thinking, but this woman had struck a chord inside him, awakened a hunger that refused to be ignored. Kissing her was a mistake, a sensuous, gorgeous mistake.

He gave over to the temptation he'd fought earlier and lifted his hands to her neck, sliding his palms over her skin to thread them into her hair. It was warm silk against the back of his hands, a raw, simple pleasure.

Her mouth opened beneath his, her tongue sliding against his, signaling a salient desire that penetrated his defenses and made him no longer care that she was in his brigade. There were no rules against them doing any of this—whatever this was—but he didn't date at work. As he lost himself in her taste and touch, he seriously reconsidered that personal rule. He captured her quiet gasp against his mouth and felt the locks turning on the chains that held his restraint.

It was a long moment before Claire eased back, nibbling on his bottom lip before she broke the tentative connection between them.

"What was that?" he asked, his voice rough and unfamiliar to his own ears.

She smiled. "A mistake." She swiped her thumb over his bottom lip. "But one I enjoyed."

She eased back until he was forced to release her. Regret settled in his belly that this would go no further. "I'll see you around, Evan."

He watched her go, the slight sway of her hips more alluring because she did not try to affect any sensuality. She simply walked, cloaked in confidence and sexual appeal.

He let her go. Because Evan Loehr knew all about mistakes, and he wasn't about to make one with Claire Montoya.

One click CARRY ME HOME now!

A MESSAGE FROM JESSICA SCOTT

Dear Reader,

Thank you so much for reading. If you'd like to make sure you never miss a new release, sign up for my newsletter at http://www.jessicascott.net/subscribe/ and please like my Facebook page at https://www.facebook.com/JessicaScottAuthor/. You can also join my reader room, affectionately known as The Pint for sneak peeks, giveaways and general all around shenanigans.

If you enjoyed the story, please consider leaving a review. Word of mouth is incredibly important for helping other readers discover new authors. I appreciate any and all reviews (whether positive or negative or somewhere in between).

Until next time!
Jess

ALSO BY JESSICA SCOTT

THE COMING HOME SERIES

Because of You

I'll Be Home for Christmas: A Coming Home Novella

Anything For You: A Coming Home Short Story

Back to You

Come Home to Me: A Coming Home Novella*

Carry Me Home*

A Place Called Home*

Take Me Home*

Homefront

After The War

Last One Home*

THE FALLING SERIES

Before I Fall

Break My Fall

After I Fall

Catch My Fall

Until We Fall

NONFICTION

To Iraq & Back: On War and Writing

The Long Way Home: One Mom's Journey Home From War

BOOKSHOTS

Dawn's Early Light

Author's Note

The Coming Home series and Homefront series were originally published as separate series. I have rebranded them to get things organized as they were originally intended.

Come Home to Me: A Coming Home Novella* was originally published as part of the Homefront series

Carry Me Home* was originally published as Until There Was You as part of the Coming Home series

A Place Called Home* was originally published as All for You as part of the Coming Home series

Take Me Home* was originally published as It's Always Been You as part of the Coming Home series

Last One Home* was originally published as Find My Way Home as part of the Homefront series

ABOUT THE AUTHOR

Jessica Scott is an Iraq war veteran, an active duty Army officer and the USA Today bestselling author of novels set in the heart of America's Army. She is the mother of two daughters, too many animals, and wife to a retired NCO.

She's also written for the New York Times At War Blog, PBS Point of View Regarding War, and IAVA. She deployed to Iraq in 2009 as part of Operation Iraqi Freedom (OIF)/New Dawn and has had the honor of serving as a company commander at Fort Hood, Texas twice.

She holds a Ph.D. from Duke in sociology and she's been featured as one of Esquire Magazine's Americans of the Year for 2012.

Photo: Courtesy of Buzz Covington Photography
Find her online at http://www.jessicascott.net

For more information,
www.jessicascott.net
jessica@jessicascott.net

This book is a work of fiction. Names, characters, places, and incidents are the product of the author's imagination or are used fictitiously. Any resemblance to actual events, locales, or persons, living or dead, is coincidental.

I'll Be Home for Christmas

Copyright © 2014 by Jessica Scott

All rights reserved. This book is a work of fiction. Names, characters, places, and incidents are the product of the authors imagination or are used fictitiously. Any resemblance to actual events, locales, or persons, living or dead, is coincidental. No part of this book may be reproduced, scanned, or distributed in any print or electronic form without permission.

Printed in the United States of America

First Printing 2014

Author photo courtesy of Buzz Covington Photography

For more information please see www.jessicascott.net

Come Home to Me

Copyright © 2013 by Jessica Dawson

Cover design by Jessica Dawson.

All rights reserved. In accordance with the U.S. Copyright Act of 1976, the scanning, uploading, and electronic sharing of any part of this book without the permission of the publisher is unlawful piracy and theft of the author's intellectual property. Thank you for your support of the author's rights.

First ebook edition: November 2013

Second ebook edition: January 2019

The publisher is not responsible for websites (or their content) that are not owned by the publisher.

Printed by Libri Plureos GmbH in Hamburg, Germany